Praise for Donna Leon's
Commissario Brunetti Mysteries:

"Leon is the ideal author for people who vaguely long for a 'good mystery'.... That Leon is also a brilliant writer should only add to the consistently comforting appeal of her Venetian procedurals, featuring Commissario Guido Brunetti, an immensely likable police detective who takes every murder to heart." —*The New York Times Book Review*

"Few detective writers create so vivid, inclusive, and convincing a narrative as Donna Leon, the expatriate American with the Venetian heart.... One of the most exquisite and subtle detective series ever."
—*The Washington Post*

"She uses the relatively small and crime-free canvas of Venice for rips about Italian life, sexual styles and—best of all—the kind of ingrown business and political corruption that seems to lurk just below the surface." —*Chicago Tribune*

"Hers is an unusually potent cocktail of atmosphere and event."
—*The New Yorker*

"For those who know Venice, or want to, Brunetti is a well-versed escort to the nooks, crannies, moods, and idiosyncrasies of what residents call *La Serenissima*, the Serene One.... Richly atmospheric, [Leon] introduces you to the Venice insiders know." —*USA Today*

"Donna Leon is the undisputed crime fiction queen.... Leon's ability to capture the social scene and internal politics [of Venice] is first-rate." —*The Baltimore Sun*

"I struggle to think of other series authors who are as dependable as the excellent Leon." —*The Philadelphia Inquirer*

"Compassionate yet incorruptible, Brunetti knows that true justice doesn't always end in an arrest or a trial." —*Publishers Weekly*

# A
# Noble
# Radiance

Also by Donna Leon

# Donna Leon

# A
# Noble
# Radiance

Grove Press
*New York*

First published in Great Britain in 1998 by William Heinemann
This edition first published in the United States in 2006 by Penguin Books

*Printed in the United States of America*
*Published simultaneously in Canada*

ISBN: 978-0-8021-4579-6

Grove Press
an imprint of Grove Atlantic
154 West 14th Street
New York, NY 10011

Distributed by Publishers Group West

groveatlantic.com

20 21 22 23    7 6 5

*Per Biba e La Bianca*

*La nobiltà ha dipinta negli occhi l'onestà*
The nobility has honesty painted in its eyes
*Don Giovanni*
Mozart

# A
# Noble
# Radiance

# 1

There was nothing much to notice about the field, a hundred-metre square of dry grass below a small village in the foothills of the Dolomites. It lay at the bottom of a slope covered with hardwood trees which could easily be culled for firewood, and that was used as an argument to increase the price when the land and the two-hundred-year-old house upon it came to be sold. Off to the north a slant-faced mountain loomed over the small town of Ponte nelle Alpi; a hundred kilometres to the south lay Venice, too far away to influence the politics or customs of the area. People in the villages spoke Italian with some reluctance, felt more at home in Bellunese dialect.

The field had lain untilled for almost half a century, and the stone house had sat empty. The immense slates that made up the roof had shifted with age and sudden changes in temperature, perhaps even with the occasional earthquake that had struck the area during the centuries the roof had protected the house from rain and snow, and so it no longer did that, for many of the slates had crashed to earth, leaving the upper rooms exposed to the elements. Because the house and property lay at the heart of a contested will, none of the eight heirs had bothered to repair the leaks, fearful that they would never get back the few hundred thousand lire the repairs would cost. So the rain and snow dripped, then flowed, in, nibbling away at plaster and floorboards, and each year the roof tilted more drunkenly towards the earth.

The field, too, had been abandoned for the same reasons. None of the presumptive heirs wanted to expend either time or money working the land, nor did they want to weaken their legal position by being seen to make unpaid use of the property. Weeds flourished, made all the more vital by the fact that the last people to cultivate the land had for decades manured it with the droppings of their rabbits.

It was the scent of foreign money that settled the dispute about the will: two days after a retired German doctor made an offer for the house and land, the eight heirs met at the home of the eldest. Before the end of the evening, they had arrived at a unanimous decision to sell the house and land; their subsequent decision was not to sell until the foreigner had doubled his offer, which would bring the selling price to four times what any local resident would—or could—pay.

Three weeks after the deal was completed, scaffolding went up, and the centuries-old, hand-cut slates were hurled down to shatter in the courtyard below. The art of laying the slates had died with the artisans who knew how to cut them, and so they were replaced with moulded rectangles of prefabricated cement that had a vague resemblance to terra cotta tiles. Because the doctor had hired the oldest of the heirs to serve as his foreman, work progressed quickly; because this was the Province of Belluno, it was done honestly and well. By the middle of the spring, the restoration of the house was almost complete, and with the approach of the first warm days, the new owner, who had spent his professional life enclosed in brightly lit operating rooms and who was conducting the restorations by phone and fax from Munich, turned his thoughts to the creation of the garden he had dreamed about for years.

Village memory is long, and it recalled that the old garden had run alongside the row of walnut trees out behind the house, so it was there that Egidio Buschetti, the foreman, decided to plough. The land hadn't been worked for most of his own lifetime, so Buschetti estimated that his tractor would have to pass over the land twice, once to cut through the metre-high weeds, and then once again to disc up the rich soil lying underneath.

At first Buschetti thought it was a horse—he remembered that the old owners had kept two—and so he continued with his tractor all the way to what he had established as the end of the field. Pulling at the broad wheel, he swung the tractor around and headed back, proud of the razor-straightness of the furrows, glad to be out in the sun again, happy at the sound and the feel of the work, sure now that spring had come. He saw the bone sticking up crookedly from the furrow he had just ploughed, the white length of it sharply visible against the nearly black earth. No, not long enough to be a horse, but he didn't remember that anyone had ever kept sheep here. Curious, he slowed the tractor, somehow reluctant to ride over the bone and shatter it.

He shifted into neutral and drew to a stop. Pulling on the hand brake, he climbed down from his high metal seat and walked over towards the cantilevered bone that jutted up towards the sky. He bent and reached out to shove it away from the path of the tractor, but a sudden reluctance pulled him upright again, and he prodded at it with the toe of his heavy boot, hoping thus to dislodge it. It refused to move, so Buschetti turned towards the tractor, where he kept a shovel clamped in back of his seat. As he turned, his eyes fell upon a gleaming white oval a bit farther along the bottom of the furrow. No horse, no sheep had ever gazed out from so round a skull, nor would they leer up at him through the sharpened carnivore teeth so frighteningly like his own.

3

# 2

The intuition of the news in just a country town never spreads faster than when it deals with death or disaster, so the news that human bones had been discovered in the garden of the old Orsez house was common knowledge throughout the village of Col di Cugnan before dinnertime. It was not since the death of the mayor's son in that automobile accident down by the cement factory seven years ago that news had spread so quickly; even the story about Graziella Rovere and the electrician had taken two days to become common knowledge. But that night the villagers, all seventy-four of them, switched off their televisions, or talked above them, during dinner, trying to think of how it could be and, more interestingly, who it could be.

The mink-sweatered news reader on RAI 3, the blonde who wore a different pair of glasses each night, went ignored as she reported the latest horrors in the ex-Yugoslavia, and no one paid the slightest heed to the arrest of the former Minister of the Interior on charges of corruption. Both were by now normal, but a skull in a ditch behind the home of the foreigner, that was news. By bedtime, the skull had been variously reported to have been shattered by a blow from an axe, or a bullet, and to display signs that an attempt had been made to dissolve it with acid. The police had determined, people were certain, that they were the bones of a pregnant woman, a young male, and the husband of Luigina Menegaz, gone off to Rome twelve years ago and

4

never heard from since. That night people in Col di Cugnan locked their doors, and those who had lost the keys years ago and never bothered about them slept less easily than did the others.

At eight the next morning, two *Carabinieri*-driven all-terrain vehicles arrived at the home of Doctor Litfin and drove across the newly planted grass to park on either side of the two long rows ploughed the day before. It was not until an hour later that a car arrived from the provincial centre of Belluno, carrying the *medico legale* of that city. He had heard none of the rumours about the identity or cause of death of the person whose bones lay in the field, and so he did what seemed most necessary: he set his two assistants to sifting through the earth to find the rest of the remains.

As this slow process advanced, both of the *Carabinieri* vehicles took turns driving across the soon-destroyed lawn and up to the village, where the six officers had coffees in the small bar, then began to ask the residents of the village if anyone was missing. The fact that the bones seemed to have been in the earth for years did not affect their decision to ask about recent events, and so their researches proved ineffective.

In the field below the village, the two assistants of Doctor Bortot had set up a fine mesh screen at a sharp angle. Slowly, they poured buckets of earth through it, bending down occasionally to pick out a small bone or anything that looked like it might be one. As they pulled them out, they displayed them to their superior, who stood at the edge of the furrow, hands clasped behind his back. A long sheet of black plastic lay spread at his feet, and as he was shown the bones, he instructed his assistants where to place them, and together they slowly began to assemble their macabre jigsaw puzzle.

Occasionally he asked one of the men to hand him a bone, and he studied it for a moment before bending to place it somewhere on the plastic sheet. Twice he corrected himself, once bending to move a small bone from the right side to the left, and another time, with a muttered exclamation, moving another from below the metatarsal to the end of what had once been a wrist.

At ten, Doctor Litfin arrived, having been alerted the previous evening to the discovery in his garden and having driven through the night from Munich. He parked in front of his house and pulled himself stiffly from the driver's seat. Beyond the house, he saw the countless deep tracks cut into the new grass he had planted with such simple joy three weeks before. But then he saw the three men standing in the field off in the distance, almost as far away as the patch of young raspberry plants he had brought down from Germany and planted at the same time. He started across the destroyed lawn but stopped in his tracks at a shouted command that came from somewhere off to his right. He looked around but saw nothing except the three ancient apple trees that had grown up around the ruined well. Seeing no one, he started again towards the three men in the field. He had taken only a few steps before two men dressed in the ominous black uniforms of the *Carabinieri* burst out from under the nearest of the apple trees, machine guns aimed at him.

Doctor Litfin had survived the Russian occupation of Berlin, and though that had happened fifty years before, his body remembered the sight of armed men in uniform. He put both of his hands above his head and stood rock-still.

They came out fully from the shadows then, and the doctor had a hallucinogenic moment of seeing the contrast of their death-black uniforms against the innocent backdrop of pink apple blossom. Their glossy boots trampled across a carpet of fresh-fallen petals as they approached him.

'What are you doing here?' the first one demanded.

6

'Who are you?' the other asked in the same angry tone. In Italian made clumsy by fear, he began, 'I'm Doctor Litfin. I'm the . . .' he said but stopped to search for the appropriate term. 'I'm the *padrone* here.'

The *Carabinieri* had been told that the new owner was a German, and the accent sounded real enough, so they lowered their guns, though they kept their fingers near the triggers. Litfin took this as permission to lower his hands, though he did that very slowly. Because he was German, he knew that guns were always superior to any claim to legal rights, and so he waited for them to approach him, but this did not prevent him from turning his attention momentarily back to the three men who stood in the newly ploughed earth, they now as motionless as he, their attention on him and the approaching *Carabinieri*.

The two officers, suddenly diffident in the face of the person who could afford the restorations to house and land evident all around them, approached Doctor Litfin, and as they drew nearer, the balance of power changed. Litfin perceived this, and seized the moment.

'What is all of this?' he asked, pointing across the field and leaving it to the policemen to infer whether he meant his ruined lawn or the three men who stood at the other side of it.

'There's a body in your field,' the first officer answered.

'I know that, but what's all this . . . ?' he sought the proper word and came up only with '*distruzione*'.

The marks of the tyre treads seemed actually to grow deeper as the three men studied them, until finally one of the policemen said, 'We had to drive down into the field.'

Though this was an obvious lie, Litfin ignored it. He turned away from the two officers and started to walk towards the other three men so quickly that neither of the officers tried to stop him. When he got to the end of the first deep trench, he called across to the man who was obviously in charge, 'What is it?'

'Are you Doctor Litfin?' asked the other doctor, who had already been told about the German, what he had paid for the house, and how much he had spent so far on restorations.

Litfin nodded and when the other man was slow to answer, asked again, 'What is it?'

'I'd say it was a man in his twenties,' Doctor Bortot answered and then, turning back to his assistants, motioned them to continue with their work.

It took Litfin a moment to recover from the brusqueness of the reply, but when he did, he stepped on to the ploughed earth and went to stand beside the other doctor. Neither man said anything for a long time as they stood side by side and watched the two men in the trench scrape away slowly at the dirt.

After a few minutes, one of the men handed Doctor Bortot another bone, which, with a quick glance, he bent and placed at the end of the other wrist. Two more bones; two more quick placements.

'There, on your left, Pizzetti,' Bortot said, pointing to a tiny white knob that lay exposed on the far side of the trench. The man he spoke to glanced at it, bent and picked it from the earth, and handed it up to the doctor. Bortot studied it for a moment, holding it delicately between his first two fingers, then turned to the German. 'Lateral cuneiform?' he asked.

Litfin pursed his lips as he looked at the bone. Even before the German could speak, Bortot handed it to him. Litfin turned it in his hands for a moment, then glanced down at the pieces of bone laid out on the plastic at their feet. 'That, or it might be the intermediate,' he answered, more comfortable with the Latin than the Italian.

8

'Yes, yes, it could be,' Bortot replied. He waved his hand down towards the plastic sheet, and Litfin stooped to place it at the end of the long bone leading to the foot. He stood up and both men looked at it. '*Ja,ja,*' Litfin muttered; Bortot nodded.

And so for the next hour the two men stood together beside the trench left by the tractor, first one and then the other taking a bone from the two men who continued to sift the rich earth through the tilted screen. Occasionally they conferred about a fragment or sliver, but generally they agreed about the identity of what was passed up to them by the two diggers.

The spring sun poured down on them; off in the distance, a cuckoo began his mating call, repeating it until the four men were no longer aware of it. As it grew hotter, they began to peel off their coats and then their jackets, all of which ended up hung on the lower branches of the trees running along the side of the field to mark the end of the property.

To pass the time, Bortot asked a few questions about the house, and Litfin explained that the exterior restorations were finished; there remained the interior work, which he estimated would take much of the summer. When Bortot asked the other doctor why he spoke Italian so well, Litfin explained that he had been coming to Italy on vacation for twenty years and, during the last, to prepare himself for the move, had been taking classes three times a week. The bells from the village above them rang out twelve times.

'I think that might be all, Dottore,' one of the men in the trench said and, to emphasize it, struck his shovel deep into the ground and rested his elbow on it. He took out a pack of cigarettes and lit one. The other man stopped as well, took out a handkerchief and wiped his face.

Bortot looked down at the patch of excavated earth, now about three metres square, then down at the bones and shrivelled organs spread out on the plastic sheeting.

9

Litfin suddenly asked, 'Why did you think it's a young man?'

Before answering, Bortot bent down and picked up the skull. 'The teeth,' he said, handing it to the other man.

But instead of looking at the teeth, which were in good condition and with no sign of the wearing-away of age, Litfin, with a small grunt of surprise, turned the skull to expose the back. In the centre, just above the indentation that would fit around the still-missing final vertebra, there was a small round hole. He had seen enough of skulls and of violent death that he was neither shocked nor disturbed.

'But why male?' he asked, handing the skull back to Bortot.

Before he answered, Bortot knelt and placed the skull back in its place at the top of the other bones. 'This: it was near the skull,' he said as he stood, taking something from his jacket pocket and handing it to Litfin. 'I don't think a woman would wear that.'

The ring he handed Litfin was a thick gold band that flared out into a round, flat surface. Litfin put the ring on to the palm of his left hand and turned it over with the index finger of his right. The design was so worn away that at first he could distinguish nothing, but then it slowly came into focus: carved in low relief was an intricate design of an eagle rampant holding a flag in its left claw, a sword in its right. 'I forget the Italian word,' Litfin said as he looked at the ring. 'A family crest?'

'*Stemma*,' Bortot supplied.

'*Sì, stemma*,' Litfin repeated and then asked, 'Do you recognize it?'

Bortot nodded.

'What is it?'

'It's the crest of the Lorenzoni family.'

Litfin shook his head. He'd never heard of them. 'Are they from around here?'

This time Bortot shook his head.

As he handed back the ring, Litfin asked, 'Where are they from?'

'Venice.'

# 3

Not only Doctor Bortot, but just about anyone in the Veneto region, would recognize the name Lorenzoni. Students of history would recall the Count of that name who accompanied the blind Doge Dandolo at the sack of Constantinople in 1204; legend has it that it was Lorenzoni who handed the old man his sword as they scrambled over the wall of the city. Musicians would recall that the principal contributor to the building of the first opera theatre in Venice bore the name of Lorenzoni. Bibliophiles recognized the name as that of the man who had lent Aldus Manutius the money to set up his first printing press in the city in 1495. But these are the memories of specialists and historians, people who have reason to recall the glories of the city and of the family. Ordinary Venetians recall it as the name of the man who, in 1944, provided the SS with the chance to discover the names and addresses of the Jews living in the city.

Of the 256 Venetian Jews who had been living in the city, eight survived the war. But that is only one way of looking at the fact and at the numbers. More crudely put, it means that 248 people, citizens of Italy and residents of what had once been the Most Serene Republic of Venice, were taken forcibly from their homes and eventually murdered.

Italians are nothing if not pragmatic, so many people believed that, if it had not been Pietro Lorenzoni, the father of the present count, it would have been someone else who revealed the hiding place of the head of the Jewish community to the SS. Others suggested that he must have been threatened into doing it: after all, since the end of the war the members of the various branches of the family had certainly devoted themselves to the good of the city, not only by their many acts of charity and generosity to public and private institutions, but by their having filled various civic posts—once even that of mayor, though for only six months—and having served with distinction, as the phrase has it, in many public capacities. One Lorenzoni had been the Rector of the University; another organized the Biennale for a period of time in the sixties; and yet another had, upon his death, left his collection of Islamic miniatures to the Correr Museum.

Even if they didn't remember any of these things, much of the population of the city recalled the name as that of the young man who had been kidnapped two years ago, taken by two masked men from beside his girlfriend while they were parked in front of the gates of the family villa outside Treviso. The girl had first called the police, not the family, and so the Lorenzonis' assets had been frozen immediately, even before the family learned of the crime. The first ransom note, when it came, demanded seven billion lire, and at the time there was much speculation about whether the Lorenzonis could find that much money. The next note, which came three days after the first, lowered the sum to five billion.

But by then the forces of order, though making no evident signs of progress in finding the men responsible, had responded as was standard in cases of kidnapping and had effectively blocked all attempts on the part of the family to borrow money or bring it in from foreign sources, and so the second demand also went unmet. Count Ludovico, the father of the kidnapped boy, went on national television and begged those responsible to free his son. He said he was willing to give himself up to them in his son's place, though he was too upset to explain how this could be done.

There was no response to his appeal; there was no third ransom demand.

That was two years ago, and since then there had been no sign of the boy, Roberto, and no further progress, at least not public progress, on the case. Though the family's assets had been unblocked after a period of six months, they remained for another year under the control of a government administrator, who had to consent to the withdrawal or liquidation of any sum in excess of a hundred million lire. Many such sums passed out of the Lorenzoni family businesses during that period, but all of them were legitimate, and so permission was given for them to be paid out. After the administrator's powers lapsed, a gentle governmental eye, as discreet as it was invisible, continued to observe the Lorenzoni business and spending, but no outlay was indicated beyond the normal course of business expenditure.

The boy, though another three years would have to pass before he could be declared legally dead, was believed by his family to be so in the real sense. His parents mourned in their fashion: Count Ludovico redoubled the energy he devoted to his business concerns, while the Contessa withdrew into private devotion and acts of piety and charity. Roberto was an only child, so the family was now perceived as having no heir, and thus a nephew, the son of Ludovico's younger brother, was brought into the business and groomed to take over the direction of the Lorenzoni affairs, which included vast and diverse holdings in Italy and abroad.

The news that the skeleton of a young man wearing a ring with the Lorenzoni family crest had been found was telephoned to the Venice police from the phone in one of the *Carabinieri* vehicles and received by Sergeant Lorenzo

Vianello, who took careful notes of the location, the name of the owner of the property, and of the man who had discovered the body.

After replacing the phone, Vianello went upstairs and knocked on the door of his immediate superior, Commissario Guido Brunetti. When he heard the shouted '*Avanti*', Vianello pushed open the door and went into Brunetti's office.

'*Buon dì*, Commissario,' he said and, not having to be invited, took his usual place in the chair opposite Brunetti, who sat behind his desk, a thick folder opened in front of him. Vianello noticed that his superior was wearing glasses; he didn't remember ever seeing them before.

'Since when do you wear glasses, sir?' he asked.

Brunetti looked up then, his eyes strangely magnified by the lenses. 'Just for reading,' he said, taking them off and tossing them down on to the papers in front of him. 'I don't really need them. It's just that it makes the fine print on these papers from Brussels easier to read.' With thumb and forefinger, he grabbed at the bridge of his nose and rubbed it, as if to remove the impression of the glasses as well as that left by what he had been reading.

He looked up at the sergeant. 'What is it?'

'We've had a call from the *Carabinieri* in a place called . . .' he began, then looked down at the piece of paper in his hand. 'Col di Cugnan.' Vianello paused but Brunetti said nothing. 'It's in the province of Belluno,' as if giving Brunetti a clear idea of the geography would be helpful. When Brunetti still said nothing, Vianello continued. 'A farmer up there has dug up a body in a field. It appears to be a young man in his early twenties.'

'According to whom?' Brunetti interrupted.

'I think it was the *medico legale*, sir.'

'When did this happen?' Brunetti asked.

'Yesterday.'

15

'Why did they call us?'

'A ring with the Lorenzoni crest was found with the body.'

Brunetti again put his fingers to the bridge of his nose and closed his eyes. 'Ah, the poor boy,' Brunetti sighed. He took his hand away and looked across at Vianello. 'Are they sure?'

'I don't know, sir,' Vianello said, answering the unspoken part of Brunetti's question. 'The man I spoke to said only that they had identified the ring.'

'That doesn't mean that it was his, doesn't even mean that the ring belonged to . . .' here Brunetti paused and tried to recall the boy's name. 'Roberto.'

'Would someone not in the family wear a ring like that, sir?'

'I don't know, Vianello. But if whoever put the body there didn't want it to be identified, they certainly would have taken the ring. It was on his hand, wasn't it?'

'I don't know, sir. All he said was that the ring was found with him.'

'Who's in charge up there?'

'The man I spoke to said he was told to call us by the *medico legale*. I've got his name here somewhere.' He consulted the paper in his hand and said, 'Bortot. That's all he gave me, didn't tell me his first name.'

Brunetti shook his head. 'Tell me the name of the place again.'

'Col di Cugnan.' Seeing Brunetti's inquisitive look, Vianello shrugged to show that he had never heard of it, either. 'It's up near Belluno. You know how strange the names of places are up there: Roncan, Nevegal, Polpet.'

'And a lot of the family names, too, if I remember it right.'

Vianello waved the paper. 'Like the *medico legale*.'

'Did the *Carabinieri* say anything else?' Brunetti asked.

'No, but I thought you should know about it, sir.'

'Yes, good,' Brunetti said, only half attentive. 'Has anyone contacted the family?'

'I don't know. The man I spoke to didn't say anything about it.'

Brunetti reached for the phone. When the operator responded, he asked to be connected with the *Carabinieri* station in Belluno. When they answered, he identified himself and said he wanted to speak to the person in charge of the investigation of the body they had found the day before. Within moments, he was speaking to Maresciallo Bernardi, who said he was in charge of the investigation there. No, he didn't know whether the ring had been on the hand of the man in the trench or not. If the *commissario* had been there, he would have seen how difficult that would be to determine. Perhaps the *medico legale* would be better able to answer his question. In fact, the Maresciallo couldn't provide much information at all, save what was already contained on the piece of paper in Vianello's hand. The body had been taken to the civil hospital in Belluno, where it was being held until the autopsy could be performed. Yes, he did have Doctor Bortot's number, which he gave to Brunetti, who had nothing else to ask.

He depressed the receiver, then immediately dialled the number the *Carabiniere* had given him.

'Bortot,' the doctor answered.

'Good morning, Doctor, this is Commissario Guido Brunetti of the Venice police.' He paused there, accustomed as he was to having people interrupt to ask him why he was calling. Bortot said nothing, so Brunetti continued. 'I'm calling about the body of the young man that was found yesterday. And about the ring that was found with him.'

'Yes, Commissario?'

'I'd like to know where the ring was.'

'It wasn't on the bones of the hand if that's what you mean. But I'm not sure that means it wasn't on the hand to begin with.'

'Could you explain, Doctor?'

'It's difficult to say just what's happened here, Commissario. There is some evidence that the body has been disturbed. By animals. That's normal enough if it's been in the ground for any length of time. Some of the bones and organs are missing, and it seems that the others have been shifted around a good deal. And so it's difficult to say where the ring might have been when he was put into the ground.'

'Put?' Brunetti asked.

'There's reason to believe he was shot.'

'What reason?'

'There is a small hole, about two centimetres in diameter, at the base of his skull.'

'Only one hole?'

'Yes.'

'And the bullet?'

'My men were using an ordinary mesh screen when they searched the site for bones, so if it was there, something as small as bullet fragments might have fallen through.'

'Are the *Carabinieri* continuing the search?'

'I can't answer that, Commissario.'

'Will you do the autopsy?'

'Yes. This evening.'

'And the results?'

'I'm not sure what sort of results you're looking for, Commissario.'

'Age, sex, cause of death.'

'I can give you the age already: in his early twenties, and I don't think anything I find during the autopsy will either contradict that or give a closer idea of the exact age. Sex is almost certainly male, given the length of the bones in the arms and legs. And I'd guess the cause of death was the bullet.'

'Will you be able to confirm that?'

'It depends on what I find.'

'What condition was the body in?'

'Does that mean how much of it was left?'

'Yes.'

'Enough to get tissue and blood samples. Much of the body tissue was gone—animals, I told you—but some of the larger ligaments and muscles, especially those on the thigh and leg, are in good condition.'

'When will you have the results, Dottore?'

'Is there need for haste, Commissario? After all, he's been in the ground for more than a year.'

'I'm thinking of his family, Dottore, not of police business.'

'You mean the ring?'

'Yes. If it's the missing Lorenzoni boy, I think they should be told as soon as possible.'

'Commissario, I'm not in possession of enough information to be able to identify him as anyone in particular, beyond what I've already told you. Until I have the dental and medical records of the Lorenzoni boy, I can't be sure of anything except age and sex and perhaps cause of death. And how long ago it happened.'

'Do you have an estimate of that?'

'How long ago did the boy disappear?'

'About two years.'

There was a long pause. 'It's possible, then. From what I saw. But I'll still need those records to make any sort of positive identification.'

'I'll contact the family, then, and ask for them. As soon as I get them, I'll fax them to you.'

'Thank you, Commissario. For both things. I don't like having to speak to the families.'

Brunetti couldn't conceive of a person who would like it, but he said nothing to the doctor more than that he would call that evening to see if the autopsy had indeed confirmed the doctor's speculations.

When he replaced the phone, Brunetti turned to Vianello. 'You heard?'

'Enough. If you want to call the family, I'll call Belluno and see if the *Carabinieri* have found the bullet. If not, I'll tell them to get back to the field where they found him and look until they do.'

Brunetti's nod served as both assent and thanks. When Vianello was gone, Brunetti pulled out the phone book from his lower drawer and flipped it open to the 'L's. He found three listings for Lorenzoni, all at the same San Marco address: 'Ludovico, *avvocato*', 'Maurizio, *ingeniere*', and 'Cornelia', no profession listed.

His hand reached out for the phone, but instead of lifting it, he got up from his desk and went down to speak to Signorina Elettra.

When he went into the small antechamber outside the office of his superior, Vice-Questore Giuseppe Patta, the secretary was talking on the phone. Seeing him, she smiled and held up one magenta-nailed finger. He approached her desk and, while she finished her conversation, he both listened to what she said and glanced down at that day's headlines, reading them upside down, a skill that had often proven most useful. *L'Esule di Hammamet*, the headline declared, and Brunetti wondered why it was that former politicians who fled the country to avoid arrest were always 'exiles' and never 'fugitives'.

'I'll see you then at eight,' Signorina Elettra said, and added, '*Ciao, caro*,' before putting down the phone.

What young man had summoned that final, provocative laugh, and who would tonight sit across from those dark eyes? 'A new flame?' Brunetti asked before he could consider how bold a question it was.

However forward the question might have been, Signorina Elettra seemed not to mind at all. '*Magari,*' she said with tired resignation. 'If only it were. No, it's my insurance agent. I meet him once a year: he buys me a drink, and I give him a month's salary.'

Accustomed as he was to the frequent excesses of her rhetoric, Brunetti still found this surprising. 'A month's?'

'Well,' she temporized, 'very close to.'

'And what is it, if you'll permit me to ask, that you insure?'

'Not my life, certainly,' she said with a laugh, and Brunetti, when he realized how deeply he meant it, bit back the gallantry of saying that no compensation could possibly be made for such a loss. 'My apartment and the things in it, my car, and since three years ago, a private health insurance.'

'Does your sister know about that?' he asked, wondering what a doctor who worked for the national health system would think of a sister who paid not to have to use that system.

'Who do you think it was that told me to get it?' Elettra asked.

'Why?'

'I suppose because she spends so much time in the hospitals, so she knows what goes on there.' She considered this a moment and added, 'Though, from what she's told me, it's probably more a case of what doesn't go on. Last week, one of her patients was in a room at the Civile with six other women. Nobody bothered to give them any food for two days, and they could never get anyone to explain why.'

'What happened?'

'Luckily, four of them had relatives who came to visit, so they divided their food among the others. If they hadn't, they wouldn't have eaten.'

Elettra's voice had risen as she spoke; as she continued, it rose even higher. 'If you want someone to change your sheets, you've got to pay to have them do it. Or to bring a bed pan. Barbara's given up on it, so she's told me to go to a private clinic if I ever have to go to the hospital.'

'And I didn't know you had a car,' he said, always surprised to learn that someone living and working in the city had one. He'd never owned one, nor had his wife, though both of them could drive, badly.

'I keep it at my cousin's in Mestre. He uses it during the week, and I get to use it on the weekends if I want to go anywhere.'

'And the apartment?' asked Brunetti, who had never bothered to insure his own.

'I went to school with a woman who had an apartment in Campo della Guerra. Remember when they had that fire there? Her apartment was one of the ones that got burned out.'

'I thought the *comune* paid for the restoration,' Brunetti said.

'They paid for *basic* restoration,' she corrected him. 'That didn't include trifles like her clothing or possessions or new furniture.'

'Would insurance be any better?' Brunetti asked, having heard countless horror stories about the difficulty of getting money out of an insurance company, regardless of how legitimate the claim.

'I'd rather try with a private company than with the city.'

'Who wouldn't?' Brunetti asked in tired resignation.

'But what can I do for you, Commissario?' she asked, waving away their conversation and, with it, the thought of loss and pain.

'I'd like you to go down to the archives and see if you can get me the file on the Lorenzoni kidnapping,' Brunetti said, returning both loss and pain to the room.

'Roberto?'

'Did you know him?'

'No, but my boyfriend at the time had a younger brother who went to school with him. The Vivaldi, I think. It was ages ago.'

'Did he ever say anything about him?'

'I don't remember exactly, but I think he didn't like him very much.'

'Do you remember why?'

She tilted her chin up at an angle and pulled her lips into a tight moue that would have subtracted greatly from the beauty of any other woman. In Elettra's case, all it did was show him the fine line of her jaw and emphasize the redness of her pursed lips.

'No,' she finally said. 'Whatever it was, it's gone.'

Brunetti didn't know how to ask the next question. 'You said your boyfriend of the time. Are you still, er, are you still in contact with him?'

Her smile blossomed, as much at his question as at the awkwardness of his phrasing.

'I'm the godmother of his first son,' she said. 'So it would be very easy to call and ask him to ask his brother what he can remember. I'll do it this evening.' She pushed herself back from her chair. 'I'll go down and see about the file. Shall I bring it up to your office?' He was grateful she didn't ask why he wanted to see it. Superstitiously, Brunetti hoped that, by not talking about it, he could prevent its turning out to be Roberto.

'Yes, please,' he said and went back up there to wait.

# 4

A father himself, Brunetti chose to delay calling the Lorenzoni family until the autopsy was completed. From what Doctor Bortot had said and from the presence of the ring, it seemed unlikely that anything he might discover during it would exclude the possibility of its being Roberto Lorenzoni, but as long as that possibility existed, Brunetti wanted to spare the family what might be unnecessary pain.

While he waited for the original file on the crime, he tried to recall what he knew about it. Since the kidnapping had taken place in the province of Treviso, the police of that city had handled the original investigation, even though the victim was Venetian. Brunetti had been busy with another case at the time, but he remembered the diffused sense of frustration that had filled the Questura after the investigation had spread to Venice and the police tried to find the men who had kidnapped the boy.

Of all crimes, Brunetti had always found kidnapping the most horrible, not only because he had two children, but because of the dirt it did on humanity, placing an entirely arbitrary price on a life and then destroying that life when the price was not met. Or worse, as in so many cases, taking the person, accepting the money, and then never releasing the hostage. He had been present when the body of a twenty-seven-year-old woman had been retrieved; she had been kidnapped and then placed in a living tomb under a metre of earth and left there to suffocate. He still remembered her hands, grown as black as the earth above her, clutched helplessly to her face in death.

He could not be said to know anyone in the Lorenzoni family, though he and Paola had once been at a formal dinner party where Count Ludovico had also been present. As is always the case in Venice, he occasionally saw the older man on the street, but they had never spoken. The *commissario* who had handled the Venetian part of the investigation had been transferred to Milan a year ago, so Brunetti could not ask him face to face about the way things had been handled or about his impression of events. Often that sort of personal, unrecorded response proved useful, especially when a case came to be reconsidered. Brunetti accepted the possibility, since the body found in the field might prove not to be that of the Lorenzoni boy, that the case would not be reopened and the body would prove to be a matter for the Belluno police. But then how explain the ring?

Signorina Elettra was at his door before he could answer his own question. 'Please come in,' he called. 'You found it very quickly.' Such had not always been the case with the Questura files, not until her blessed arrival. 'How long have you been with us now, Signorina?' he asked.

'It will be three years this summer, Commissario. Why do you ask?'

It was on his lips to say, 'So that I might better count my joys,' but that sounded to him too much like one of her own rhetorical flights. Instead, he answered, 'So I can order flowers to celebrate the day.'

She laughed at this and they both remembered his original shock when he learned that one of her first actions upon taking the position as Vice-Questore Patta's secretary had been to order a bi-weekly delivery of flowers, often quite spectacular flowers, and never fewer than a dozen. Patta, who was concerned only that his expense allotment from the city extend to his frequent lunches—usually quite as spectacular as the flowers—never thought to question the expense, and so her antechamber had become a source of pleasure to the entire Questura. It was impossible to tell if the staff's delight resulted from what Signorina Elettra decided to wear that day, the flowers in the small room, or from the fact that the government was paying for them. Brunetti, who took equal delight in all three, found a line, he thought from Petrarch, running through his memory, where the poet blessed the month, the day, and the hour when he first saw his Laura. Saying nothing about any of this, he took the file and placed it on the desk in front of him.

He opened the file when she left and began to read. Brunetti had remembered only that it happened in the autumn; September 28th, sometime before midnight on a Tuesday. Roberto's girlfriend had stopped her car (there followed the year, make, and licence number) in front of the gates of the Lorenzoni family villa, rolled down the window, and punched the numerical code into the digital lock that controlled them. When the gates failed to open, Roberto got out of the car and walked over to see what was wrong. A large stone lay just inside the gates, and its weight prevented them from opening.

Roberto, the girl said in the original police report, bent to try to move the rock, and when he was stooped down, two men emerged from the bushes beside him. One put a pistol to the boy's head, while the other came and stood just outside her window, pointing his pistol at her. Both wore ski masks.

She said that, at first, she thought it was a robbery, and so she put her hands in her lap and tried to remove the emerald ring she was wearing, hoping to drop it to the floor of the car, safe from the thieves. The car radio was playing, so she couldn't hear what the men said, but she told the police she realized it wasn't a robbery when she saw Roberto turn and walk into the bushes in front of the first man.

The second man remained where he was, outside her window, pointing his gun at her but making no attempt to speak to her for another few moments, and then he backed into the bushes and disappeared.

The first thing she did was to lock the door of the car. She reached between the seats of the car for her *telefonino,* but its batteries had run down, and it was useless. She waited to see if Roberto would come back. When he didn't—she didn't know how long she waited—she backed away from the gate, turned, and drove towards Treviso until she came to a phone booth at the side of the highway. She dialled 113 and reported what had happened. Even then, she said, it didn't occur to her that it could be a kidnapping; she had even thought it might be a joke of some sort.

Brunetti read through the rest of the report, looking to see if the officer who spoke to her had asked why she would think such a thing could be a joke, but the question didn't appear. Brunetti opened a drawer and looked for a piece of paper; finding none, he leaned down and pulled an envelope from his wastepaper basket, turned it over and made a note on the back, then went back to the report.

The police contacted the family, knowing no more than that the boy had been taken away at gunpoint. Count Ludovico arrived at the villa at four that morning, driven there by his nephew, Maurizio. The police were, by then, treating it as a probable kidnapping, so the mechanism to block all the family funds had been put into motion. This could be done only with those funds in the country, and the family still had access to their holdings in foreign banks. Knowing this, the *commissario* from the Treviso police who was heading the investigation attempted to impress upon Count Ludovico the futility of giving in to ransom demands. Only by blocking any attempt to give the kidnappers what they demanded could they be dissuaded from future crimes. Most times, he told the Count, the person was never returned, often never found.

Count Ludovico insisted that there was no reason to believe that this was a kidnapping. It could be a robbery, a prank, a case of mistaken identity. Brunetti was well familiar with the need to deny the horrible and had often dealt with people who could not be made to believe that a member of their family was endangered or, often, dead. So the Count's insistence that it was not, could not be, a kidnapping was entirely understandable. But Brunetti wondered, again, at the suggestion that it could be some sort of prank. What sort of young man was Roberto that the people who knew him best would assume this?

That it was not was proven two days later, when the first note arrived. Sent express from the central post office in Venice, probably dropped into one of the slots outside the building, it demanded seven billion lire, though it did not say how the payment was to be arranged.

By then the story was splashed all over the front pages of the national newspapers, so there could have been no doubt on the kidnappers' part that the police were involved. The second note, sent from Mestre a day later, dropped the ransom to five billion and said that the information about how and when to pay it would be phoned to a friend of the family, though no one was named. It was upon receipt of this note that Count Ludovico made his televised appeal to the kidnappers to release his son. The text of the message was attached to the report. He explained that there was no way he could raise the money, all of his assets having been frozen. He did say that, if the kidnappers would still contact the person they intended calling and tell him what to do, he would gladly exchange places with his son: he would obey any command they gave. Brunetti made a note on the envelope, telling himself to see if he could get a tape of the Count's appearance.

Appended was a list of the names and addresses of everyone questioned in connection with the case, the reason the police had questioned them, and their relationship to the Lorenzonis. Separate pages held transcripts or summaries of these conversations.

Brunetti let his eye run down the list. He recognized the names of at least a half dozen known criminals, but he was unable to see any common thread connecting them. One was a burglar, another a car thief, and a third, Brunetti knew, having put him there, was in prison for bank robbery. Perhaps these were some of the people the Treviso police used as informers. All led nowhere.

Some other names he recognized, not because of their criminality, but because of their social position. There was the parish priest of the Lorenzoni family, the director of the bank where most of their funds were held, and the names of the family lawyer and notary.

Doggedly, he read through every word in the file; he studied the block printing on the plastic-covered ransom notes and the lab report that accompanied them, saying that there were no fingerprints and that the paper was too widely sold to be traceable; he examined the photos of the opened gate to the villa taken both from a distance and close up. This last included a photo of the rock that had blocked the gate. Brunetti saw that it was so large that it could not have fitted through the bars of the gate: whoever had put it there would have to have done so from inside. Brunetti made another note.

The last papers contained in the file had to do with the finances of the Lorenzonis and included a list of their holdings in Italy, as well as others they were known to possess in foreign countries. The Italian companies were more or less familiar to Brunetti, as they were to every Italian. To say 'steel' or 'cotton' was pretty much to pronounce the family name. The foreign holdings were more diverse: the Lorenzonis owned a Turkish trucking company, beet processing plants in Poland, a chain of luxury beach hotels in the Crimea, and a cement factory in the Ukraine. Like so many businesses in Western Europe, the interests of the Lorenzoni family were expanding beyond the confines of the continent, many of them following the path of victorious capitalism towards the East.

It took him more than an hour to read through the file, and when he finished, he took it down to Signorina Elettra's office. 'Could you make me a copy of everything here?' he asked as he placed it on her desk.

'The photos, too?'

'Yes, if you can.'

'Has he been found, the Lorenzoni boy?'

'Someone has,' Brunetti answered but then, conscious of this minor evasion, added, 'It's probably him.'

She pulled in her lips and raised her eyebrows, then shook her head and said, 'Poor boy. Poor parents.' Neither of them said anything for a moment, and then she asked, 'Did you see him when he appeared on television, the Count?'

'No, I didn't.' He couldn't remember why, but he knew he hadn't seen it.

'He was wearing full make-up, the way the newscasters do. I know about that sort of thing. I remember thinking at the time that it was a strange thing for a man to be made to do especially in those circumstances.'

'How did he seem to you?' Brunetti asked.

She thought about this for a moment and then answered, 'He seemed without hope, absolutely certain that, whatever he begged or pleaded, it wasn't going to be given to him.'

'Despair?' Brunetti asked.

'You'd think that, wouldn't you?' She looked away from him and paused again. Finally she answered, 'No, not despair. A sort of tired resignation, as if he knew what was going to happen and knew he couldn't do anything to stop it.' She looked back at Brunetti and gave a combination smile and shrug. 'I'm sorry I can't explain it better than that. Perhaps if you looked at it yourself, you'd see what I mean.'

'How could I get a copy?' he asked.

'I suppose RAI must have it in their files. I'll call someone I know in Rome and see if I can get a copy.'

'Someone you know?' Brunetti sometimes wondered if there were a man in Italy between the ages of twenty-one and fifty that Signorina Elettra didn't know.

'Well, really someone Barbara knows, an old boyfriend of hers. He works in the news department in RAI. They graduated together.'

'Then he's a doctor?'

'Well, he has a degree in medicine, though I don't think he's ever practised. His father works for RAI, so he was offered a job as soon as he got out of university. Because they can say he's a doctor, they use him to answer medical questions that come up—you know the sort of thing they do: when they have a programme about dieting or sunburn and they want to be sure that what they tell people is true, they set Cesare to doing the research. Sometimes he even gets interviewed, Dottor Cesare Bellini, and he tells people what the latest medical wisdom is.'

'How many years did he spend in medical school?'

'Seven, I think, just like Barbara.'

'To be interviewed about sunburn?'

Again the smile appeared, just as quickly to be shrugged away. 'There are too many doctors already; he was lucky to get the job. And he likes living in Rome.'

'Well, then, call him if you would.'

'Certainly, Dottore, and I'll bring you the copies of the report as soon as I make them.'

He saw that there was still something she wanted to say. 'Yes?'

'If you are going to reopen the investigation, would you like me to make a copy for the Vice-Questore?'

'It's a bit early to say we're going to reopen the investigation, so a single copy for me would suffice,' Brunetti said in his most oblique voice.

'Yes, Dottore,' came Signorina Elettra's non-committal answer, 'and I'll see that the originals get back into the file.'

'Good. Thank you.'

'Then I'll call Cesare.'

'Thank you, Signorina,' Brunetti said and went back up to his office, thinking of a country that had too many doctors but where it grew more difficult year by year to find a carpenter or a shoemaker.

# 5

Though the man in Treviso who had headed the Lorenzoni kidnapping was unknown to Brunetti, he well remembered Gianpiero Lama, who had been in charge of that part of the investigation handled by the Venice police. Lama, a Roman who had come to Venice heralded by the successful arrest and subsequent conviction of a Mafia killer, had worked in the city for only two years before being promoted to the position of Vice-Questore and sent to Milan, where Brunetti believed him still to be.

He and Brunetti had worked together, but neither of them had much enjoyed the experience. Lama had found his colleague too timid in the pursuit of crime and criminals, unwilling to take the kind of risks which Lama believed necessary. Since Lama had also thought it perfectly acceptable that the law sometimes be ignored, or even bent, in order to effect an arrest, it was not uncommon that the people he arrested were later released on some technicality discovered by the *magistratura*. But as this usually happened some time after Lama's original handling of the case, his behaviour was seldom viewed as the cause of the subsequent dismissal of the charges or the overturning of a conviction. The perceived audacity of Lama's behaviour had ignited his career, and like a flaring rocket he rose higher and ever higher, each promotion preparing the way for the next.

Brunetti recalled that it was Lama who had interviewed the Lorenzoni boy's girlfriend, he who had failed to follow up either her or the father's suggestion that the kidnapping could have been a joke. Or if he had questioned them about it, Lama had failed to make any mention of it in his report.

Brunetti pulled the envelope towards him and began another list, this time of those people who might help him learn more, if not about the actual kidnapping, then about the Lorenzoni family. At the top of the list he automatically put the name of his father-in-law, Count Orazio Falier. If anyone in the city would be sensitive to the delicate spider's web where nobility, business, and enormous wealth were interwoven, it was Count Orazio.

Signorina Elettra's entrance distracted him momentarily from the list. 'I called Cesare,' she said as she placed a folder on his desk. 'He took a look in his computer and found the date, so he says he'll have no trouble in getting a copy of the tape. He'll send it up by courier this afternoon.' Even before he could ask how she did it, Signorina Elettra answered. 'It has nothing to do with me, Dottore. He said he's coming to Venice next month, and I think he wants to use his having spoken to me as an excuse to get in touch with Barbara again.'

'And the courier?' Brunetti asked.

'He said he'll put it down against the report RAI's doing on the airport road,' she said, reminding Brunetti of one of the most recent scandals. Billions had been paid to friends of the government officials who had arranged the planning and construction of the useless *autostrada* out to Venice's tiny airport. Some of them had subsequently been convicted of fraud, but the case was now caught up in the endless appeal process, while the ex-Minister who had made a fortune by masterminding the whole thing continued not only to receive his state pension, rumoured to be in excess of ten million lire a month, but was said to be off in Hong Kong, amassing yet another fortune.

He pulled himself back from this reverie and looked up at Signorina Elettra. 'Please thank him for me,' Brunetti finally said.

'Oh, no, Dottore, I think we should let him think we're the ones doing him a favour, giving him an excuse to get in touch with Barbara again. I even told him I'd say something to her about it, so he'd have an excuse to call her.'

'And why is that?' Brunetti asked.

She seemed surprised that Brunetti would not have seen it. 'In case we need him again. You never know, do you, when we might want to make use of a television network?' Remembering the last shambles of an election, when the owner of three of the largest television networks had used them shamelessly to advance his campaign, he waited for her comment. 'I think it's time the police, rather than the others, made use of them.'

Brunetti, always wary of political discussions, thought it best to demur, and so pulled the copy of the file towards him and thanked her as she left.

The phone rang before Brunetti could do anything more than think about making calls. When he answered it, he heard the familiar voice of his brother.

'*Ciao*, Guido, *come stai*?'

'*Bene*,' Brunetti answered, wondering why Sergio would call him at the Questura. His mind, and then his heart, fled to his mother. 'What's wrong, Sergio?'

'Nothing, nothing at all. It's not about *Mamma* that I'm calling.' As it had managed to do since their childhood, Sergio's voice calmed him, assured him that all was well or soon would be. 'Well, not about her directly.'

Brunetti said nothing.

'Guido, I know you've gone to see *Mamma* the last two weekends. No, don't even say anything. I'm going on Sunday. But I want to ask you if you'd go the next two.'

'Of course,' Brunetti said.

Sergio went on as though he hadn't heard. 'It's important, Guido. I wouldn't ask unless it were.'

'I know that, Sergio. I'll go.' Having said that, Brunetti felt embarrassed to ask the reason.

Sergio continued. 'I got a letter today. Three weeks to get a letter here from Rome. *Puttana Eva,* I would *walk* here from Rome in less time than that. They had the fax number of the laboratory, but did they think to send a fax? No, the idiots sent it through the mails.'

From long experience, Brunetti knew that Sergio had to be headed off once he got on to the subject of any of the state's variously incompetent services. 'What was in the letter, Sergio?'

'The invitation, of course. That's why I'm calling you.'

'For the conference on Chernobyl?'

'Yes, they've asked us to read our paper. Well, Battestini will read it, since his name is on it, but he's asked me to explain my part of the research and to help answer questions afterwards. I didn't know until I got the invitation that we'd go. That's why I didn't call you until now, Guido.'

Sergio, a researcher in a medical radiology lab, had been talking about this conference, it seemed, for years, though it was really no more than months. The damages wrought by the incompetencies of yet another state system could now no longer be hidden, and this had given rise to endless conferences on the effects of the explosion and subsequent fall-out, this latest one to be held in Rome next week. No one, Brunetti thought in his more cynical moments, dared to suggest that no further nuclear reactors be built or tests performed—here he silently cursed the French—but all rushed to the endless conferences to engage in collective hand-wringing and the exchange of terrible information.

'I'm glad you're getting the chance to go, Sergio. Congratulations. Can Maria Grazia go with you?'

'I don't know yet. She's almost finished with the place on the Giudecca, but someone's asked her to make plans and give an estimate for a complete restoration in a four-floor *palazzo* over in the Ghetto, and if she doesn't get them done by then, I doubt she'll be able to come.'

'She trusts you to go to Rome by yourself?' Brunetti asked, knowing, even as he asked it, how foolish the question was. Similar in many things, *i fratelli* Brunetti shared a common uxoriousness which was often a source of humour among their friends.

'If she gets the contract, I could go to the moon by myself, and she wouldn't even notice.'

'What's your paper about?' Brunetti asked, knowing he was unlikely to understand the answer.

'Oh, it's technical stuff, about fluctuations in red and white blood cell counts during the first weeks after exposure to fall-out or intense radiation. There are some people in Auckland we've been in touch with who are working on the same thing, and it seems that their results are identical to ours. That's one of the reasons I wanted to go to the conference—Battestini would have gone anyway, but this way someone else pays for us, and we get to see them and talk to them and compare results.'

'Good, I'm happy for you. How long will you be gone?'

'The conference lasts six days, from Sunday until Friday, and then I might stay on in Rome for two days more and not get back until Monday. Wait a minute; let me give you the dates.' Brunetti heard the flipping of pages, and then Sergio's voice was back. 'From the eighth until the sixteenth. I should be back the morning of the sixteenth. And, Guido, I'll go the next two Sundays.'

'Don't be silly, Sergio. These things happen. I'll go while you're away, and then you go the Sunday after you get back, and I'll go the next one. You've done the same for me.'

'I just don't want you to think I don't want to go and see her, Guido.'

'Let's not talk about that, all right, Sergio?' Brunetti asked, surprised how painful he still found the thought of his mother. He had tried for the last year, with singular lack of success, to tell himself that his mother, that bright-spirited woman who had raised them and loved them with unqualified devotion, had moved off to some other place, where she waited, still quick-witted and eager to smile, for that befuddled shell that was her body to come and join her so that they could drift off together to a final peace.

'I don't like asking you, Guido,' his brother repeated, reminding Brunetti as he did of how careful Sergio had always been not to abuse his position as elder brother or the authority that position invested him with.

Brunetti recalled a term his American colleagues were in the habit of using, and he 'stonewalled' his brother. 'Tell me about the kids, Sergio.'

Sergio laughed outright at the way they'd fallen into the familiar pattern: his need to justify everything; his younger brother's refusal to find that necessary. 'Marco's almost finished with his military service; he'll be home for four days at the end of the month. And Maria Luisa's speaking nothing but English so she'll be ready to go to the Courtauld in the autumn. Crazy, isn't it, Guido, that she's got to go to England to study restoration?'

Paola, Brunetti's wife, taught English Literature at the University of Cà Foscari. There was little his brother could tell him about the insanity of the Italian university system that Brunetti did not already know.

'Is her English good enough?' he asked.

'Better be, huh? If it isn't, I'll send her to you and Paola for the summer.'

'And what are we supposed to do, speak English all the time?'

'Yes.'

'Sorry, Sergio, we never use it unless we don't want the kids to know what we're saying. Both of them have taken so much of it in school that we can't even do that anymore.'

'Try Latin,' Sergio said with a laugh. 'You were always good at that.'

'I'm afraid that was a long time ago,' said Brunetti sadly.

Sergio, ever sensitive to things he couldn't name, caught his brother's mood. 'I'll call you before I leave, Guido.'

'Good, *stammi bene,*' Brunetti said.

'*Ciao,*' Sergio answered and was gone.

During his life, Brunetti had often heard people begin sentences with, 'If it weren't for him . . .' and he could not hear the words without substituting Sergio's name. When Brunetti, always the acknowledged scholar of the family, was eighteen, it was decided that there was not enough money to allow him to go to university and delay the time when he could begin to contribute to the family's income. He yearned to study the way some of his friends yearned for women, but he assented to this family decision and began to look for work. It was Sergio, newly engaged and newly employed in a medical laboratory as a technician, who agreed to contribute more to the family if it would mean that his younger brother would be allowed to study. Even then, Brunetti knew that it was the law he wanted to study, less its current application than its history and the reasons why it developed the way it had.

Because there was no faculty of law at Cà Foscari, it meant that Brunetti would have to study at Padova, the cost of his commuting adding to the responsibility Sergio agreed to assume. Sergio's marriage was delayed for three years, during which time Brunetti quickly rose to the top of his class and began to earn some money by tutoring students younger than himself.

Had he not studied, Brunetti would not have met Paola in the university library, and he would not have become a policeman. He sometimes wondered if he would have become the same man, if the things inside of him that he considered vital would have developed in the same way, had he, perhaps, become an insurance salesman or a city bureaucrat. Knowing idle speculation when he saw it, Brunetti reached for the phone and pulled it towards him.

# 6

Just as Brunetti had always thought it vulgar to ask Paola how many rooms there were in her family's *palazzo* and hence remained ignorant of that number, so too had he no idea of the exact number of phone lines going into Palazzo Falier. He knew three of the numbers: the more or less public one that was given out to all friends and business associates; the one given only to members of the family; and the Count's private number, which he had never found it necessary to use.

He called the first, as this was hardly an emergency or a matter of great privacy.

'Palazzo Falier,' a male voice Brunetti had never heard responded on the third ring.

'Good morning. This is Guido Brunetti. I'd like to speak to . . .' here he paused for an instant, uncertain whether to call the Count by his title or to refer to him as his father-in-law.

'He's on the other line, Dottor Brunetti. May I have him call you in . . .' It was the other man's turn to pause. 'The light's just gone out. I'll connect you.'

There followed a soft click, after which Brunetti heard the deep baritone of his father-in-law's voice, 'Falier.' Nothing more.

'Good morning. It's Guido.'

The voice, as it had done of late, softened. 'Ah, Guido, how are you? And how are the children?'

'We're all well. And both of you?' He couldn't call her 'Donatella', and he wouldn't call her 'the Countess'.

'Both well, thank you. What is it I can do for you?' The Count knew there could be no other reason for Brunetti's call.

'I'd like to know whatever you can tell me about the Lorenzoni family.'

During the ensuing silence, Brunetti could all but hear the Count sorting through the decades of information, scandal, and rumour which he possessed about most of the notables of the city. 'Why is it you're interested in them, Guido?' the Count asked, and then added, 'If you're at liberty to tell me.'

'The body of a young man's been dug up near Belluno. There was a ring in the grave with him. It has the Lorenzoni crest.'

'It could be the person who stole it from him,' the Count volunteered.

'It could pretty well be anyone,' Brunetti agreed. 'But I've been looking through the file of the original investigation of the kidnapping, and there are a few things I'd like to clear up if I could.'

'Such as?' the Count asked.

In the more than two decades that Brunetti had known the Count, he had never known him to be indiscreet; further, nothing Brunetti had to say could not be told to anyone interested in the investigation. 'Two people said they thought it was a joke. And the stone that was blocking the gate had to have been placed there from inside.'

'I don't have a very clear memory of it, Guido. I think we were out of the country when it happened. It happened at their villa, didn't it?'

'Yes,' Brunetti answered, and then from something in the Count's voice, asked, 'Have you been there?'

'Once or twice.' The Count's tone was absolutely non-committal.

'Then you know the gates,' Brunetti said, not wanting to ask directly about the Count's familiarity with the Lorenzonis. Not yet, at any rate.

'Yes,' the Count answered. 'They open inward. There's a call box on the wall, and all a visitor has to do is push the bell and then announce himself. The gates can be opened from the house.'

'Or from the outside if you have the code,' Brunetti added. 'That's what his girlfriend tried to do, but the gates wouldn't open.'

'The Valloni girl, wasn't it?' the Count asked.

The name was familiar from the report. 'Yes. Francesca.'

'A pretty girl. We went to her wedding.'

'Wedding?' Brunetti asked. 'How long ago was that?'

'A little more than a year ago. She married that Salviati boy. Enrico, Fulvio's son; the one who likes speedboats.'

Brunetti grunted in acknowledgement of a vague memory he had of the boy. 'Did you know Roberto?'

'I met him a few times. I didn't think very much of him.'

Brunetti wondered if it was the Count's social position that allowed him to speak ill of the dead, or the fact that the boy had been gone for two years. 'Why not?'

'Because he had all the pride of his father and none of his talent.'

'What sort of talent does Count Ludovico have?'

He heard a noise from the other end of the phone, as though a door had closed, and then the Count said, 'Excuse me a moment, Guido.' A few seconds passed, after which he returned to the phone and said, 'I'm sorry, Guido, but a fax has just come in, and I'm afraid I have to make some calls while my agent in Mexico City is still in the office.'

Brunetti wasn't sure, but he thought Mexico City was

about half a day behind them. 'Isn't it the middle of the night there?'

'Yes. He's paid to be there, and I want to get him before he leaves.'

'Oh, I see,' Brunetti said. 'When may I call you again?'

The Count's answer came quickly. 'Is there any chance we could meet for lunch, Guido? There are some things I've been wanting to talk to you about. Perhaps we could do both.'

'Gladly. When?'

'Today. Is that too soon?'

'No, not at all. I'll call Paola and tell her. Would you like her to come?'

'No,' the Count said, almost sharply, and then added, 'Some of the things I want to discuss concern her, so I'd prefer she not be there.'

Confused, Brunetti said only, 'All right. Where shall we meet?' expecting the Count to name one of the famous restaurants in the city.

'There's a place over near Campo del Ghetto. The daughter of a friend of mine and her husband run it, and the food's very good. If it's not too far for you, we could meet there.'

'Fine. What's it called?'

'La Bussola. It's just off San Leonardo, heading towards Campo del Ghetto Nuovo. One o'clock?'

'That'll be fine. I'll see you there. At one.' Brunetti hung up and pulled the phone book back towards him. He flipped through it until he came to the 'S's. He found a number of Salviatis, but only one Enrico, listed as a 'consulente', a term that always amused Brunetti as much as it confused him.

The phone rang six times before a woman's voice, already annoyed at the caller, answered, 'Pronto.'

'Signora Salviati?' Brunetti asked.

The woman was panting, as though she'd run to answer the phone. 'Yes, what is it?'

'Signora Salviati, this is Commissario Guido Brunetti. I'd like to ask you a few questions about the Lorenzoni kidnapping.' From beyond her, he heard the high wailing of a baby's scream, that genetically pitched howl no human can ignore.

He heard the phone slam down on a hard surface, thought he heard her tell him to wait, and then all sound was swallowed up in the wail, which rose up to a sudden squeal and, as suddenly as it had started, stopped.

She was back at the phone again. 'I told you everything about that years ago. I don't even remember it very clearly now. So much time has passed, so much has happened.'

'I realize that, Signora, but it would be a great help to us if you could spare me a little time. I guarantee it wouldn't take long at all.'

'Then why can't we do it on the phone?'

'I'd prefer to do it in person, Signora. I'm afraid I don't like the phone very much.'

'When?' she asked in sudden concession.

'I saw that your address is in Santa Croce. I've got to be over there this morning'—he didn't, but it was close to the *traghetto* at San Marcuola and so he could quickly get to San Leonardo and lunch with the Count—'so it would be very easy for me to stop by. If that's convenient with you, of course.'

'Let me look at my schedule,' she said, putting the phone down again.

She had been seventeen when the kidnapping happened, so she was not even twenty now, and with what sounded like a very young baby. Schedule?

'If you came at quarter to twelve, we could talk. But I've got an engagement for lunch.'

45

'That's perfect for me, Signora. I'll see you then; he said quickly and hung up before she could change her mind or check her schedule again.

He called Paola and told her that he couldn't come home for lunch. As usual, she accepted this with such equanimity that Brunetti wondered for an instant if she had already made other plans. 'What will you do?' he asked.

'Hmm?' she asked. 'Oh, read.'

'And the children? What about them?'

'I'll feed them, Guido, don't worry. You know how they wolf their food down if the two of us aren't there to exert a civilizing influence on them, so I'll have plenty of time to myself.'

'Will you eat, too?' he asked.

'Guido, you're obsessed with food. You do know that, don't you?'

'Only because of the frequency with which you remind me of it, my treasure,' he said with a laugh. He thought of telling her she was obsessed with reading, but Paola would just take that as a compliment, so he told her he'd be home for supper and hung up.

He left the Questura without bothering to tell anyone where he was going and was careful to take the back steps and so avoid Vice-Questore Patta, who, given the fact that it was after eleven, might safely be assumed to be in his office.

Outside, Brunetti, who was wearing both a woollen suit and a light coat in response to the early morning chill, was surprised at how warm it had become. He started along the embankment and was just turning left into the trail of streets that would take him out to Campo Santa Maria Formosa and, from there, to the Rialto, when he suddenly stopped and took off his coat. He turned and went back towards the Questura. When he got to the building the guards inside recognized him and pressed the switch that opened the large glass doors. He went into the small office on the right and saw Pucetti at the desk, talking on the phone. Seeing his superior, Pucetti said something and hung up, then quickly got to his feet.

'Pucetti,' Brunetti said, making a pushing gesture with one hand to force the young man to sit down again. 'I'd like to leave this here for a few hours. I'll pick it up when I get back.'

Pucetti, instead of resuming his seat, came forward and took the coat from his hands. 'I'll put it up in your office, if I might, Dottore.'

'No, it's fine here. Don't bother.'

'I'd rather, sir. We've had a number of things disappear down here during the last few weeks.'

'What?' Brunetti asked with real surprise. 'From the guard room of the Questura?'

'It's them, sir,' Pucetti said, nodding in the direction of the interminable line that stretched back from the door of the Ufficio Stranieri, on which it seemed like hundreds of people waited to fill out the forms that would legalize their residence in the city. 'We're getting a lot of Albanians and Slavs, and you know what thieves they are.'

Had Pucetti said such a thing to Paola, she would have been all over him in an instant, calling him a bigot and a racist, and pointing out that *all* Albanians and *all* Slavs weren't anything. But as she wasn't there and as Brunetti, in general, tended to agree with Pucetti's sentiments, he did nothing more than thank the young man and leave the building.

# 7

As he was leaving Campo Santa Maria Formosa, Brunetti suddenly remembered something he had seen last autumn in Campo Santa Marina, so he cut through to the smaller *campo* and turned right just as he entered it. The metal cages were already hung outside the windows of the pet shop. Brunetti drew closer to see if the *merlo indiana* was still there. Surely that was it, up in the top cage, feathers black and gleaming, one jet eye turned towards him.

Brunetti approached the cage, leaned forward, and said, '*Ciao.*' Nothing. Undaunted, he repeated, '*Ciao,*' careful to draw the word out to two syllables. The bird hopped nervously from one parallel bar to the other, turned, and regarded Brunetti with the other eye. He glanced around and noticed that a white-haired woman had stopped in front of the *edicola* in the middle of the *campo* and was giving him a very strange look. He ignored her and turned his attention back to the bird. '*Ciao,*' he said again.

It suddenly occurred to Brunetti that this might be a different bird; after all, one medium-sized mynah bird looked pretty much like any other. He tried once more, '*Ciao.*' Silence. Disappointed, he turned away, smiling weakly at the woman, who stood still, staring across the *campo* at him.

Brunetti had gone only two steps when, from behind him, he heard his own voice call out, '*Ciao,*' the last vowel much prolonged, in the manner of birds.

He turned around immediately and went back to his place in front of the cage. '*Come ti stai?*' he asked this time, paused a moment, then put the question again. He felt, rather than saw, a presence beside him and turned to see the white-haired woman standing there. He smiled, and she smiled back. '*Come ti stai?*' he asked the bird again, and with absolute vocal fidelity, it asked him right back,' *Come ti stai?*' in a voice eerily like his own.

'What else can he say?' the woman asked.

'I don't know, Signora. That's all I've ever heard it say.'

'Wonderful, isn't it?' she asked, and when he looked at her smile of simple delight, he saw that the years had dropped away from her.

'Yes, wonderful,' he said, and left her there in front of the store, saying '*Ciao, ciao, ciao*', to the bird.

He cut through to Santi Apostoli and up Strada Nuova as far as San Marcuola, where he took the *traghetto* across the Grand Canal. The reflection from the water was so intense that Brunetti wished he had his sunglasses, but who, that foggy, damp morning of early spring, would have thought such splendour had been in store for the city?

On the other side, he cut to the right, then to the left, and then back to the right, following unconscious instructions that were programmed into him during decades of walking the city streets to visit friends, take girls home, get a coffee, or to do any of those thousand things a young man did without any conscious thought of destination or route. Soon he came out in Campo San Zan Degola. To the best of Brunetti's knowledge, no one knew whether it was the decapitated body of San Giovanni or his missing head which was venerated in the church. It seemed to him to make little difference.

The Salviati she had married was the son of Fulvio, the notary, so Brunetti knew the house had to be down the second *calle* on the right, third house on the left. And so it proved: the number was the same as the one in the phone book, though three different Salviatis lived here. The bottom bell had the initial E, and so Brunetti rang it, wondering if they got to move to the higher floors of the building as the older members of the family died and left the apartments vacant.

The door snapped open and he went in. In front of him was a narrow walkway, leading across a courtyard to a flight of steps. Cheerful-looking tulips lined the walkway on both sides, and a brave magnolia was just coming into blossom in the centre of the grass to the left of the path.

He walked up the steps and, as he reached the door at the top, he heard the lock release. On the other side were more steps, these leading to a landing on which stood two doors.

At the top, the door on the left opened and a young woman came out to the landing. 'Are you the policeman?' she asked. 'I've forgotten your name.'

'Brunetti,' he said as he walked up the remaining steps towards her. She stood in front of the door, no expression whatsoever on what would otherwise have been a very pretty face. If the baby was indeed hers, and if it was as young as his information suggested, then she had lost no time in getting back her trim young body, which was dressed in a tight red skirt and an even tighter black sweater. Her bland face was surrounded by a cloud of curly black hair that fell to her shoulders, and she looked at him with surprising lack of interest.

When he reached the top of the steps, he said, 'Thank you for agreeing to talk to me, Signora.'

She didn't bother to answer this or to acknowledge that he had spoken, but turned to lead him back into the apartment, ignoring his muttered, '*Permesso.*'

'We can go in here,' she said over her shoulder, leading him into a large living room on the left. On the walls Brunetti saw etchings depicting scenes of such violence that they had to be Goyas. Three windows looked down on an enclosed space which he assumed was the narrow courtyard he had come through; the enclosing wall was uncomfortably close. She sat down in the centre of a low sofa and crossed her legs, exposing more thigh than Brunetti was accustomed to see displayed by young mothers. Waving to a chair that stood opposite her, she asked, 'What is it you'd like to know?'

Brunetti tried to assess the emotion that was emanating from her and knew that his instincts sought nervousness. But he found nothing other than irritation.

'I'd like you to tell me how long you knew Roberto Lorenzoni.'

She pushed at a lock of hair with the back of her hand, probably unconscious of how impatient the gesture made her seem. 'I told all that to the other policeman.'

'I know that, Signora. I've read the report, but I'd like you to tell me in your own words.'

'I'd like to think it's my own words that are in the report,' she said curtly.

'I'm sure they are. But I'd like to hear for myself what you have to say about him. It might give me a better understanding of what sort of man he was.'

'Have you found the people who took him?' she asked with the first sign of real curiosity she had displayed since he arrived.

'No.'

She seemed disappointed at this but said nothing.

'Could you tell me how long you knew him?'

'I went out with him for a year or so. Before it happened, that is.'

'And what sort of person was he?'

'What do you mean, "What sort of person was he?" He was someone I went to school with. We had things in common, liked to do the same things. He made me laugh.'

'Is that why you thought it might be a joke, the kidnapping?'

'Why I what?' she asked with real confusion.

'It says in the original report,' Brunetti explained, 'that you first thought it might be a joke. When it happened, that is.'

She looked away from Brunetti, as if listening to music played so softly in another room that only she could hear it. 'I said that?'

Brunetti nodded.

After a long pause, she said, 'Well, I suppose I could have. Roberto had some very strange friends.'

'What sort of friends?'

'Oh, you know, students from the university.'

'I'm not sure I understand why they would be strange,' Brunetti said.

'Well, none of them worked, but they all had a lot of money.' As if she knew how weak this sounded, she continued, 'No, that's not it. They said strange things, about how they could do anything they wanted to in life or with their lives. Things like that. The sort of things students say.' Seeing the look of polite expectation on Brunetti's face, she added, 'And they were very interested in fear.'

'Fear?'

'Yes, they read those horror books, and they were always going to see movies that had lots of violence and things like that in them.'

Brunetti nodded and made a non-committal noise.

'In fact, that was one of the reasons I had pretty much decided to stop seeing Roberto. But then it happened, and

I didn't have to tell him.' Was that relief he heard in her voice?

The door opened, and a middle-aged woman came into the room, carrying a baby which had its mouth open, poised to scream. When she saw Brunetti, the woman stopped, and sensing her motion, the baby closed its mouth and turned to look at the source of the woman's surprise.

Brunetti stood.

'This is the policeman, *Mamma*,' the young woman said, paying no attention at all to the baby, and then asked, 'Did you want something?'

'No, no, Francesca. But it's time for the feeding.'

'It'll have to wait, won't it?' the girl answered as though the idea gave her some satisfaction. She looked at Brunetti and then back at the woman she called *Mamma*. 'Not unless you want the policeman to watch me nurse.'

The woman made an inarticulate noise and grabbed the baby more tightly. It—Brunetti could never tell if the tiny ones were boys or girls—continued to stare at him and then turned towards its grandmother and gave a bubbling laugh.

'I suppose we can wait ten minutes,' the older woman said and turned and left the room, the baby's laugh following behind her like the wake of a ship.

'Your mother?' Brunetti asked, though he was doubtful about this.

'My husband's,' she answered curtly. 'What else do you want to know about Roberto?'

'Did you, at the time, think that some of his friends might have engineered this?'

Before she answered, she brushed again at her hair. 'Will you tell me why you want to know?' she asked. The tone of her question took years from her previous manner and reminded Brunetti that she couldn't yet be twenty.

'Will that help you answer the question?' he asked.

'I don't know. But I still know a lot of these people, and I don't want to say anything that might . . .' She allowed her sentence to trail off, leaving Brunetti to wonder what sort of answer she might give.

'We've found what might be his body,' he said and offered no further explanation.

'Then it couldn't have been a joke,' she said instantly.

Brunetti smiled and nodded in what he wanted her to believe was agreement, not bothering to tell her how often he had witnessed the violent consequences of what had begun as nothing more than a joke.

She looked down at the cuticle of her right forefinger and began to pick at it with the fingers of her left. 'Roberto always said he thought his father loved his cousin, Maurizio, more than he did him. So he did things that would force his father to pay attention to him.'

'Such as?'

'Oh, getting in trouble at school, being rude to the teachers, little things. But once he had some friends hot-wire his car and steal it. He had them do it when he was parked in front of one of his father's offices in Mestre and he was inside, talking to his father: that way, his father couldn't think he'd left the keys in it or lent it to someone.'

'What happened?'

'Oh, they drove it to Verona and left it in a parking garage there, then took the train back. It wasn't found for months, and when it was, the insurance had to be paid back, and the parking fees had to be paid.'

'How is it that you know about this, Signora?'

She started to answer, paused, and then said, 'Roberto told me about it.'

Brunetti resisted the impulse to ask when he had told her. His next question was more important.

'Are these the same friends who might have played a joke like this?'

'Like what?'

'A false kidnapping?'

She looked down at her finger again. 'I didn't say that. And if you've found his body, then there's no question of that, is there? That it was a joke?'

Brunetti left that alone for a moment and asked, instead, 'Could you give me their names?'

'Why?'

'I'd like to talk to them.'

For a moment, he thought she was going to refuse, but she gave in and said, 'Carlo Pianon and Marco Salvo.'

He remembered the names from the original file. Because they were Roberto's best friends, the police had wondered if they were the people the kidnappers said they would contact to use as intermediaries. But both of them were enrolled in a language course in England when Roberto was kidnapped.

He thanked her for the names and added, 'You said that was one of the reasons you had decided not to go out with him any more. Were there others?'

'Oh, there were lots of reasons,' she answered vaguely.

Brunetti said nothing, allowing her weak response to echo in the room. Finally she added, 'Well, he wasn't much fun any more, not the last week or so. He was tired all the time, and he said he didn't feel well. It got so all he could talk about was how tired he felt, and how weak. I didn't like having to listen to him complain all the time. Or have him fall asleep in the car and things like that.'

'Did he go to a doctor?'

'Yes. That was right after he started saying he couldn't smell anything any more. He always complained about smoking—he was worse than an American about that—but then he said he couldn't even smell smoke.' Her own nose twitched in response to the absurdity of this. 'So he decided to go to some specialist.'

'What did the doctor say?'

'That there was nothing wrong with him.' She paused a moment after that, then added, 'Except for diarrhoea, but the doctor gave him something for that.'

'And?' Brunetti asked.

'I suppose it stopped,' she said dismissively.

'But did he continue to be tired, the way you've described?'

'Yes. He kept saying he was sick, and the doctors kept saying that there was nothing wrong with him.'

'Doctors? Did he go to more than one?'

'I think so. He talked about a specialist in Padova. That's the one who finally told him he was anaemic and gave him some pills to take. But soon after that, it happened, and he was gone.'

'Do you think he was sick?' Brunetti asked.

'Oh, I don't know,' she answered. She crossed her legs, displaying even more thigh. 'He liked to have attention.'

Brunetti attempted to phrase it delicately. 'Did he give you reason to believe he really was sick or anaemic?'

'What do you mean, did he give me reason?'

'Was he less, er, energetic than usual?'

She looked across at him, as though Brunetti had just walked into the room from some other century. 'Oh, you mean sex?' He nodded. 'Yes, he lost interest in it; that's another reason I wanted it to end.'

'Did he know this, that you wanted things to end between you?'

'I never got a chance to tell him.'

Brunetti considered that and then asked, 'Why were you going to the villa that night?'

'We'd been to a party in Treviso, and Roberto didn't want to have to drive all the way back to Venice. So we were going to spend the night at the villa and go back in the morning.'

'I see,' Brunetti said and then asked, 'Aside from being tired, was his behaviour different in any way in the weeks before it happened?'

'What do you mean?'

'Did he seemed especially nervous?'

'No, not that I could say. He was short tempered with me, but he was short tempered with everyone. He had an argument with his father, and he had one with Maurizio.'

'What was the argument about?'

'I don't know. He never told me things like that. And it's not that I was very interested.'

'Why were you interested in him, Signora?' Brunetti asked and, catching her glance, added, 'If I might ask.'

'Oh, he was good company. At least at the beginning he was. And he always had a lot of money.' Brunetti thought the order of importance of those two remarks might better be reversed, but he said nothing.

'I see. Do you know his cousin?'

'Maurizio?' she asked, Brunetti thought rather unnecessarily.

'Yes.'

'I met him a couple of times. At Roberto's house. And once at a party.'

'Did you like him?'

She looked across at one of the etchings and, as if its violence had somehow inspired her, said, 'No.'

'Why?'

She shrugged dismissively at a memory from so long ago. 'I don't know. He seemed arrogant to me.' Hearing this, she added, 'Not that Roberto couldn't be like that sometimes, but Maurizio was just . . . well, he always has to tell everyone what to do. Or that's how it seemed to me.'

'Have you seen him since Roberto disappeared?'

'Of course,' she answered, surprised at the question. 'Just after it happened, he was there with Roberto's parents. All the time, when the notes came. So I saw him.'

'I mean after that, after the notes stopped.'

'No, not to talk to, if that's what you mean. I see him on the street sometimes, but we don't have anything to say to one another.'

'And Roberto's parents?'

'No, not them, either.' Brunetti doubted if the parents of the kidnapped boy would remain in contact with his former girlfriend, especially after her marriage to another man.

Brunetti had nothing else to ask her, but he wanted her to remain open to the possibility of answering more questions, should they arise. 'I don't want to keep you from your baby, Signora,' he said, glancing down at his watch.

'Oh, that's all right, I don't mind,' she answered, and Brunetti was surprised at how much he believed her and at how much that fact made him dislike her.

He got to his feet quickly. 'Thank you very much, Signora. I think that will be all for now.'

'For now?'

'If it does turn out to be Roberto's body, then the investigation will have to be reopened, Signora, and I suspect that everyone who had any knowledge of the original kidnapping will be questioned again.'

She pulled her lips together in a tight grimace of irritation at how much all of this was intruding on her time.

He went towards the door so as not to give her the chance to complain. 'Again, thank you, Signora,' he said.

She got up from the sofa and came towards him. Her face fell back into the curious immobility he had noticed when he first met her, and the beauty she'd shown disappeared.

She saw him to the door, and as she opened it, the baby wailed out from somewhere at the back of the apartment. Ignoring it, she said, 'Would you let me know if it really is Roberto?'

'Of course, Signora,' Brunetti answered.

He started down the steps. The baby's cry was cut off by the closing of the door.

# 8

Brunetti glanced at his watch as he left the Salviati house. It was twenty to one. He took the *traghetto* again, and when he came out at San Leonardo, he crossed the *campo* and took the first left. A few empty tables stood in the shade in front of the restaurant.

Inside, a counter stood to his left, a few demijohns of wine on a shelf in back of it, long rubber tubes flowing from their tops. To the right, two arched doors opened into another room, and there, at a table against the wall, he saw his father-in-law, Count Orazio Falier. The Count sat, a glass of what looked like prosecco in front of him, reading the local paper, *Il Gazzettino*. Brunetti was surprised to see him with such a newspaper, which meant either that his opinion of the Count was higher than he realized, or of the local newspaper, lower.

'*Buon dì*,' Brunetti said as he approached the table.

The Count peered over the top of his paper and got to his feet, leaving the pages spread before him.

'*Ciao*, Guido,' the Count said, extending his hand and clasping Brunetti's. 'I'm glad you could come.'

'I asked to talk to you, remember,' Brunetti answered.

Reminded, the Count said, 'The Lorenzonis, eh?'

Brunetti pulled out the chair opposite the Count and sat. He looked down at the paper, and, although the body was still unidentified, he found himself wondering if the story could somehow already be printed.

The Count interpreted his glance. 'Not yet.' He took the time to fold the paper neatly in two, and then in two again. 'It's become so bad, hasn't it?' he asked, holding the paper up between them.

'Not if you like cannibalism, incest, and infanticide,' Brunetti answered.

'Did you read it today?' When Brunetti shook his head, the Count explained. 'There was a story this morning about a woman in Tehran who killed her husband, ground up his heart, and ate it in something called *ab goosht*.' Before Brunetti could register either surprise or disgust, the Count went on, 'But then they opened a parenthesis and gave the recipe for *ab goosht*: tomatoes, onions, and chopped meat.' He shook his head. 'Who are they writing for? Who wants to know that sort of thing?'

Brunetti had long ago abandoned any faith he had ever had in the taste of the general public, and so he answered, 'The readers of *Il Gazzettino*, I'd say.'

The Count looked across at him and nodded. 'I suppose you're right.' He tossed the paper on to the next table. 'What is it you want to know about the Lorenzonis?'

'This morning, you said that the boy had none of the father's talent. I'd like to know what that talent is.'

'*Ciappar schei*,' the Count answered, slipping into dialect.

Immediately at ease at the sound of Veneziano, Brunetti asked, 'Making money how?'

'In any way he can: steel, cement, shipping. If it can be moved, the Lorenzonis can take it there for you. If it can be built, the Lorenzonis can sell you the materials to build it.' The Count thought about what he had just said and added, 'Be a good slogan for them, wouldn't it?' When Brunetti nodded, the Count added, 'Not that the Lorenzonis need to advertise. At least not anywhere in the Veneto.'

'Do you have dealings with them? The firm, that is.'

'In the past, I used their trucks to take textiles to Po-land and to bring back—I'm not sure about this; it was at least four years ago—but I think it was vodka. But with the loosening of border controls and customs regulations, I'm finding it cheaper to move things by rail, so I don't have any business with them any more.'

'Do you know them socially?'

'No more than I know a few hundred people in the city,' the Count said and looked up as the waitress approached their table.

She wore a man's shirt tucked into crisply pressed jeans and had hair cut as short as a boy's. Though she wore no make-up, the impression she gave was anything but boy-ish, for the jeans curved over her hips, and the open top three buttons of the shirt suggested that she wore no bra but might have been well advised to do so. 'Count Orazio,' she said in a deep contralto full of warmth and promise, 'it's a pleasure to see you here again.' She turned to Brunetti and included him in the warmth of her smile.

Brunetti remembered that the Count had told him the daughter of a friend ran this place, so perhaps it was as an old family friend that the Count asked, '*Come stai,* Valeria?' His use of the familiar 'tu', however, sounded anything but avuncular, and Brunetti watched the young woman to see how she responded.

'*Molto bene,* Signor Conte. *E Lei?*' she answered, the for-mality of the words wildly at odds with her tone.

'Fine, thank you, my dear.' He waved an open hand to-wards Brunetti. 'This is my son-in-law.'

'*Piacere,*' he said to the young woman, and she returned the same word, adding only a smile.

'What do you recommend for us today, Valeria?' the Count asked.

'To start with, we've got sarde in saor,' she said, 'or

latte di seppie. We made the sarde last night, and the seppie came from Rialto this morning.'

Probably frozen if they did, Brunetti thought. It was too early for fresh cuttlefish roe, but the sardines would be fresh. Paola seemed never to have time to clean the sardines and marinate them in onions and raisins, so they would be a treat.

'What do you think, Guido?'

'Sarde,' he said without hesitation.

'Yes. For me too.'

'Spaghetti alle vongole,' the young woman said, not so much recommending as giving their order.

Both men nodded.

'And after,' Valeria said, 'I'd recommend the rombo or perhaps the coda di rospo. Both are fresh.'

'How are they cooked?' the Count asked.

'The rombo's grilled, and the coda's baked with white wine, zucchini, and rosemary.'

'Is it good, the coda?' the Count asked.

Instead of answering, she put the knuckle of the first finger of her right hand into her cheek and turned it, smacking her lips as she did.

'That settles it, then,' the Count said, smiling up at her.

'How about you, Guido?'

'No, I'll take the rombo,' Brunetti said, thinking the other dish sounded too fussy, the sort of thing that would share a plate with a piece of carrot carved to look like a rose, or a sprig of mint arranged at a clever angle.

'Wine?' she asked.

'Do you have that Chardonnay your father makes?'

'It's what we drink ourselves, Conte, but we usually don't serve it.' She saw his disappointment, so she added, 'I can bring you a carafe.'

'Thank you, Valeria. I've had it at your father's. It's excellent.'

She nodded in acknowledgement of this truth, then added, as though it were a joke, 'Just don't say anything about it if the Finanza comes in.'

Before the Count could comment, a shout rang out from the other room. She turned and was gone.

'No wonder this country is an economic cripple,' the Count said with sudden fury. 'Best wine they make, and they can't serve it, probably because of some legal nonsense about the alcoholic content, or because some idiot in Brussels has decided it's too similar to another kind of wine made in Portugal. God, we're ruled by morons.'

Brunetti, who had always considered his father-in-law one of those rulers, found this a strange position for him to be taking. Before he could ask him about it, however, Valeria was back with a litre carafe of pale white wine and, though she hadn't been asked to bring it, a bottle of mineral water.

The Count poured two glasses of wine and pushed one towards Brunetti. 'Tell me what you think.'

Brunetti took it and sipped. He'd always hated remarks about wine and its taste, all the chatter about 'woody richness', the 'scent of crushed raspberries', so all he said was, 'Very good.' He set the glass down on the table. 'Tell me more about the boy. You said you didn't like him.'

The Count had had twenty years to grow accustomed to his son-in-law and his techniques, so he took a sip of his wine and answered, 'As I said, he was dull and full of himself, a very tedious combination.'

'What sort of work did he do for the company?'

'I think he was given the title of "*consulente*", though I haven't an idea of what he would consult about. When they needed to take a client to dinner, Roberto would come along. I suppose Ludovico hoped that his exposure to clients and talk of business would make him more serious or at least take the business more seriously.'

Brunetti, who had worked all of the summers of his university years, asked, 'But surely he didn't just go to dinner and call that his job?'

'Sometimes, if there were important deliveries or pick-ups to be made, they'd send Roberto. You know, if contracts had to get to Paris or a new book of samples for the textile factories had to be delivered in a hurry, Roberto would take them, and then he'd get to spend a weekend in Paris or Prague or wherever it was.'

'Nice work,' Brunetti said. 'What about the university?'

'Too lazy. Or too dumb,' was the Count's dismissive explanation.

Brunetti was about to remark that, from what Paola had said about the students at the university, neither of those served as much of an impediment, but he stopped when Valeria came towards their table, carrying two plates loaded with the small sardines, oil and vinegar glistening on their skins.

'*Buon appetito,*' she wished them and moved away to answer a wave from someone at another table.

Neither man bothered to bone the tiny fish, but forked them up, dripping oil, sliced onions, and raisins, and ate them whole.

'*Bon,*' the Count said. Brunetti nodded but said nothing, delighted with the fish and the sharp tang of vinegar. He'd once been told that, centuries ago, Venetian fishermen had been forced to eat the fish this way, chopping them up and pickling them to keep them from rotting, just as he'd been told that the vinegar was poured in against scurvy. He had no idea if either story was true, but if it was, he thanked the fishermen.

When the sardines were gone, Brunetti took a piece of bread and wiped his plate clean with it. 'Did he do anything else, Roberto?'

'You mean in the business?'

'Yes.'

The Count poured them each another half glass of wine. 'No. I think that's all he was either capable of doing or interested in doing.' He took another sip. 'He wasn't a bad boy, just dull. The last time I saw him, in fact, I felt sorry for him.'

'When was that? And why?'

'It must have been a few days before he was kidnapped. His parents were having a party for their thirtieth anniversary and invited me and Donatella. Roberto was there.' The Count paused after he said this and after a time, added, 'But it was almost as if he weren't there.'

'I don't understand,' Brunetti said.

'He seemed invisible. No, that's not what I mean. He looked thinner, and he had already begun to lose his hair. It was summer, but he looked like he hadn't been out of the house since winter. And he's the one who was always on the beach or playing tennis.' The Count looked off, recalling the evening. 'I didn't speak to him, and I didn't want to say anything to his parents. But he looked strange.'

'Sick?'

'No, not that, well, not really. Just very pale and thin, like he'd been on a diet and stayed on it too long.'

As if called on to put an end to all talk of diet, Valeria arrived just at that moment with two heaped plates of spaghetti topped with scores of tiny clams still in their shells. The perfume of the oil and garlic wafted ahead of her.

Brunetti dug his fork into the spaghetti and began to twirl up the interwoven strands. When he had what he thought a sufficient forkful, he raised it to his lips, encouraged by the warmth and the pervasive scent of garlic. Mouth full, he nodded at the Count, who smiled in return and began to eat his own.

It wasn't until Brunetti's pasta was almost gone and he had begun to break open the clams, that he asked the Count, 'What about the nephew?'

'I'm told he's a natural for the business. He's got the charm to work with the customers and the brains to calculate estimates and hire the right people.'

'How old is he?' Brunetti asked.

'He's two years older than Roberto, so that would make him about twenty-five.'

'Do you know anything else about him?'

'What sort of thing?'

'Anything you can think of.'

'That's very broad.' Before Brunetti could explain, the Count asked, 'To know if he could have done this? Assuming that it's been done?'

Brunetti nodded and continued with his clams.

'His father, Ludovico's younger brother, died when Maurizio was about eight. The parents were already divorced, and the mother apparently wanted nothing to do with the boy, so when she saw the chance, she gave him to Ludovico and Cornelia, and they raised him: he might just as well have been Roberto's brother.'

Thinking of Cain and Abel, Brunetti asked, 'Do you know this or have you been told this?'

'Both,' was the Count's terse answer. 'I'd say it's unlikely that Maurizio was involved in any way.'

Brunetti shrugged and tossed his last clam shell on to the pile that had accumulated on his plate. 'I don't even know if it's the Lorenzoni boy.'

'Then why all the questions?'

'I told you: two people thought it was a joke or a stunt. And the stone that was blocking the gate was placed there from inside.'

'They could have climbed the wall,' the Count suggested.

Brunetti nodded. 'Perhaps. I just don't like the feel of the whole thing.'

The Count gave him a curious glance, as if he found the conjunction of Brunetti and intuitive feelings a strange one. 'Aside from what you've just told me, what else is it that you don't like?'

'That no one followed up on the remark that they thought it was a joke. That there is no interview with his cousin in the file. And the rock: no one asked about that.'

The Count placed his fork on top of the uneaten spaghetti that still lay in the bottom of his plate, and just as he did so, Valeria arrived to clear the table. 'Didn't you like the spaghetti, Count?'

'It was delicious, my dear, but I need to save some room for the coda.'

She nodded and removed his plate, then Brunetti's. The Count was adding wine to their glasses when she returned. Brunetti was satisfied to see that he had been right about the coda. It was decorated with sprigs of rosemary, and a radish.

'Why do they do that to food?' he asked, pointing with his chin to the Count's plate.

'Is that a real question or a criticism of the service?' the Count asked.

'Just a question,' Brunetti answered.

The Count picked up knife and fork and separated the fish to see if it was cooked all through. Seeing that it was, he said, 'I remember when, for a few thousand lire, you could get a good meal at any *trattoria* or *osteria* in the city. Risotto, fish, a salad, and good wine. Nothing fancy, just the good food that owners probably ate at their own table. But that was when Venice was a city that was alive, that had industry and artisans. Now all we have is tourists, and the rich ones are accustomed to fancy stuff like this. So to appeal to their tastes, we get food that's been made to look pretty.' He took a bite of the fish. 'At least this is good, as well as pretty. How's yours?'

'Very good,' Brunetti answered. He placed a small bone to the side of his dish and said, 'You wanted to talk to me about something?'

His head bent over the fish, the Count said, 'It's about Paola.'

'Paola?'

'Yes, Paola. My daughter. Your wife.'

Brunetti was swept with a sudden wave of anger at the Count's dismissive tone, but contained it and replied, his own voice distant with mirrored sarcasm, 'And the mother of my children. Your grandchildren. Don't forget that.'

Placing his knife and fork on his plate, the Count pushed it away from him. 'Guido, I don't mean to offend . . .'

Brunetti cut him off. 'Then don't patronize me.'

The Count picked up the wine carafe and poured half of the remainder into Brunetti's glass, the rest into his own. 'She's not happy.' He looked across at Brunetti to see how he took this, paused, and when Brunetti said nothing, said, 'She's my only child, and she's not happy.'

'Why?'

The Count lifted the hand that wore the ring with the Falier crest. Seeing it, Brunetti thought immediately of the body in the field and whether it would turn out to be the Lorenzoni boy. If so, who should he speak to next, the father, the nephew, perhaps the mother? How could he intrude on a grief that would be resurrected by the discovery of the body?

'Are you listening?'

'Of course I'm listening,' answered Brunetti, who had not been. 'You said Paola's not happy, and I asked you why.'

'And I've been telling you, Guido, but you've been off somewhere with the Lorenzoni family and the body that's been found, wondering how you can arrive at justice.' He paused and waited for Brunetti to say something. 'One of the reasons I've been trying to explain to you is just that, that your pursuit of what you construe as justice takes up . . .' Here he paused and moved his empty wine glass back and forth on the table, holding it between the knuckles of his first and second finger. He looked up at Brunetti and smiled, though the sight of his smile made Brunetti sad. 'It takes up too much of your spirit, Guido, and I think Paola suffers from that.'

'You mean it takes up too much of my time?'

'No. I mean what I said. You get involved in these crimes and with the people who commit them or suffer them, and you forget about Paola and the children.'

'That's not true. I'm seldom gone from them when I should be there. We do things together.'

'Please, Guido,' the Count said in a softer voice. 'You're too intelligent a man to believe, or to expect me to believe, that just being in a place or with a person means all of you is there. Remember, I've been around you when you've been working on something, and I know what you're like. Your spirit disappears. You talk and listen, go places with the children, but you're not really there.' The Count poured some mineral water into his glass and drank it. 'In a way, you're like the Lorenzoni boy was that last time I saw him: distracted and distant and not really there.'

'Did Paola tell you this?'

The Count looked almost surprised. 'Guido, I have no reason to expect you to believe me, but Paola would never speak a word against you, not to me and not to anyone else.'

'Then why are you so sure she's unhappy?' Brunetti struggled to keep the anger from his voice as he asked the question.

Absently, the Count's fingers reached out for a small piece of bread that lay to the left of his plate and began to crumble it into smaller pieces. 'When Paola was born, Donatella had a very bad time and was sick for a long while after the birth, so much of the care of the baby fell to me.' He saw Brunetti's surprise and laughed out loud. 'I know, I know. It must be hard to picture me feeding a baby or changing her nappy, but that's what I did for the first few months, and then when Donatella was home again, well, it had become a habit, so I continued to do it. If you've changed a baby's nappy for a year, and fed her, and sung her to sleep, then you know when she's happy or sad.' Before Brunetti could object, the Count continued, 'And it makes no difference whether the baby is four months or forty years old or if the cause is colic or an uneasy marriage. You know. So I know she's not happy.'

Brunetti's protestations of innocence or ignorance died there. He'd change nappies himself and spent many nights holding the children in his lap, reading to them, while they cried or fell off to sleep, and he'd always believed it was those nights, more than anything else, that had given him a kind of radar that responded to the state of their—he had to use the Count's word here—spirits.

'I don't know how else to do what I do; he finally said in a tone which held no anger.

The Count went on. 'I've always wanted to ask you: why is it so important to you?'

'Why is what so important to me? That I arrest the person who committed a crime?'

The Count waved this away. 'No, I don't think that's what's important to you. Why do you have to see that justice is done?'

Valeria chose this moment to appear at their table, but neither man was interested in dessert. The Count ordered two grappas and turned his attention back to Brunetti.

'You've read the Greeks, haven't you?' Brunetti finally asked.

'Some of them, yes.'

'Critias?'

'So long ago as to have only the vaguest of memories of what he wrote. Why?'

Valeria appeared, set the glasses in front of them, and left silently.

Brunetti picked up his and took a small sip. 'I'm probably quoting him badly, but somewhere he says that the laws of the state will take care of public crimes, and that's why we need religion, so that we can believe divine justice will take care of private crime.' He paused and took another sip. 'But we don't have religion any more, do we, not really?' The Count shook his head. 'So maybe that's what I'm after, not that I've ever talked about it or, for that fact, much thought about it. If divine justice won't take care of private crime any more, then it's important that it be seen to, by someone.'

'What do. you mean, private crime? As distinct from public crime, that is.'

'Giving someone bad advice so that you can later profit from their error. Lying. Betraying a confidence.'

'None of those things is necessarily illegal,' the Count said.

Brunetti shook his head. 'That's not the point. That's why they came to mind.' He paused for a moment and then continued. 'Maybe the politicians provide better examples: giving contracts to their friends, basing government decisions on personal desires, giving jobs to members of their family.'

The Count cut him off. 'Business as usual in Italian politics, you mean?'

Brunetti gave a weary nod.

'But you can't decide those things are illegal and start punishing people, can you?' the Count asked.

'No. I suppose what I'm trying to say is that I get caught up in trying to find the people responsible for bad things, not just for illegal things, or I keep thinking about the difference and believing both are wrong.'

'And your wife suffers. Which gets us back to my original remark.' The Count reached across the table and placed his hand on Brunetti's arm. 'I know how offensive you must find this. But she's my baby and always will be, so I wanted to say something to you. Before she does.'

'I'm not sure I can thank you for this,' Brunetti confessed.

'That hardly matters. My only concern is Paola's happiness.' The Count paused and considered what to say next. 'And though you may find this hard to believe, Guido, your own.'

Brunetti nodded, finding himself suddenly too moved to speak. Seeing this, the Count waved towards Valeria and made motions of writing a bill. When he turned his attention back to Brunetti, he asked in an entirely normal voice, 'Well, what do you think of the food?'

Matching his tone, Brunetti answered, 'Excellent. Your friend can be proud of his daughter. And you can be proud of yours.'

'I am,' the Count said simply. He paused, looked across at Brunetti, and said, 'And though there's no reason you should believe this, I'm also proud of you.'

'Thank you. I had no idea.' Before he spoke, Brunetti had thought it would be difficult to say, but the words had come easily and painlessly.

'No, I didn't think you did.'

# 9

Brunetti didn't get back to the Questura until after three. As he came in, Pucetti emerged from the office near the door, but he did not come to give Brunetti his overcoat, which was nowhere in evidence.

'One of them steal it?' Brunetti asked with a smile, nodding in the direction of the door to the Officio Stranieri, in front of which the line no longer stood, it having closed at 12:30.

'No, sir. But the Vice-Questore called down to tell us that he wanted to see you when you got back from lunch.' Even the transmission of someone as well-disposed towards Brunetti as Pucetti failed to disguise the anger in Patta's message.

'Is he back from lunch himself?'

'Yes, sir. About ten minutes ago. He asked where you were.' A person did not have to be a cryptographer to break the code used at the Questura: Patta's question bespoke something stronger than his normal dissatisfaction with Brunetti.

'I'll go and see him now,' Brunetti said, heading towards the front steps.

'Your overcoat's in the cupboard of your office, sir,' Pucetti called after him, and Brunetti raised a hand in acknowledgement.

Signorina Elettra was at her desk outside Vice-Questore Patta's office. When he came in, she looked up from the newspaper on her desk and said, 'The report from the autopsy's on your desk.' Though he was curious, he didn't ask her what it contained, sure that she would have read it. If he didn't know the results, there would be no reason for him to mention the autopsy to Patta.

He recognized the pale orange pages of *Il Sole Ventiquattro Ore,* the financial newspaper. 'Working on your portfolio?' he asked.

'In a manner of speaking, I suppose.'

'Meaning?'

'A company I've invested in has decided to open a pharmaceutical factory in Tadzhikistan. There's an article in the paper about opening markets in what used to be the Soviet Union, and I wanted to get an idea of whether I should stay with them or pull my money out.'

'And?'

'I think it all stinks is what I think,' she answered, closing the paper with a sweeping gesture.

'Why?'

'Because these people seem to have jumped from the Middle Ages into advanced capitalism. Five years ago, they were bartering hammers for potatoes, and now they've all become businessmen with *telefonini* and BMWs. From what I've read, they have the morals of pit vipers, and I think I don't want to have anything to do with them.'

'Too risky?'

'No, quite the contrary,' she said quite calmly. 'I think it's probably going to be a very profitable investment, but I prefer not to have my money used by people who will deal in anything, buy and sell anything, do anything in order to profit.'

'Like the bank?' Brunetti asked. She'd come to the Questura some years ago, leaving her job as secretary to the president of the Banca d'Italia, because she'd refused to take dictation of a letter going to a bank in Johannesburg. The UN obviously didn't believe in its own sanctions, but Signorina Elettra had thought it necessary to uphold them, even at the cost of her job.

She looked up, eyes brightening, a cavalry horse who had just heard the trumpets sound the charge. 'Exactly.' But if he expected her to expand upon this, or make the comparison between the two cases, he was disappointed.

She looked significantly at Patta's door. 'He's waiting for you.'

'Any idea?'

'None,' she said.

Brunetti had a sudden vision of a painting he'd seen reproduced in his fifth grade history book, of a Roman gladiator turning to salute the Emperor before turning to join in battle with an enemy who had both a larger sword and a ten kilo edge. '*Ave atque vale,*' he said, smiling.

'*Morituri te salutant,*' she responded, as casually as if she were reading out the times on a train schedule.

Inside, the Latinate theme continued, with Patta poised in profile and showing off his truly imperial nose. When he turned to face Brunetti, the imperial evaporated and was replaced by something faintly porcine, caused by the tendency of Patta's dark brown eyes to sink ever deeper into the eternally tanned flesh of his face.

'You wanted to see me, Vice-Questore?' Brunetti asked in a neutral voice.

'Are you out of your mind, Brunetti?' Patta asked with no introduction.

'Should I learn that something is troubling my wife and fail to do anything about it, I surely would be,' he said, but only to himself. To Patta he answered, instead, 'About what particular subject, sir?'

'About these recommendations for promotion and commendation,' Patta said, bringing his outspread palm down heavily on a folder that lay closed in front of him. 'I've never seen a worse case of prejudice and favouritism in my life.'

As Patta was a Sicilian, he must have seen more than his fair share of both, Brunetti reflected, but said only, 'I'm not sure I understand, sir.'

'Of course you understand. You've recommended only Venetians: Vianello, Pucetti, and what's his name?' he said, looking down and pulling back the covers of the folder. He ran his eyes down the first page, flipped it over, and started to read the second. Suddenly he stabbed at the page with a blunt forefinger. 'Here. Montisi. How can we promote a boat pilot, for God's sake?'

'The way we'd promote any other officer, I believe, by raising him one grade and giving him the higher salary that goes with it.'

'For what?' Patta asked rhetorically and looked down at the page again. '"For conspicuous bravery in the pursuit of a fleeing criminal",' he read with the emphasis of sarcasm. 'You want to promote him because he chased after someone in his boat?' Patta paused and when Brunetti failed to answer, he added, sarcasm even more pronounced, 'And they didn't even catch the men they were chasing, did they?'

Brunetti paused a few seconds before he answered, and when he did, his voice was as calm as Patta's had not been. 'No, sir, not because Montisi chased after someone in his boat. But because he stopped the boat while he was under fire from the men in the other boat and went into the water to rescue another officer who had been shot and had fallen into the water.'

'It wasn't a serious wound,' Patta said.

'I'm not sure Officer Montisi paused to reflect upon that, sir, when he saw the other man in the water.'

'Well, it's impossible. We can't promote someone who is only a pilot.'

Brunetti said nothing.

'As to Vianello, perhaps we can allow that,' Patta conceded with a singular lack of enthusiasm. Vianello had been in Standa early one Saturday afternoon when a man armed with a knife came in, waved the cashier away from her place, and began to pull money from the cash register nearest the door. The sergeant, who had gone into the store to buy a pair of sunglasses, ducked down behind the counter and, when the man made towards the door, tackled him, disarmed him, and arrested him.

'And don't even talk about Pucetti,' Patta said angrily. Six weeks ago, Pucetti, a dedicated cyclist, had been in the mountains north of Vicenza when he'd almost been run off the road by a car driven by what turned out to be a drunken man. A few minutes later, he'd come upon the same car, crashed into a tree at the side of the road and already in flames. He'd dragged the driver from the car, burning his hands seriously in the process. 'It happened out of our jurisdiction, so there can be no thought of a commendation,' Patta added by way of clarification.

He flipped the folder to the side and looked up at Brunetti. 'But that's not why I want to see you, Brunetti,' he said.

If it was his other recommendations that Patta had been reading, then Brunetti knew what was coming.

'You've not only failed to recommend Lieutenant Scarpa for promotion, but you've suggested that he be transferred,' Patta said, barely containing his rage. Patta had brought the Lieutenant with him when he was transferred to Venice some years before; since then, the Lieutenant had served as the Vice-Questore's assistant, and spy.

'That's correct.'

'I can't allow that.'

'Can't allow what, Vice-Questore? That the Lieutenant be transferred or that I suggest it?'

'Either. Both.'

Brunetti remained silent, waiting to see how far Patta would go in defence of his creature.

'You know that I have the authority to refuse to pass on these recommendations?' Patta asked and then added, 'all of them.'

'Yes, I know that.'

'Then, before I make my own recommendations to the Questore, I suggest you retract the remarks you've made about the Lieutenant.' When Brunetti said nothing, Patta asked, 'Did you hear me, Commissario?'

'Yes.'

'And?'

'There is little that will make me change my opinion of the Lieutenant and nothing that will make me change my recommendation.'

'You know nothing will come of your recommendation, don't you?' Patta asked, pushing the folder to the side, freeing himself from the risk of contamination.

'But it will be in his file,' Brunetti said, even though he knew how easily things could be made to disappear from files.

'I don't see what purpose that will serve.'

'I like history. I like things to be recorded.'

'So far as Lieutenant Scarpa is concerned, the only thing to be recorded is that he is an excellent officer and a man worthy of my trust.'

'Then perhaps you can record that, sir, and I'll record my own judgement. And then, as always happens when history is read, future readers will determine which of us was correct.'

'I don't know what you're talking about, Brunetti, about future readers of history or things needing to be recorded. What we need is mutual support and trust.'

Brunetti said nothing to this, not wanting to encourage Patta in his usual platitudes about the pursuit of justice and the enforcement of the law, which two things Patta saw as identical. The Vice-Questore, however, needed no encouragement and devoted a few minutes to this particular theme, while Brunetti wondered what questions to ask of Maurizio Lorenzoni. Regardless of the outcome of the autopsy, he wanted to continue to take a closer look at the kidnapping; the nephew, the golden boy of the family, seemed a good place to try next.

Patta's raised voice cut into his reverie. 'If I'm boring you, Dottor Brunetti, just tell me and you can leave.'

Brunetti got suddenly to his feet, smiled but did not speak, and left Patta's office.

# 10

When he got back to his office, the first thing Brunetti did was open his window and spend a moment looking down at the place where Montisi's boat was usually moored, and only after that did he go to his desk and open the autopsy report. Over the years, he had become accustomed to the idiosyncratic style of these reports. The terminology was all medical, naming bones, organs, and pieces of connecting tissue; the grammar was almost exclusively subjunctive and conditional: 'If we were dealing with the body of a person in good health', 'Had the body not been moved', 'If I were asked to give an estimate.'

Young, male, probably in his early twenties, evidence of orthodontal work. Estimated height 180 centimetres, weight probably not more than sixty kilos. The cause of death was most likely a bullet to the brain: attached was a photo of the hole in the skull, its lethal roundness in no way diminished by its smallness. A scratch on the inner surface of the left eye socket might have been left by the exit of the bullet.

Here Brunetti paused and reflected upon the eternal caution of pathologists. A person could be found with a dagger through the heart, and the report would read, 'The cause of death appears to be . . .' He regretted that someone other than Ettore Rizzardi, the *medico legale* of Venice, had done the autopsy: after years of working with him, Brunetti could usually get Rizzardi to commit himself beyond the bland, speculative language of the reports he wrote, had once or twice even lured the pathologist into speculating on the possibility that the cause of death might be different from that suggested by the autopsy.

Because the tractor had disturbed some bones and broken others, there was no way of determining whether the ring that was found with the body had been worn by the deceased. The first officers on the scene had found it but had not marked its exact location before giving it to the *medico legale,* so it was impossible to tell where it had lain in relation to the body, which had itself been further disturbed by their arrival.

As well as a pair of black leather shoes, size 42, and dark cotton socks, the man had been wearing only blue wool slacks and a white cotton shirt when he was buried. Brunetti recalled the police report which stated that Lorenzoni had been wearing a blue suit when he disappeared. Because there had been heavy rains in the province of Belluno the previous autumn and winter and because the field lay at the base of two hills and hence tended to retain water, the decomposition of both fabric and flesh had been faster than normal.

Toxicological examinations were being performed on the organs and would be ready within a week, as would the results of some further tests that were to be performed on the bones. Though the fragments of lung tissue were too badly deteriorated to make the conclusion reliable, there was evidence he had been a heavy smoker. Brunetti thought of what Roberto's girlfriend had said, and despaired of the usefulness of autopsies. A complete set of dental X-rays were contained in a transparent plastic folder.

'The dentist, then,' Brunetti said aloud and reached for the phone. While he waited for an outside line, he flipped open his copy of the Lorenzoni file and found Count Ludovico's phone number.

'*Pronto,*' a male voice answered on the third ring.

'Conte Lorenzoni?' Brunetti asked.

'Signor Lorenzoni,' the voice corrected, giving no indication of whether this was the nephew or the Count asserting solidarity with democracy.

'Signor Maurizio Lorenzoni?' Brunetti asked.

'Yes.' Nothing more.

'This is Commissario Guido Brunetti. I'd like to speak to you or your uncle, if possible, sometime this afternoon.'

'What is this in relation to, Commissario?'

'Roberto, your cousin Roberto.'

After a long pause, he asked, 'Have you found him?'

'A body has been found in the province of Belluno.'

'Belluno?'

'Yes.'

'Is it Roberto?'

'I don't know, Signor Lorenzoni. It could be: it's the body of a young man about twenty, about 180 centimetres tall . . .'

'That description would fit half the young men in Italy,' Lorenzoni said.

'A ring with the Lorenzoni crest was found with him,' Brunetti added.

'What?'

'A signet ring with the family crest was found with him.'

'Who identified it?'

'The *medico legale*.'

'Is he sure?' Lorenzoni asked.

'Yes. Unless the crest has been changed recently,' Brunetti added in a level voice.

Lorenzoni's question came after another long pause. 'Where was this?'

'In a place called Col di Cugnan, not far from Belluno.'

The next pause was longer. Then Lorenzoni asked, in a far softer voice, 'Can we see him?'

Had the voice not softened, Brunetti would have answered that there wasn't much to see; instead, he said, 'I'm afraid the identification will have to be done by other means.'

'What does that mean?'

'The body that was found has been in the ground for some time, and so there has been considerable decomposition.'

'Decomposition?'

'It would help us if we could get in touch with his dentist. There's evidence that there was considerable orthodontal work.'

'*Oh Dio,*' the young man whispered, and then said, 'Roberto wore braces for years.'

'Can you give me the name of the dentist?'

'Francesco Urbani. His office is in Campo San Stefano. He's the same dentist we all go to.'

Brunetti made a note of the name and address. 'Thank you, Signor Lorenzoni.'

'When will you know? Should I tell my uncle?' And after a pause, he added, but it wasn't a question, 'And my aunt.'

Brunetti picked up the white-bordered dental X-rays. He could send Vianello to Doctor Urbani with them this afternoon. 'I should be able to give you some information today. I'd like to speak to your uncle, and your aunt, if that's possible. This evening?'

'Yes, yes,' he answered distractedly. 'Commissario, is there a chance that this isn't Roberto?'

That chance, if it ever existed, seemed to be growing smaller with each added piece of information. 'I don't think it's very likely, but you might want to wait until we've spoken to the dentist before you tell your uncle.'

'I don't know how I can tell him,' Lorenzoni said. 'And my aunt, my aunt.'

Whatever the dentist said would only confirm what Brunetti's instincts knew was true. He decided he would speak to the Lorenzonis, all of them, and do it soon. 'I'll come and speak to them if you'd like me to.'

'Yes, I think that's better. But what if the dentist says it isn't Roberto?'

'In that case, I'll call you and tell you. At this number?'

'No, let me give you the number of my cellular,' he answered. Brunetti made a note.

'I'll be there at seven,' Brunetti said, intentionally omitting any qualification about what he'd do if the dental records didn't match.

'Yes, at seven,' Lorenzoni said and hung up without bothering to give the address or instructions about how to get there. Presumably, in Venice the name would suffice.

Brunetti immediately called down to Vianello's office and asked him to come up and get the dental X-rays. When the sergeant came in, Brunetti told him where Doctor Urbani's office was and asked Vianello to call from there with the results.

What would it be like to have a child kidnapped? What if the victim had been Raffi, his own son? The very thought of it made Brunetti's stomach tighten with fear and disgust. He remembered the rash of kidnappings that had taken place in the Veneto during the 1980s and the burst of business it had provided for private security firms. That gang had been broken up a few years ago, and the leaders sentenced to life imprisonment. With a twinge of guilt, Brunetti found himself thinking that this was not severe enough to punish them for what they had done, though the topic of capital punishment was such a red flag in his own family that he didn't pursue the logical consequences of this judgement.

He'd need to see the wall, to see how easy it would be to climb over it, or to see how else the stone might have been put behind the gates. He'd have to contact the Belluno police to ask about kidnappings in the area: he'd always thought it the most crime-free province in the country, but perhaps that was the Italy of memory. Enough time had passed, so the Lorenzonis, if they had managed to borrow enough money to pay the ransom, might be willing to say so now. And if they had, how had they paid it, and when?

Years of experience warned him that he was assuming the boy's death without final proof; the same years told him that final proof was unnecessary here. Intuition would suffice.

His thoughts shifted to his conversation with Count Orazio and his reluctance to accept the other man's intuition. In the past, Paola had sometimes said that she felt old, that the best of life was past, but Brunetti had always been able to lure her away from such ideas. He didn't know anything about menopause: the very word embarrassed him. But could this be a sign that something like that was happening? Weren't there hot flashes? Strange cravings for food?

He realized that he wished it would be something like that, something physical and, therefore, something for which he was in no way responsible and about which he could do nothing. As a schoolboy, he had been told by the priest who gave religious instruction that it was necessary, before confession, to examine his conscience. There were, the priest had explained, sins of omission and sins of commission, but even then Brunetti had found it difficult to distinguish between the two. Now that he was a man, the distinction was even more difficult to grasp.

He found himself thinking that he should take Paola flowers, take her out to dinner, ask her about her work. But even as he considered such gestures, he realized how transparently false they were, even to him. If he knew the source of her unhappiness, he might have some idea of what to do.

It wasn't anything at home, where she was as consistently explosive as she'd always been. Work, then, and from what Paola had been saying for years, he could not imagine an intelligent person who would not be driven to despair by the Byzantine politics of the university. But usually the situation there enraged her, and no one embraced battle as joyously as did Paola. The Count had said she was unhappy.

Brunetti's thoughts went from Paola's happiness to his own, and he surprised himself by realizing that it had never before occurred to him to wonder whether he was happy or not. In love with his wife, proud of his children, capable of doing his job well, why would he worry about happiness, and what more than these things could happiness be comprised of? He dealt every day with people who believed they weren't happy and who further believed that by committing some crime—theft, murder, deceit, blackmail, even kidnapping—they would find the magic elixir that would transform the perceived misery of their lives into that most desired of states: happiness. Brunetti found himself too often forced to examine the consequences of those crimes, and what he saw was often the destruction of all happiness.

Paola frequently complained that no one at the university listened to her, indeed that few people ever bothered to listen to what anyone else said, but Brunetti had never included himself in that denunciation. But did he listen to her? When she railed on about the plummeting quality of her students and the grasping self-interest of her colleagues, was he attentive enough? No sooner had he asked himself this, than the thought snaked into his mind: did she listen to him when he complained about Patta or about the various incompetencies that were part of his daily life? And surely the consequences of what he observed were far more serious than those of some student who didn't remember who wrote *I Promessi Sposi* or didn't know who Aristotle was.

Suddenly disgusted with the futility of all of this, he got up and went over to the window. Montisi's boat was back at its moorings, but the pilot was nowhere in sight. Brunetti knew that his refusal to recommend Lieutenant Scarpa for promotion had cost Montisi his promotion, but Brunetti's near certainty that the Lieutenant had betrayed a witness and caused her death made it difficult to be in the same room with him, impossible for him to go on record as approving of his behaviour. He regretted that the price of his contempt for Scarpa would have to be paid by Montisi, but Brunetti could see no way clear of it.

The thought of Paola returned, but he pushed it away and turned from the window. He went downstairs and into Signorina Elettra's office. 'Signorina,' he said as he went in, 'I think it's time to begin taking another look at the Lorenzoni case.'

'Then it was the boy?' she asked, looking up from her keyboard.

'I think so, but I'm waiting for Vianello to call me. He's checking the dental records.'

'The poor mother,' Elettra said and then added, 'I wonder if she's religious.'

'Why?'

'It helps people when terrible things happen, when people die.'

'Are you?' Brunetti asked.

'*Per carità,*' she said, pushing the idea back towards him with raised hands. 'The last time I was in church was for my confirmation. It would have upset my parents if I hadn't done it, which was pretty much the same for all my friends. But since then I've had nothing to do with it.'

'Then why did you say that it helps people?'

'Because it's true,' she said simply. 'The fact that I don't believe in it doesn't prevent it from helping other people. I'd be a fool to deny that.'

And Signorina Elettra was no fool, well he knew that. 'What about the Lorenzonis?' Brunetti asked, and before she could ask, he clarified the question. 'No, I'm not interested in their religious ideas. I'd like to know anything I can about them: their marriage, their businesses, where they have homes, who their friends are, the name of their lawyer.'

'I think a lot of this would be in *Il Gazzettino*,' she said. 'I can see what's in the files.'

'Can you do this without leaving fingerprints, as it were?' he asked, though he wasn't sure why he didn't want to make it evident that he was looking into the family.

'Like the whiskers of a cat,' she said with what sounded like real pleasure, or pride. She nodded down at the keyboard of her computer.

'With that?' Brunetti asked.

She smiled. 'Everything's in here.'

'Like what?'

'Whether any of them has ever had any trouble with us,' she answered, and he wondered if she was aware of how entirely unconscious her use of that pronoun had been.

'I suppose you could,' Brunetti said. 'I hadn't thought of that.'

'Because of his title?' she asked, one eyebrow raised, the opposite side of her mouth curved up in a smile.

Brunetti, recognizing the truth of this, shook his head in silent negation. 'I don't remember ever hearing their name mixed up with anything. Aside from the kidnapping, that is. Do you know anything about them?'

'I know that Maurizio has a temper that sometimes works to other people's cost.'

'What does that mean?'

'That he doesn't like not to get his way, and when he doesn't, his behaviour is unpleasant.'

'How do you know?'

'I know it the way I know many things about the physical health of people in the city.'

'Barbara?'

'Yes. Not because she was the doctor involved—I don't think she'd tell me then. But we were at dinner with another doctor, the one who substitutes for her when she's on vacation, and he said that he had a female patient whose hand had been broken by Maurizio Lorenzoni.'

'He broke her hand? How?'

'He slammed his car door on it.'

Brunetti raised his eyebrows. 'I see what you mean by "unpleasant".'

She shook her head. 'No, it wasn't as bad as it sounds, not really. Even the girl said he didn't intend to do it. They'd had an argument. Apparently they'd been to dinner out on the mainland somewhere, and he'd invited her to the villa, the one where the other boy was kidnapped. She refused and asked him to drive her back to Venice. He was very angry, but he did finally drive her back. When they got to the garage at Piazzale Roma, someone was in his parking space, so he had to park right up against the wall. That meant she had to get out on the driver's side. But he didn't realize that and slammed his door just as she was reaching up to grab on to the frame to help pull herself out.'

'She was sure he didn't see her?'

'Yes. In fact, when he heard her scream and saw what he had done, he was terrified, almost to tears, or so she told Barbara's friend. He got her downstairs and called a water taxi and took her to the *pronto soccorso* at the civil hospital,

90

and the next day he drove her up to a specialist in Udine who set her hand.'

'Why was she seeing this other doctor?'

'She had some sort of skin infection under the cast. He was treating her for that. So of course he asked her how she had broken her hand.'

'And that's the story she gave?'

'That's what he said. He apparently thought she was telling the truth.'

'Did she bring a civil suit against him for damages?'

'No, not that I know of.'

'Do you know her name?'

'No, but I can get it from Barbara's friend.'

'Please do,' Brunetti asked. 'And see what else you can find out about any of them.'

'Only criminal things, Commissario?'

Brunetti's impulse was to agree to this, but then he thought of the apparent contradiction in Maurizio, said to have flown into a rage when a woman refused his invitation, yet to have been moved almost to tears when he saw her broken hand. He began to grow curious about what other contradictions might be lurking amidst the Lorenzoni family. 'No, let's see what we can find out about them, anything.'

'All right, Dottore,' she said, turning her chair to bring her hands over the keys of her computer. 'I'll start with Interpol, then see what *Il Gazzettino* might have.'

Brunetti nodded towards her computer. 'You really can do it with that, instead of the telephone?'

She looked at him with infinite patience, just the sort of look his high school chemistry teacher used to give him after each unsuccessful experiment. 'The only people who ring me today are the ones who make obscene calls.'

'And everyone else uses that?' he said, indicating the little box on her desk.

'It's called a modem, sir.'

'Ah, yes, I remember. Well, see what it can tell you about the Lorenzonis.'

Before Signorina Elettra, newly appalled at his ignorance, could begin to explain to him just what a modem was and how it worked, Brunetti turned and left her office. Neither viewed his precipitate departure as a lost opportunity for the advancement of human understanding.

# 11

His phone was ringing when he got to his office; he half ran across the room to pick it up. Even before Brunetti could give his name, Vianello said, 'It's Lorenzoni.'

'The X-rays match?'

'Yes, perfectly.'

Though Brunetti had expected this, he found himself adjusting his mind to the certainty. It was one thing to tell someone that there was every possibility the body of his cousin had been found; how vastly different to tell parents that their only child was dead. Their only son. '*Gesù, pietà,*' he whispered and then in a louder voice asked Vianello, 'Did the dentist have anything to say about the boy?'

'Nothing directly, but he seemed sad to learn that he was dead. I'd say he liked him.'

'What makes you say that?'

'From the way he spoke of him. After all, the boy was a patient for years, from when he was fourteen. In a sense, the dentist watched him grow up.' When Brunetti said nothing, Vianello asked, 'I'm still in his office. Do you want me to ask anything else?'

'No, no, don't bother, Vianello. I think you'd better come back here. I want you to go up to Belluno tomorrow morning, and I want you to read through the whole file before that.'

'Yes, sir,' Vianello said and, with no further questions, hung up.

Twenty-one years old and dead with a bullet in his brain. At twenty-one, life hasn't been lived, hasn't even been properly begun; the person who will emerge from the cocoon of youth is still almost entirely dormant. And this boy was dead. Brunetti thought of his own father-in-law's tremendous wealth and again thought that it might just as easily have been his only grandson, Raffi, who had been kidnapped and murdered. Or it might have been his granddaughter. That possibility drove Brunetti from his office, from the Questura, and towards his home, filled with an irrational concern for his family's safety: like St Thomas, he could believe only what his hands could touch.

Though he was not aware of climbing the stairs more quickly than he usually did, he was so winded when he got to the bottom of the last flight that he had to lean against the wall for a minute until his breath came back to him. He pushed himself away and up the last steps, taking his keys from his pocket as he did.

He let himself in and stood just inside the door, listening to see if he could locate all three of them and know them to be safe within the walls he had given them. From the kitchen, he heard the clang of metal as something fell to the floor and then Paola's voice, 'It doesn't matter, Chiara. Just wash it off and put it back on the pan.'

He turned his attention to the back of the apartment, towards Raffi's room, and coming from it he heard the heavy bass of some dreadful noise, known to younger people as music. And never had melody, though he could discern none here, had a sweeter sound.

He hung his coat in the cupboard in the hall and went down the long corridor towards the kitchen. Chiara turned towards him as he came in.

'*Ciao, Papà. Mamma*'s teaching me how to make ravioli. We're going to have them tonight.' She held her flour-covered hands behind her back and came a few steps towards him. He leaned down and she kissed him on both cheeks; he wiped a long smear of flour from her left cheek. 'Filled with *funghi*, right *Mamma*?' she asked, turning to Paola, who stood at the stove, stirring the mushrooms in a large frying pan. She nodded and kept stirring.

Behind them on the table lay a few crooked piles of oddly shaped pale rectangles. 'Are those the ravioli?' he asked, remembering the neat geometry of the squares his mother used to cut and fill.

'They will be, *Papà*, as soon as we get them filled.' She turned to Paola for confirmation. 'Won't they, *Mamma*?'

Paola stirred and nodded, turned to Brunetti and accepted his kisses without comment.

'Won't they, *Mamma*?' Chiara repeated, voice a tone higher.

'Yes. Just a few more minutes for the mushrooms and we can start to fill them.'

'You said I could do it myself, *Mamma*,' Chiara insisted.

Before Chiara could turn to Brunetti to witness this injustice, Paola conceded the point. 'If your father will pour me a glass of wine while the mushrooms finish, all right?'

'Would you like me to help you to fill them?' Brunetti asked, half joking.

'Oh, *Papà*, don't be silly. You know you'd make a mess.'

'Don't talk to your father that way,' Paola said.

'What way?'

'That way.'

'I don't understand.'

'You do so understand.'

'White or red, Paola?' Brunetti interrupted. He walked past Chiara, and seeing that Paola had turned back to the stove, he narrowed his eyes at Chiara and gave a small shake of his head while motioning towards Paola with his chin.

Chiara pursed her lips, shrugged, but then nodded. 'All right, *Papà*, if you want to, you can.' Then, after a grudgingly long pause, 'So can *Mamma* if she wants to.'

'Red,' Paola said and stirred the mushrooms around the pan.

Brunetti walked past her and stooped to open the cabinet under the sink. 'Cabernet?' he asked.

'Uh, huh,' Paola agreed.

He opened the wine and poured out two glasses. When she reached out a hand to take the glass, he took her hand, pressed her palm to his lips, and kissed it. Surprised, she looked up at him. 'What's that for?' she asked.

'Because I love you with all my heart,' he said and handed her the glass.

'Oh, *Papà*,' Chiara moaned. 'Only people in the movies say things like that.'

'You know your father doesn't go to the movies,' Paola said.

'Then he read it in a book,' Chiara said, already losing whatever little interest she had in the sort of things grown-ups found to say to one another. 'Aren't the mushrooms done yet?'

Glad of the distraction provided by her daughter's impatience, Paola said, 'one more minute and they're done. But you've got to wait until they're cool.'

'How long will that take?'

'Ten or fifteen minutes.'

Brunetti stood with his back to them, looking out of the window and off to the mountains to the north of Venice.

'Can I come back then and do it?'

'Of course.'

He heard Chiara leave the kitchen and go down the hall towards her room.

'Why did you say that?' Paola asked when she was gone.

'Because it's true,' Brunetti said, still looking out of the window.

'But why did you say it now?'

'Because I never say it.' He sipped at his wine. It occurred to him to ask if she didn't believe him or if she didn't like hearing it, but he said nothing, took another sip of wine.

Before he heard her move, he felt Paola come up beside him. She wrapped her left arm around his waist and pulled herself close to him. Saying nothing, she stood beside him, looking out of the window with him. 'I can't remember the last time it was this clear. Is that the Nevegal, do you think?' she asked, raising her right hand to point to the closest of the mountains.

'That's up near Belluno, isn't it?' he asked.

'I think so, yes. Why?'

'I might have to go up there tomorrow.'

'What for?'

'They've found the Lorenzoni boy's body. Up near Belluno.'

It was a long time before she said anything. 'Oh, the poor boy. And his parents. Terrible.' After another long pause, she asked, 'Do they know?'

'No, I have to tell them now. Before dinner.'

'Oh, Guido, why do you always have to do these awful things?'

'If other people wouldn't do awful things, I wouldn't have to, Paola.'

For an instant, he feared she would take offence at his reply, but she ignored it and leaned even closer to him. 'I don't know them, but I'm sorry for them. What a horrible thing to happen.' And he felt her grow tense as the thought came to her that it might have been her child, her son. Their son. 'How awful. How awful to do a thing like that. How can they?'

He had no answer to this, just as he had no answer to any of those big questions about why people committed crimes or savaged one another. He had answers only to the smaller questions. 'They do it for money.'

'All the worse,' was her immediate reply. 'Oh I hope they get them,' and then, as she remembered, she said, 'I hope you get them.'

So did he, he realized, surprised by the strength of his desire to find the people who had done this. But he didn't, not now, want to talk of this; instead, he wanted to answer her question about why he had said he loved her. He was not a man accustomed to speaking of his emotions, but he wanted to tell her, to bind her to him anew with the power of his words and his love. 'Paola,' he began, but before he could say anything further, she pulled herself roughly away from him, shocking him to silence.

'The mushrooms,' she said, pulling the pan from the flame with one hand and opening the window with the other. And talk of love, with the mushrooms, went up in smoke.

# 12

When he finished his wine, he went down the hall and knocked at Raffi's door. Hearing nothing but the continued boom boom boom of the music from inside, Brunetti pushed open the door. Raffi lay on his bed, a book open on his chest, sound asleep. Thinking of Paola, Chiara, the neighbours, and human sanity in general, Brunetti walked to the small stereo on Raffi's bookcase and turned the volume down. He looked at Raffi, who didn't move, and turned it down even more. Moving closer to the bed, he glanced at the title of the book: *Calculus*. No wonder he slept.

Chiara was in the kitchen, muttering dark threats at the pieces of ravioli which refused to maintain the shape into which she squeezed them. He said goodbye and went down the hall to Paola's study. He stuck his head inside and said, 'If it's necessary, we can always go over to Gianni's for a pizza.'

She glanced up from her papers. 'No matter what she does to those poor ravioli, we are going to eat every one she puts on our plates, and you are going to ask for seconds.' Before he could protest, she cut him off, pointing a threatening pencil at him. 'It's the first dinner she's cooked, all by herself, and it's going to be wonderful.' She saw him start to speak and cut him off again. 'Burned mushrooms, pasta that will have the consistency of wallpaper glue, and a chicken that she's chosen to marinate in soy sauce and which will consequently have the salt content of the Dead Sea.'

'You make it sound inviting.' Well, Brunetti thought, she can't do anything with the wine. 'What about Raffi? How are you going to get him to eat it?'

'Don't you think he loves his little sister?' she asked with the false indignation he knew so well.

Brunetti said nothing.

'All right,' Paola admitted, 'I promised him ten thousand lire if he ate everything.'

'Me too?' Brunetti asked and left.

As he walked down Rughetta towards Rialto, Brunetti realized that he felt better than at any time since his lunch with his father-in-law. He still had no idea what was bothering Paola, but the ease of their last interchange had convinced him that, whatever it was, the substratum of their marriage would survive. Up and down, up and down the bridges he walked, just as his spirits had gone up and down all day, first with the excitement of a new case, then the Count's upsetting confidence, and the peace given by Paola's confession that she had bribed their son.

To get through the interview with the Lorenzonis, he had only the hope of the dinner which awaited him, yet how willingly he would have eaten a month of Chiara's dinners, if he could have avoided being the bearer of grief and misery once again.

The *palazzo* was near the Municipio, though he had to cut past the Cinema Rossini and come back towards the Grand Canal to get to it. He paused for a moment on Ponte del Teatro and studied the rebuilt foundations of the buildings that lined the canal on either side. When he was a boy, the canals had undergone a perpetual process of cleaning, and the waters were kept so clear that people could swim in them. Now, the cleaning of a canal was a major event, so rare that it was greeted with headlines and talk of good city management. And contact with their waters was an experience many people might choose not to survive.

When he found the *palazzo*, a looming four-storey building whose front windows looked out over the Grand Canal, he rang the bell, waited a minute, then rang it again. A man's voice came through the intercom, 'Commissario Brunetti?'

'Yes.'

'Please come in,' the voice said, and the door snapped open. Brunetti walked through and found himself in a garden far larger than he would have expected to see in this part of the city. Only the most wealthy could have afforded to build their *palazzo* around so much empty space, and only descendants of equal wealth could continue to maintain it.

'Up here,' a voice called from a door at the top of a flight of stairs to his left. He turned and started to climb. At the top waited a young man in a double-breasted blue suit. He had dark brown hair with a pronounced widow's peak, which he attempted to hide by brushing his hair across his forehead. As Brunetti approached, he extended his hand and said, 'Good evening, Commissario. I'm Maurizio Lorenzoni. My uncle and aunt expect you.' His grip was one of those limp contacts which always left Brunetti wanting to wipe his palm on his trousers, but it was offset by the young man's glance, which was direct and even. 'Have you spoken to Dottore Urbani?' As neat a way of asking as Brunetti could imagine.

'Yes, we have, and I'm afraid the identification has been confirmed. It's your cousin, Roberto.'

'There can't be any question?' he asked in a voice that already knew the answer.

'No. None.'

The young man jammed his fists into the pockets of his jacket and pressed down, pulling the jacket forward on his shoulders. 'This will kill them. I don't know what my aunt will do.'

'I'm sorry,' Brunetti said, meaning it. 'Would it be better if you told them?'

'I don't think I could do that,' Maurizio answered, eyes on the ground.

In all the years he had been bearing news like this to the families of the slain, he had never encountered a person who was willing to do it for him. 'Do they know I'm here? Who I am?'

The young man nodded and looked up. 'I had to tell them. So they know what to expect. But it's . . .'

Brunetti finished the sentence for him: 'It's different to expect and then to have it confirmed. Perhaps you could take me to your aunt and uncle.'

The young man turned and led Brunetti into the building, leaving the door open behind them. Brunetti stepped back and closed it, but the young man didn't notice. He led Brunetti down a marble-floored corridor to an immense pair of walnut doors. Without knocking, he pushed them open and stepped back to allow Brunetti to go into the room before him.

Brunetti recognized the Count from photos he had seen of him: the silver hair, the erect posture, and the square jaw that he must have long since tired of hearing compared to Mussolini's. Although Brunetti knew the Count to be in his late fifties, the air of vibrant masculinity that emanated from him created the aura of a man almost a decade younger. The Count stood in front of a large fireplace, staring down at the spray of dried flowers that filled it, but turned to look at Brunetti when he came in.

Dwarfed by the armchair in which she huddled, a sparrow-like woman stared across at Brunetti as though he were the devil come to take her soul away. As indeed he had, Brunetti thought, filled with sudden pity by the sight of the thin hands nervously folded in her lap. Although the Countess was younger than her husband, the agony of the last two years had drained all youth and all hope from her and left behind an old woman who might more easily have been the Count's mother than his wife. Brunetti knew she had been one of the great beauties of the city: certainly the elegant bones of her face were still perfect. But there was little other than bone visible in her face.

Even before her husband could speak, she asked, voice so soft it would have been lost in the room had it not been the only sound, 'Are you the policeman?'

'Yes, Contessa, I am.'

The Count came forward from the fireplace then and extended his hand to Brunetti. His grasp was as firm as his nephew's was limp, forcing Brunetti's fingers against one another. 'Good evening, Commissario. Excuse me if I don't offer you something to drink. I think you'll understand.' His voice was deep but surprisingly soft, almost as soft as his wife's had been.

'I bring you the worst of news, Signor Conte,' Brunetti said.

'Roberto?'

'Yes. He's dead. His body has been found near Belluno.'

From across the room, the boy's mother asked, 'Are you sure?' Brunetti looked towards her and was amazed to see that she appeared to have grown even smaller in the few moments that had passed, sat even more deeply huddled between the two tall wings of the chair.

'Yes, Contessa. We've shown X-rays of his teeth to his dentist, and he confirms that they are the same as Roberto's.'

'X-rays?' she asked. 'What about his body? Hasn't anyone identified it?'

'Cornelia,' her husband said softly, 'let him finish, and then we can ask questions.'

'I want to know about his body, Ludovico. I want to know about my baby.'

Brunetti turned his attention back to the Count, looking for a sign that he should proceed, and how. The Count nodded at Brunetti, who continued, 'He was buried in a field. It looks like he's been there for some time, more than a year.' He stopped, hoping that they would understand what happened to a body in a year under the earth and not make him have to tell them.

'But why the X-rays?' the Contessa demanded. Like so many people Brunetti had encountered in the same circumstances, there were things she did not want to understand.

Before Brunetti could mention the ring, the Count interrupted, looking across at his wife. 'It means that the body has deteriorated, Cornelia, and they have to identify it that way.'

Brunetti, who was watching the Countess as her husband spoke, saw the instant when his explanation penetrated whatever defences she had left. Perhaps it was the word 'deteriorated' that did it; whatever it was, at the moment when she understood, she put her head against the back of the chair and closed her eyes. Her lips moved, either in prayer or protest. The Belluno police would give them the ring, Brunetti knew, and so he spared himself the pain of telling them about it.

The Count turned away from Brunetti and redirected his attention to the flowers in the fireplace. For a long time, no one in the room said anything, until finally the Count asked, not looking at Brunetti, 'When can we have him back?'

'You'll have to contact the authorities in Belluno, sir, but I'm sure they'll do whatever you want.'

'How do I contact them?'

'If you call the Questura in Belluno,' Brunetti started to say but then offered, 'I can do it for you. Perhaps it would be easier that way.'

Maurizio, who had been silent through all of this, interrupted, addressing the Count, 'I'll do it, *Zio.*' Catching Brunetti's eye, he nodded towards the door, but Brunetti ignored him.

'Signor Conte, as soon as possible, I'd like to speak to you about the original kidnapping.'

'Not now,' the Count said, still not looking at him.

'I realize how terrible this is, sir,' Brunetti said, 'but I will need to talk to you.'

'You'll talk to me when I please, Commissario, and not before,' the Count said, still not bothering take his eyes from the contemplation of the flowers.

In the silence created by this, Maurizio moved away from the door and went over to his aunt's chair. He bent down and placed a hand briefly on her shoulder. Straightening, he said, 'I'll show you out, Commissario.'

Brunetti followed him from the room. In the hall, he told the young man how to go about reaching the people in Belluno who would see to releasing Roberto's body and returning it to Venice. Brunetti did not ask him when he might speak to Count Ludovico again.

# 13

The dinner, when they finally sat down to eat it, lived up to his every expectation, which fact he bore with a stoicism that would have done credit to his favourite Roman writers. He both asked for and ate a second helping of ravioli, covered in something he thought had once been butter, charred sage leaves mashed about in its midst. The chicken was as salty as threatened, so much so that he found himself opening a third bottle of mineral water before the meal was finished. For once, Paola said nothing when he opened a second bottle of wine and did more than her fair share to help him finish it.

'What's for dessert?' he asked, earning the most tender look he'd seen on Paola's face in weeks.

'I didn't have time to make anything,' Chiara said, failing to see the look that passed among the other three people at the table. No doubt the Donner Party had exchanged such a glance at hearing the first calls of the men come to rescue them.

'I think there's still some *gelato*,' Raffi volunteered, living up to his part of the bargain with his mother.

'No, I finished it this afternoon,' Chiara confessed.

'Would you two like to go over to Campo Santa Margarita and get some more?' Paola asked. 'And bring it back here?'

'But what about the dishes, *Mamma*?' Chiara asked. 'You said because I cooked dinner, Raffi had to do them.'

Even before Raffi could protest, Paola said, 'If you two will go and get the ice cream, I'll do the dishes.' Amidst their shouted acceptance, Brunetti took out his wallet and handed Raffi twenty thousand lire. They left, already negotiating over flavours.

Paola got up from the table and started to gather the plates. 'You think you'll survive?' she asked.

'If I can drink another litre of water before we go to bed, and if I get to keep a bottle by the bed tonight.'

'Pretty dreadful, wasn't it?' Paola conceded.

'She was happy,' Brunetti temporized and then added, 'But it really is another strong argument in favour of the education of women, isn't it?'

Paola laughed at this and stacked the dishes in the sink. Easily, then, they discussed the dinner, both taking pleasure in the fact that Chiara had been so thoroughly pleased with herself, sure proof of the success of familial deception. And, he found himself thinking, familial love.

When the dishes were done and slotted above the sink to drain, he said, 'I think I'll go up to Belluno with Vianello tomorrow.'

'The Lorenzoni boy?'

'Yes.'

'How was it for them, when you told them?'

'Bad, especially for the mother.'

He realized that a mother's loss of her only son wasn't something Paola wanted to contemplate. As usual, she used details to divert. 'Where did they find him?'

'In a field.'

'A field? Where?'

'In one of those places with one of those strange Bellunese names—Col di Cugnan, I think.'

'But how did they find it?'

'A farmer was ploughing his field and turned up the bones.'

'God, how terrible,' she said, and then immediately added, 'And you had to tell them that, and then come home to that awful dinner.'

He couldn't keep himself from laughing at this.

'What's so funny?'

'That the first thing you think about is food.'

'I get it from you, my dear,' she said with what sounded like polite disdain. 'Before I married you, I hardly gave food a second thought.'

'Then how'd you learn to cook so well?'

She waved this away, but he detected both embarrassment and a desire to have the truth coaxed from her, and so he persisted, 'No, tell me: how did you learn to cook? I thought you'd been doing it for years.'

Speaking very quickly, she said, 'I bought a cookbook.'

'A cookbook? You? Why?'

'When I knew that I liked you as much as I did, and I saw how important food was to you, I decided I had better learn how to cook.' She looked at him, waited for him to comment, but when he didn't, she continued, 'I started to cook at home, and, believe me, some of the first things I cooked were even worse than what we had tonight.'

'Hard to believe,' Brunetti said. 'Go on.'

'Well, I knew I liked you, and I suppose I knew I wanted to be with you. So I kept at it, and I just sort of . . .'

She broke off and gave a gesture that encompassed the entire kitchen. 'I suppose I learned.'

'From a book?'

'And with some help.'

'From whom?'

'Damiano. He's a good cook. And then my mother. And then, after we were engaged, from yours.'

'My mother? She taught you how to cook?' Paola nodded and Brunetti said, 'She never told me.'

'I made her promise not to.'

'Why?'

'I don't know, Guido,' she said, obviously lying. He said nothing, knowing from long experience that she'd explain. 'I guess I wanted you to think I could do everything, even cook.'

He leaned forward in his chair and grabbed her around the waist, pulling her towards him. She tried half-heartedly to twist away. 'I feel so silly, telling you after all this time,' she said, leaning against him, bending to kiss the top of his head. Suddenly, the idea came upon her from nowhere, and she said, 'My mother knows her.'

'Who?'

'Countess Lorenzoni. I think they're on the board of some charity together, or some . . .' She broke off. 'I can't remember, but I know she knows her.'

'Has she ever said anything about her?'

'No, not anything I'd remember. Except for this thing about her son. It destroyed her, or that's what *Mamma* says. She used to be involved in lots of things: the Friends of Venice, the theatre, raising money for the restoration of La Fenice. But when this happened, she stopped everything. My mother says she never goes out, doesn't accept calls from anyone. No one sees her any more. I think *Mamma* said it was not knowing what happened to him that did this to her, that she could probably accept his death. But this way, not knowing if he's alive or dead . . . I can't imagine anything more horrible. Even knowing he's dead is better than that.'

Brunetti, who usually voted in favour of life, ordinarily would have disputed this, but it was not a subject he wanted to drag into discussion tonight. He'd spent the day thinking about the disappearance and death of children, and he wanted nothing more to do with it. Blatantly, he changed the topic. 'How are things at the idea factory?' he asked.

She moved away from him, took the cutlery from the side of the sink, and began to wipe it dry. 'About on the same level as dinner,' she finally answered. Piece by piece, she dropped the knives and forks into a drawer. 'The chairman of the department has insisted that we begin to pay attention to colonial literature.'

'What's that?' Brunetti asked.

'Well might you ask,' she replied, wiping a serving spoon. 'Those people who grew up in cultures where English is not the native language but who write in English.'

'What's wrong with that?'

'He's asked some of us to teach this stuff next year.'

'You?'

'Yes,' she answered, dropping the last spoon into the drawer and slamming it closed.

'What class?'

'"The Voice of Caribbean Women."'

'Because you're a woman?'

'Not because I'm Caribbean,' she answered.

'And?'

'And I've refused to teach it.'

'Why?'

'Because they don't interest me. Because I'd teach it reluctantly and badly.' He sensed equivocation here and waited for her to confess it. 'And because I won't let him tell me what to teach.'

'Is this what's been bothering you?' he asked casually.

Though the look she gave him was sharp, her answer was as off-handed as his question. 'I didn't know that anything was bothering me.' She started to add to this, but the door slammed open, the children were back with the ice cream, and his question remained unanswered.

That night, indeed, Brunetti woke up at least twice, and each time he drank two glasses of mineral water. The second time was just after dawn, and when he turned back from putting the glass down on the floor beside his bed, he propped himself up on his elbow and studied Paola's face. A lock of hair curved down under her chin, and a few strands stirred softly with her breathing. Eyes closed, all animation erased, her face revealed only bones and character. Secret and separate, she lay beside him, and he studied her face for some sign that would help him to know her more absolutely. With sudden urgency, he wanted what Count Orazio had told him to be untrue, wanted desperately for her, and for their life, to be happy and tranquil.

Mocking this desire, the bells of San Polo rang out six times, and the sparrows who had decided to build a nest between the loose bricks of the chimney called out that it was daylight and time to get to work. Brunetti ignored them and put his head back down on his pillow. He closed his eyes, sure he'd never get back to sleep, but soon discovered how easily he could ignore the call to return to work.

# 14

That morning, Brunetti decided it would be wise to present Patta with what little information he had about the Loren-zoni murder—it could be called that now—and he did so soon after the Vice-Questore got to the Questura. Brunetti feared that there would be repercussions from his own behaviour towards Patta the previous day, but there were none; at least no obvious ones. Patta had seen the newspa-per accounts and expressed formulaic concern about the death, his greatest regret apparently that it should have happened to a member of the nobility.

Brunetti explained that, as he'd just happened to answer the call confirming the identification of the dental records, he had taken it upon himself to inform the parents. From long experience, he was careful to display no interest in the case, asked almost casually whom the Vice-Questore wanted to assign to it, even going so far as to suggest one of his colleagues.

'What are you working on now, Brunetti?'

'The dumping out at Marghera,' Brunetti answered promptly, making pollution sound more important than murder.

'Ah, yes,' Patta answered: he'd heard of Marghera. 'Well, I think that's something the uniformed branch can handle.'

'But I've still got to interview the Captain of the Port,' Brunetti insisted. 'And someone's got to check the records of that tanker from Panama.'

'Let Pucetti do it,' Patta said dismissively.

Brunetti remembered a game he used to play with the children, when they were much younger. They would drop a handful of spaghetti-length wooden sticks and then see how many they could pick up individually without moving any of the other sticks. The trick was to move extremely gently; one false move could bring everything tumbling down.

'You don't think Mariani would do?' Brunetti suggested, naming one of the other two *commissari*. 'He's just back from vacation.'

'No, I think you should handle this. After all, your wife knows people like this, doesn't she?'

'People like this' was a phrase Brunetti had for years heard hurled about as a pejorative, usually racist, yet here it was, newly sprung from the lips of the Vice-Questore himself, sounding for all the world like the highest possible praise. Brunetti nodded vaguely, uncertain of the sort of people his wife might know or what she might know about them.

'Good, then your association with her family might help you here,' Patta said, suggesting that the power of the state or the authority of the police counted for nothing at all with 'people like this'. Which, Brunetti reflected, might well be the case.

He dragged out a very reluctant, 'Well,' and then gave in, anything that could be construed as enthusiasm carefully banished from his voice. 'If you insist, Vice-Questore, then I'll speak to Pucetti about Marghera.'

'Keep me or Lieutenant Scarpa up to date on what you're doing, Brunetti,' Patta added almost absently.

'Of course, sir,' he said, as empty a promise as he'd made in quite some time. Seeing that Patta had nothing further to say to him, Brunetti got to his feet and left the office.

When he emerged, Signorina Elettra asked, 'Did you persuade him to give it to you?'

'Persuade?' Brunetti repeated, amazed that Signorina Elettra, even after all this time with Patta, could actually believe that Patta was open to reason or persuasion.

'By telling him how busy you were with other things, of course,' she said, hitting a key on her computer and sparking her printer into life.

Brunetti couldn't help smiling down at her. 'I thought for a moment I'd have to use violence in refusing to accept,' Brunetti said.

'You must be very interested in it, Commissario.'

'I am.'

'Then perhaps this will interest you,' she said, reaching forward and taking a few pages out of the slot beneath the printer's mouth. She passed them to him.

'What is it?'

'A list of every time one of the Lorenzonis has come to our attention.'

'Our?'

'The forces of order.'

'Which includes?'

'Us, the *Carabinieri,* the Customs Police, and the finance Police.'

Brunetti put a look of false astonishment on his face. 'No access to the Secret Service, Signorina?'

Her look was bland. 'Not until it's really necessary, sir. That's a contact I don't want to abuse by overuse.'

Brunetti studied her eyes, looking for a sign that she was joking. He was uncertain which would be more unsettling: the discovery that she was telling the truth or the fact that he couldn't tell the difference.

In the face of her continued equanimity, he chose not to pursue this line of questioning and looked at the papers. The first listing dated from October of three years before: Roberto arrested for drunken driving. Small fine: case dismissed.

Before he could read further, she interrupted him. 'I didn't include anything there having to do with the kidnapping, sir. I'm having a separate list compiled to deal with that. I thought it would be less confusing.'

Brunetti nodded and left, reading as he climbed the stairs to his office. The Christmas of that same year—Christmas Day, in fact—a truck belonging to the Lorenzoni transportation company had been hijacked from State Highway 8, near Salerno. The truck had been carrying a quarter of a billion lire in German-made laboratory equipment; the cargo was never recovered.

Four months later, a random customs inspection of a Lorenzoni truck discovered that its cargo manifest declared only half the number of Hungarian binoculars actually contained in the truck. A fine was imposed and quickly paid. There was a lull of a year, during which the Lorenzonis were not subject to the attentions of the police, but then Roberto was involved in a fight at a disco. No criminal charges were brought, but a civil suit was settled when the Lorenzonis paid twelve million lire to a boy whose nose was broken in the fight.

And that was it: nothing more. During the eight months that ensued between the fight in the disco and his kidnapping, neither Roberto, his family, nor any of its wide-flung businesses existed in any way whatsoever for the many police powers which surveilled the country and its citizens. And then, like a bolt from quiet skies, the kidnapping. Two notes, a public appeal to the kidnappers, and then silence. Until the body of the boy was found in a field near Belluno.

Even as he thought this, Brunetti asked himself why he was thinking of Roberto, and had done so from the very beginning, as a 'boy'. After all, the young man, at the time of the kidnapping and presumably at the time of his death, which seemed to have happened soon thereafter, had been twenty-one. Brunetti tried to recall how various people had spoken of Roberto: his girlfriend had mentioned his practical jokes and selfishness; Count Orazio had been almost condescending; and his mother had mourned her baby.

His thoughts were interrupted by the entrance of Vianello. 'I've decided I want to go up to Belluno with you, Vianello. You think you could see about getting us a car?'

'I can do better than that,' the sergeant answered with a broad smile. 'In fact, that's what I've come about.'

Knowing he was supposed to, Brunetti asked, 'What does that mean?'

'Montisi,' was the sergeant's cryptic reply.

'Montisi?'

'Yes, sir. He can get us there.'

'I didn't know they'd built a canal.'

'His daughter, sir.'

Brunetti knew that Montisi's greatest source of pride was the fact that the three children he had sent to the university had become a doctor, a psychologist, and an archaeologist. 'Which one?' he asked.

'Renata, the psychologist,' Vianello answered, and before Brunetti could ask, explained, 'She's also a pilot. A friend of hers keeps a Cesna out at the Lido. If we want, she'll drop us off up there this afternoon and then go on to Udine.'

'Let's do it,' Brunetti said, catching from Vianello's tone the excitement of a day's outing.

She turned out to be just as good a pilot as her father. Brunetti and Vianello, still caught up in the enthusiasm and novelty of the idea, kept their noses pressed against the small windows of the plane for most of the twenty-five minute flight. During it Brunetti learned two things he hadn't known: that two airlines had refused to hire her as a pilot because she had a degree in psychology and would 'embarrass the other pilots' with her level of culture; and that vast stretches of land around Vittorio Veneto were listed by the military as 'Pio XII', slang for 'Proibito', and hence could not be flown over. So the small plane carried them along the Adriatic coast and then sharply to the northwest, over Pordenone and then to Belluno. Below them, the earth changed from tan to brown to green and back again as they flew over still-fallow fields or vast swathes of new plantings; every so often a stand of fruit trees exploded in pastel blossoms or a sudden gust of wind could be seen to hurl great handfuls of petals up towards the plane.

Ivo Barzan, the *commissario* who had seen to the removal of Roberto Lorenzoni's body from the field to the hospital and who had then contacted the Venice police, was waiting for them when the plane landed.

He took them, first, to Doctor Litfin's house and walked with them to the dark rectangle near the stand of trees. A single beige chicken pecked busily at the freshly turned earth of the shallow pit, not at all disturbed by the snapping of the wind in the strips of red and white tape which surrounded it. No bullet had been found, Barzan told them, though the *Carabinieri* had twice gone over the field with metal detectors.

As he looked down into the pit and heard the chicken scraping and pecking, Brunetti wondered what this place had been like when the boy died, if indeed he had died here. In winter, it would have been grim and bleak; in the autumn, at least there would still have been living things. And, at the stupidity of that thought, he reviled himself. If death waits at the end of the field, it hardly matters if the earth is strewn with mud or flowers. Hands in his pockets, he turned away from the pit.

Barzan told them that none of the neighbours had anything helpful to tell the police. One old woman insisted that the dead man was her husband, poisoned by the mayor, a Communist. No one remembered anything unusual, though Barzan did have the grace to add he thought it unlikely anyone could be very helpful when the police were no more specific than to ask if anyone had seen something strange about two years ago.

Brunetti spoke to the people across the road, an old couple well into their eighties, who tried to make up for their inability to remember seeing anything by offering coffee and, when all three policemen accepted, lacing it generously with sugar and grappa.

Doctor Bortot, who was waiting for them in his office at the hospital, said there was little he could add to the report he had already sent to Venice. It was all there: the deadly hole at the base of the skull, the lack of a clearly defined exit hole, the extensive damage to and deterioration of the internal organs.

'Damage?' Brunetti asked.

'The lungs, from what I could see. He must have smoked like a Turk, this boy, and been smoking for years,' Bortot said and paused to light a cigarette. 'And the spleen,' he started and then paused. 'The damage might have been from natural exposure, but it doesn't explain why it's so small. But it's hard to tell when he's been in the ground so long.'

'More than a year?' Brunetti asked.

'That's what I'd guess, yes. Is it the Lorenzoni boy?' he asked.

'Yes.'

'Well, the time's about right, then. If they killed him soon after they took him, it would be a bit less that two years, and that's about what I would guess.' He crushed out his cigarette. 'You have children?' he asked, making the question general.

All three policemen nodded.

'Well, then,' Bortot said inconclusively and excused himself, explaining that he had three more autopsies to perform that afternoon.

Barzan, with remarkable generosity, offered to have his driver take them back to Venice, and, tired by the site of death, Brunetti agreed. Neither he nor Vianello had much to say as they sped south, though Brunetti was struck by how much less interesting the scenery was, seen from the window of a car. From the ground, as well, no warning was given about what places were '*Zona Proibita*'.

# 15

The morning papers, as Brunetti had anticipated, fell upon the Lorenzoni story with vulpine avidity. Because of their assumption that the reading public was incapable of recalling even the most important details of a story that had appeared eighteen months before—in which assumption Brunetti believed them to be correct—each story began by retelling the story of the original kidnapping. In them, Roberto was variously described as 'the oldest son', 'the nephew', and 'the only son' of the Lorenzoni family, and the kidnapping was reported to have taken place in Mestre, Belluno, and Vittorio Veneto. Not only the readers seemed to have forgotten the details.

Doubtless due to their failure to obtain a copy of the autopsy report, the ghoulish delight the press usually took in cases of exhumation was strangely absent from the accounts, the writers contenting themselves with the lacklustre 'advanced stage of decomposition' and 'human remains'. Reading the stories, Brunetti found himself uncomfortable with his own disappointment at the tepid language, worried that his palate had become accustomed to richer fare.

On his desk when he reached his office was a video cassette in a padded brown envelope which carried his name. He called down to Signorina Elettra. 'Is this the tape from RAI?' he asked.

'Yes, Dottore. It got here yesterday afternoon.'

He looked down at the envelope, but it seemed to be unopened. 'Did you watch it at home?' he asked.

'No. I don't have a cassette player.'

'Or you would have?'

'Of course.'

'Shall we go down to the lab and have a look at it?' he suggested.

'I'd like that, sir,' she said and hung up.

She was waiting for him at the door of the ground-floor laboratory, today dressed in a pair of jeans that had been ironed to within an inch of their life. The casual note was re-inforced by a pair of what he thought must be cowboy boots with dangerous toes and slanted heels. A silk crepe blouse re-established a professional tone, as did the severe chignon into which her hair was pulled today.

'Is Bocchese here?' he asked.

'No, he's giving evidence today.'

'Which case?'

'The Brandolini robbery.'

Neither of them bothered to shake their heads at the fact that this four-year-old robbery, which had been followed two days later by an arrest, was getting to trial only now. 'But I asked him yesterday if we could use the lab to watch it, and he said it was all right,' she explained.

Brunetti opened the door and held it for her. Signorina Elettra went over to the VCR and switched it on as though she were entirely at home in the lab. He slipped in the tape. They waited for a few moments until the screen lit up with the RAI logo and test pattern, quickly followed by the date and a few lines of what Brunetti assumed was technical information.

'Do we have to send this back?' he asked, moving away from the screen and seating himself on one of the wooden folding chairs that faced it.

She came and sat in the chair next to him. 'No. Cesare said it's a copy. But he'd prefer that no one else finds out he sent it.'

Brunetti's reply was cut off by the voice of the announcer, giving the then-new facts of the Lorenzoni kidnapping and telling his viewers that RAI was bringing them an exclusive message from Count Ludovico Lorenzoni, the father of the victim. He explained, while the screen showed footage of the predictable tourist sites in Venice, that the Count had made the appeal that afternoon and that it would be shown exclusively on RAI in hopes that the kidnappers would heed the appeal of a bereaved parent. Then, with the screen lingering on a low angle shot of the façade of San Marco, the announcer handed over to the RAI crew in Venice.

A man in a dark suit and serious expression stood in the broad hallway of what Brunetti recognized to be the Lorenzoni palace. Behind him could be seen the double doors to the study in which Brunetti had spoken to the family. He summarized what the other man had said, then turned and opened one of the doors to the study. It swung open to allow the camera to focus on, then draw near, Count Ludovico, who sat behind a desk Brunetti did not remember being in the room.

At first, the Count looked down at his hands, but as the camera drew closer, he raised his eyes and looked directly at it. A few seconds passed, the camera found the right distance and stopped moving, and the Count began to speak.

'I address my words to the persons who are responsible for the disappearance of my son, Roberto, and I ask that they listen to me with attention and charity. I am willing to pay any sum at all for the return of my son, but the agencies of the state have prevented that: I no longer have access to any of my assets, and there is no way I can hope to raise the sum demanded, either here in Italy or abroad. If I could do this, I swear upon my honour that I would, and I further swear that I would gladly give that sum, any sum, to assure the safe return of my son.'

Here the Count paused and looked down at his hands. After a moment, he returned his eyes to the camera. 'I ask these people to have compassion on me and on my wife, who joins me in my entreaty. I appeal to their feelings of humanity and I ask them to free my son. If they wish, I will gladly exchange places with him: they have but to tell me what they want me to do, and it will be done. They have said that they will contact me through a friend of mine whom they have not named. All they need to do is contact this person and leave instructions. Whatever they ask, I will do, and do gladly, if it will assure me the return of my beloved son.'

The Count paused here, but briefly. 'I appeal to their sense of compassion and ask that they have mercy on my wife and on me.' The Count stopped, but the camera remained on his face until he glanced to the left of the camera for a second, then back into its lens.

The screen gradually darkened, to be replaced in a moment by the studio announcer. He reminded the viewers that this had been a RAI exclusive and added that anyone having information about Roberto Lorenzoni should call the number listed at the bottom of the screen. Apparently because this was a file copy and not one that was shown on the RAI stations, no number appeared.

The screen went dark.

Brunetti got up and turned down the sound, leaving the television on. He pushed the 'rewind' button and waited until the tape stopped humming. When he heard it click to a stop, he turned to Signorina Elettra. 'What do you think?'

'I was right about the make-up,' she said.

'Yes,' Brunetti agreed. 'Anything else?'

'The language?' she suggested.

123

Brunetti nodded. 'You mean that he referred to them as "they" and not as "you"?' he asked.

'Yes,' she answered. 'That seems strange. But maybe it was too difficult for him to address them directly, given what they'd done to his son.'

'Possible,' Brunetti agreed, trying to imagine how a father would react to this, the greatest of horrors.

He reached out and hit the 'play' button again. The tape began once more, but this time there was no sound.

He glanced at Signorina Elettra, who raised her eyebrows. 'I never take the headphones on planes,' he explained. 'It's remarkable, what you seen in films if there's no sound to distract you.'

She nodded, and together they watched the tape play through again. This time, they could see the eyes of the announcer flit across the script that was playing somewhere just to the left of the camera. The other one, outside the door to the Count's study, seemed to know his lines by heart, though the seriousness of his face seemed forced and unnatural.

If Brunetti had expected the Count's nervousness or anger to come through more clearly this way, he was mistaken. Viewed in silence, he seemed to be without emotion. When he looked down at his hands, any viewer would doubt that the Count could ever find the will to look up again, and when his eyes flashed for that fleeting moment to the side of the camera, it was a gesture utterly devoid of curiosity or impatience.

When the screen again darkened, Signorina Elettra said, 'Poor man, and he had to sit there while they put make-up on his face.' She shook her head, eyes closed, as though she'd walked in on an indecent act.

Again, Brunetti pressed the 'rewind' button, and again the tape reversed itself and wound to a stop. He pressed the 'reject' button, and the tape sprang out. Brunetti slipped it into its box and the box into the pocket of his jacket.

'Something horrible should happen to them,' she said with sudden ferocity.

'Execution?' Brunetti asked, bending forward to turn off both the VCR and the television.

She shook her head. 'No. No matter how horrible these people are, no matter what people do, we can't allow any government to have that power.'

'Because they can't be trusted?' Brunetti asked.

'Would you trust this government?' she asked.

Brunetti shook his head.

'Can you name a government that you would trust?' she continued.

'To decide about the life and death of a citizen?' He shook his head, and asked, 'But then how punish people who do things like this?'

'I don't know. I want them to be destroyed, want them to die. I'd be a liar to deny that. But it's too dangerous a power to be given to . . . to anyone.'

He remembered something Paola had once said; he no longer recalled the context. Whenever people want to argue dishonestly, she'd said, they pull out a specific example so overwhelming as to render disagreement impossible. But no matter how compelling specific cases were, she always insisted, law was about principle and about universals. In-dividual cases proved themselves and nothing else. Since he had so often seen the individual horror of the aftermath of crime, Brunetti well understood the impulse to call for new laws, more punitive laws. As a policeman, he knew that the rigour of the law was most often exercised on the weak and the poor, and he further knew that the law's severity was no impediment to crime. He knew all of this as a policeman, but as a man and as a father, he still longed to see the people who had snuffed out the life of this young man brought to justice and brought to suffering.

He walked over and opened the door to the lab, and they left, returning to their jobs and to the world where crime was something to be stopped, not the subject of philosophical speculation.

# 16

Good sense told Brunetti it was foolish to expect the Lorenzoni family to talk to him before the boy was buried, but it was charity which prevented his asking. The newspaper accounts had given Monday as the day for the funeral, the church of San Salvador its place. Before then, however, there was still a good deal of information Brunetti wanted to obtain about Roberto.

Back at his desk, he called the office of Doctor Urbani and asked the dentist's secretary if the name of Roberto's family doctor was on record. It took her a few minutes to check, but it turned out the name was listed, given on the original file that was opened for Roberto when he first went to Doctor Urbani's office ten years ago.

The doctor's name, Luciano De Cal, was vaguely familiar to Brunetti; he had gone to school with a De Cal, but his name was Franco, and he was a jeweller. The doctor, when Brunetti called him in his office and explained the reason of his call, said that, yes, Roberto had been his patient for most of his life, ever since the original family doctor of the Lorenzonis had retired.

When Brunetti began to ask about Roberto's health in the months before his disappearance, Doctor De Cal excused himself for a moment and went to get the boy's file. He had come in about two weeks before his disappearance, Doctor De Cal said, complaining about lethargy and continuing stomach pain. The doctor had first thought it was colic, to which Roberto was prone, especially in the first weeks of cool weather. But when he didn't respond to treatment, De Cal had suggested he see an internist.

'Did he see that doctor?' Brunetti asked.

'I don't know.'

'Why not?'

'I went on holiday, to Thailand, soon after I gave him Dottor Montini's name, and when I got back, he had been kidnapped.'

'Did you ever have cause to speak to this Doctor Montini about him?'

'About Roberto?'

'Yes.'

'No, never. He's not someone I know socially: he's a professional colleague.'

'I see,' Brunetti answered. 'Could you give me his number?'

De Cal set the phone down, and came back with the number. 'It's in Padova,' he explained and gave Brunetti the number.

Brunetti thanked him and asked, 'You thought it might be colic, Dottore?'

Brunetti heard the rustle of a page. 'Well, it could have been.' Again, the sound of turning pages came down the line. 'I have it recorded here that he came to see me three times in a period of two weeks. That was in September, the tenth, the nineteenth and the twenty-third.'

The last appointment, then, would have been five days before he was kidnapped.

'How did he seem?' Brunetti asked.

'I have a note here that he seemed irritated and nervous, but I really don't have a clear memory of it.'

'What sort of a boy did he seem to you, Doctor?' Brunetti asked suddenly.

De Cal answered after a moment. 'I suppose he was pretty typical.'

'Of what?' Brunetti asked.

'Of that sort of family, that social circle.'

He remembered now that his classmate, Franco, had been a committed Communist. That sort of thing very often ran in families, so he asked the doctor, 'You mean of the wealthy and idle?'

De Cal had the grace to laugh at Brunetti's tone. 'Yes, I suppose I do. Poor boy, there was no bad in him. I knew him since he was about ten, so there was little I didn't know about him.'

'Such as?'

'Well, he wasn't very bright. I think it was a disappointment to his father, that Roberto should be so slow.'

Brunetti sensed that there was an unsaid half to that sentence, and so he suggested a way to end it.

'Unlike his cousin?'

'Maurizio?

'Yes.'

'Have you met him?' De Cal asked.

'Once.'

'And what did you think?'

'You couldn't say he isn't bright.'

De Cal laughed and Brunetti smiled at the answer.

'Is he your patient as well, Doctor.'

'No, only Roberto. I'm really a paediatrician, you know, but Roberto kept coming to me when he got older, and I never had the heart to suggest he start seeing another doctor.'

'Not until Doctor Montini,' Brunetti reminded him.

'Yes. Whatever it was, it wasn't colic. I thought it might be Crohn's Disease—I've even made a note of it in the file here. That's why I sent him to Montini. He's one of the best men around here for Crohn's.'

Brunetti had heard of the disease but could remember nothing. 'What are the symptoms?' he asked.

'Intestinal pain to begin with. Then diarrhoea, blood in the stool. It's very painful. Very serious. He had all of those symptoms.'

'And did you ever have your diagnosis confirmed?'

'I told you, Commissario. I sent him to Montini, but when I got back from vacation, he had been kidnapped, so I didn't pursue it. You could ask Montini.'

'I will, Dottore,' Brunetti said and bade the doctor a polite farewell.

He immediately called the Padova number. Doctor Montini was making his rounds at the hospital and wouldn't be back in his office until the following morning at nine. Brunetti left his name, office and home numbers, and asked that the doctor call him as soon as he could. There was no special need for haste, but Brunetti felt a dull impatience with not knowing what he was looking for or what was important, and he thought that haste would at least disguise that ignorance.

His phone rang as soon as he set it down. It was Signorina Elettra, saying that she'd prepared a file on the Lorenzoni businesses, both in Italy and abroad, and wondered if he would like to see it. He went downstairs to get it.

The file was as thick as a package of cigarettes. 'Signorina,' he began, 'how did you manage to accumulate something like this in so little time?'

'I spoke to some friends who are still working at the bank and asked if they could ask around.'

'You did all this since I asked you?'

'It's easy, sir. It all comes to me through that.' As had by now become ritual, she waved in the direction of her computer, the screen of which glimmered behind her.

'How long would it take a person to learn to use one of them, Signorina?'

'You, sir?' she asked.

'Yes.'

'It would depend on two things, no, three.'

'And what are they?'

'How intelligent you are. How much you want to learn. And who teaches you.'

Modesty prevented his asking her assessment of the first, uncertainty kept him from answering the second. 'Could you teach me?'

'Yes.'

'Would you?'

'Certainly. When would you like to begin?'

'Tomorrow?'

She nodded, then smiled.

'How much time will it take?' Brunetti asked.

'That depends, as well.'

'On what?'

Did her smile grow even wider? 'On the same three things.'

He started to read while still on the steps, and by the time he was again at his desk, he had read through lists of holdings that totalled billions of lire, and he had begun to understand why the kidnappers would have chosen the Lorenzonis. Little order had been imposed upon the papers in the file, but Brunetti made an attempt at that by separating them into piles, placing the papers in rough correspondence to their location on the map of Europe.

Trucks, steel, plastics factories in the Crimea: he followed a trail of perpetual expansion to meet new markets, a veritable explosion towards the East, as more and more of the Lorenzoni interests and holdings slipped behind the place where the Iron Curtain no longer stood. In March, two clothing factories in Vercelli had been closed, only to reopen two months later in Kiev. A half hour later, he set the last paper down on his desk and saw that most of them lay to his right, even though he was vague about the exact location of many of the places to which the Lorenzoni interests were expanding.

It did not take Brunetti long to remember the stories that had recently filled the press about the so-called Russian Mafia, the bands of Chechens, who, if these accounts were to be believed, had taken over most business in Russia, both legitimate and illegitimate. It was a short leap from there to the possibility that these men could somehow have been responsible for the kidnapping. After all, the men who took Roberto had not spoken at all, had merely shown him their guns and led him away.

But then how would they have ended up in that field below Col di Cugnan, a place so small that even most Venetians had probably never heard of it? He pulled out the file on the kidnapping and paged through it until he found the plastic-covered ransom notes. Though the block letters could have been printed by anyone, there were no errors in the Italian, though Brunetti admitted to himself that that proved nothing.

He had no idea of what Russian crime would feel like, but all his instincts told him that this wasn't one. Whoever had kidnapped Roberto would have had to know about the villa, been able to wait there undetected until he turned up. Unless, of course, Brunetti added to himself, they already knew when Roberto would appear. This, in fact, was yet another one of those questions that had not been asked during the original investigation. Who had known of Roberto's plans for the evening and of his intention to go to the villa?

As often happened, Brunetti was struck by restlessness as he read the reports prepared by other people, in this instance people no longer involved in the case.

Feeling not a little uncomfortable at the ease with which he succumbed to his feelings, he picked up the phone and dialled the internal number for Vianello. When the sergeant answered, Brunetti said, 'Let's go look at the gate.'

# 17

Although Brunetti was as urban a man as could be imagined, never having lived anywhere but in a city, he took a peasant's delight in the abundance of nature and in any sign of its beauty. Since childhood he had loved the springtime most, felt for it a passion that was tangled up with memories of the joy that came with the first warm days after the endless cold of winter. And there was, too, delight at the return of colour: the bold yellow of forsythia, the purple of crocuses, and the happy green of new leaves. Even from the rear window of the car that sped north on the *autostrada*, he could see these colours, and he gloried in them. Vianello, riding in the passenger seat beside Pucetti, discussed with him the strangely mild winter, far too warm to have frozen and thus destroyed the seaweed in the *laguna*, which in its turn meant that the beaches would be filled with it this summer.

They turned off at Treviso, then doubled back on the state highway in the direction of Roncade. After a few kilometres, they saw a sign on the right, directing them towards the church of Sant Ubaldo.

'It's down here, isn't it?' Pucetti asked, having checked the map before they set off from Piazzale Roma.

'Yes,' Vianello answered, 'supposed to be on the left in about three kilometres.'

'Never been up here,' Pucetti said. 'Pretty.'

Vianello nodded but said nothing.

After a few minutes, a turn in the narrow road brought them within sight of a thick stone tower up ahead on their left. A high wall ran off at right angles from two sides of the tower and was soon lost among the budding trees that stood on either side of it.

At a tap on his shoulder from Brunetti, Pucetti slowed as they reached the wall, and they drove along it for a few hundred metres. When Brunetti saw gates ahead of them, he tapped Pucetti on the shoulder again, signalling him to stop. He pulled on to the broad arc of gravel in front of the gates, angling the front of the car towards them. The three men got out.

The file on the kidnapping had reported that the stone which blocked the gates on the inside was twenty centimetres wide at its narrowest point, yet the distance between the iron rungs of the gates, Brunetti saw when he held up his hand to measure them, was just a bit broader than his palm, no more than ten centimetres. He moved off to the left, following the wall, with was half again as tall as he.

'If they had a ladder, I suppose,' Vianello called from where he stood, hands on hips and head bent back, looking up at the top of the gates. Before Brunetti could answer, he heard the sound of a car approaching from his left. A small white Fiat with two men in the front seat came into view. It slowed at the sight of Brunetti and the others, and the men in the car made no attempt to disguise their curiosity at the sight of the uniformed men and the blue and white police car. They moved off slowly, just as another car came from the right and passed them. This car, too, slowed to allow the occupants to stare at the police in front of the Lorenzoni villa.

A ladder, Brunetti reflected, meant a van. Roberto had been kidnapped on the twenty-eighth of September, so the autumn foliage on the bushes at the side of the road could have provided sufficient cover for a vehicle of any kind, even a van.

Brunetti went back to the gate and stood in front of the control panel of the alarm system attached to the column on the left. He pulled a small slip of paper from his pocket and glanced at it. Reading the numbers from it, he punched out a five-figure code on the control box. The red light on the front of the panel went out, and a green one at the bottom came on. A mechanical hum sounded from the back of the column, and the iron gates started to swing open.

'How'd you know that?' Vianello asked.

'It was in the original report,' Brunetti answered, not without a certain satisfaction at having thought to write the numbers down. The humming stopped: the gates stood fully open.

'It's private property, isn't it?' Vianello asked, leaving it to Brunetti to make the first step and, with it, give the order.

'Yes, it is,' Brunetti answered. He walked through the gates and started up the gravel-covered driveway.

Vianello motioned to Pucetti to stay outside and himself followed Brunetti through the gates and up the drive. Box hedges grew on either side, placed so close together as to create almost solid walls of green between them and the gardens that were sure to stand behind them. After about fifty metres, stone arches opened on either side, and Brunetti went through the one on the right. When Vianello came through behind him, he found Brunetti standing still, hands in the pockets of his trousers, coat flung back on either side. Brunetti studied the ground in front of them, a series of raised flowerbeds set within ordered gravel paths.

Saying nothing, he turned and crossed the central path and went through the other arch, where he again stopped and looked around him. The meticulous order of path and flowerbeds was repeated here; a mirror image of the garden on the opposite side. Hyacinths, lilies of the valley, and crocuses basked in the sun, looking as though they, too, would like to put their hands in their pockets and have a look around.

Vianello came to stand beside Brunetti. 'Well, sir?' he asked, not at all sure why Brunetti did nothing more than stand and study the flowers.

'No stones, are there, Vianello?'

Vianello, who hadn't paid attention, not really, to his surroundings, answered, 'No, sir. There aren't. Why?'

'Assuming the layout hasn't changed much, that means that they'd have to bring it with them, doesn't it?'

'And carry it over the wall with them?'

Brunetti nodded. 'The local police did at least patrol the inside of the wall, the whole thing. Nothing was disturbed on the ground under it.' Turning to Vianello, he asked, 'What do you think that stone weighed?'

'Fifteen kilos?' Vianello guessed. 'Ten?'

Brunetti nodded. Neither had to comment on the difficulty of getting something that heavy over the wall.

'Shall we have a look at the villa?' Brunetti asked, though neither he nor Vianello heard it as a question.

Brunetti went back through the arch; Vianello followed him. Side by side, they started up the gravel pathway, which curved to the right. Off ahead of them a bird sang out joyously, and the rich scent of loam and heat filled the air.

Vianello, who was looking at his feet while he walked, was at first conscious only of small stones splashing up towards his ankles and then of dust falling on to the tops of his shoes. The sound of the shot registered only after this. It was quickly followed by another, and the spurt of stones a metre behind where Vianello had been standing showed that this one would have found its target. But as the pebbles flew into the air, Vianello was already lying at the right side of the path, knocked there by Brunetti, the force of whose lunging push propelled him, still running, a few metres beyond the fallen sergeant.

Without conscious thought, Vianello pushed himself to his feet and, crouching low, ran towards the hedge. The solid wall of branches provided no hiding place, only a dark green wall against which his blue uniform would be less visible than again the white gravel.

Another shot burst out, and then another. 'Back here, Vianello,' Brunetti shouted, and without looking to see where Brunetti was and still crouching low, Vianello ran towards the sound of his voice, vision dimmed by panic. Suddenly someone grabbed him by the left arm and dragged him off his feet. He saw an opening in the hedge and lurched through it like a beached seal, capable in his panic only of pushing himself forward with elbows and knees.

His wild thrusts forward were stopped by something hard: Brunetti's knees. He rolled away, stumbled to his feet, and drew his revolver. His hand trembled.

In front of him, Brunetti stood at a narrow opening left in the hedge by the removal of one of the bushes, his own revolver in his hand. Brunetti pulled himself back from the opening. 'You all right, Vianello?' he asked.

'Yes,' was all he could think to say. Then, 'Thank you, sir.'

Brunetti nodded, then crouched low and stuck his head out briefly from behind the protective branches of the trees.

'You see anything?' Vianello asked.

Brunetti gave a negative double grunt. Behind them, from the direction of the gates, the sharp double bleat of the police siren ripped through the air. Both men turned towards it, listening to see if it drew any closer, but the noise seemed to remain stationary. Brunetti got to his feet.

'Pucetti?' Vianello asked, thinking it unlikely that the local police could have got there so quickly.

For a moment, Brunetti was willing to set out towards the villa in search of whoever it was that had fired at them, but then the sound of the siren slipped into his consciousness again, and good sense intervened. 'Let's go back,' he said, turning towards the entrance and starting towards it, the path studded by the ranks of raised flowerbeds. 'He's probably called for help.'

They kept close to the hedge, and even when it curved sharply to the left and thus out of the line of fire from the villa, they kept inside of it, both of them reluctant to set foot on to the gravel path. Only when they were within sight of the stone wall did Brunetti feel safe enough to push his way, not without difficulty, through the thick branches and back on to the path.

The gates were closed, but the police car was now parked directly in front, its passenger door touching the gates and effectively blocking the exit.

When they got to within a few metres of the gate, Brunetti called out, shouting above the continuing sound of the car's pealing siren, 'Pucetti?'

An answering call came from behind the car, but there was no sign of the young policeman.

'Pucetti?' Brunetti called again.

'Hold up your gun, sir,' came Pucetti's voice from behind the car.

Understanding instantly, Brunetti raised his fist into the air, careful to show that he was still holding the revolver.

When Pucetti saw it, he came out from behind the car, his own gun in his hand, though pointed at the ground. He reached in through the open window of the car, and the noise of the klaxon stopped. In the sudden silence, he said, 'I wanted to be sure, sir.'

'Good,' Brunetti answered, wondering if he would have thought to eliminate the possibility of a hostage situation. 'You call the locals?'

'Yes, sir. There's a *Carabinieri* station outside of Treviso. They should be here soon. What happened?'

'Someone started to shoot at us as we were walking up the driveway.'

'You see them?' Pucetti asked.

Brunetti shook his head andVianello said, 'No.'

The young officer's next question was cut off by the sound of a new siren, this one coming from the direction of Treviso.

Above that noise, Brunetti called out the numbers of the gate's code, and Pucetti punched them in. The gate started to swing open, and even before Brunetti could suggest it, Pucetti got into the car and angled it back, then drove it halfway through the gates. He pulled the front sharply to the left and turned the car so that it would block the gates with its front fender while still allowing them enough room to pass through the gates on the other side.

The jeep that pulled up behind their car held two *Carabinieri*. They stopped behind the police car and the driver rolled down his window. 'What is it?' he asked, directing the question at all three of them. Thin-faced and sallow, he sounded quite calm, as though it were an everyday occurrence to be asked to respond to a call that the police were under fire.

'Someone up there started shooting,' Brunetti explained.

'They know who you are?' the *Carabiniere* asked. This time his accent was clearer. Sardinian. Perhaps he was accustomed to answering calls like this. He made no attempt to get out of the vehicle.

'No,' Vianello answered. 'What difference does that make?'

'They've had three robberies out here. And then there was that kidnapping. So if they saw someone coming up the driveway, it makes sense they'd start shooting. I would.'

'At this?' Vianello said, rather dramatically pounding his open palm on the chest of his uniform jacket.

'At that,' the *Carabiniere* shot back, pointing to the revolver that was still in Brunetti's hand.

Brunetti interrupted them. 'We've still been shot at, officer.' He bit back saying anything else.

Instead of answering, the *Carabiniere* pulled his head back inside the jeep, wound up the window, and picked up a cellular phone. Brunetti watched him press in a number, and from behind him Pucetti whispered, '*Gesù bambino.*'

There was a short telephone conversation, and then the *Carabiniere* dialled another number. After a moment's pause, he started to speak and went on speaking for a while. He nodded twice, pushed another button, and leaned forward to replace the phone on the dashboard.

He opened the window. 'You can go in now,' he said, gesturing beyond the gate with his chin.

'What?' Vianello asked.

'You can go in. I called them. I told them who you are, and they said you can go in.'

'Who did you talk to?' Brunetti asked.

'The nephew, what's his name?'

'Maurizio,' Brunetti volunteered.

'Yes. He's up there, but he said he won't fire again now that he knows who you are.' When none of them made a move, the *Carabiniere* urged them, 'Go ahead. It's safe. They won't shoot any more.'

Brunetti and Vianello exchanged a glance, and then Brunetti signalled with his hand for Pucetti to remain by the car. Saying nothing to the *Carabiniere*, the two men went back through the gate and again up the gravel drive. This time, Vianello looked ahead of him, eyes sweeping from side to side as they moved away from the gate.

Neither man spoke as they moved up the driveway.

From around the curve ahead of them, a man walked into view. Brunetti recognized him instantly as the nephew, Maurizio. He was not carrying a gun.

The distance between the three men closed. 'Why didn't you say anything?' Maurizio called out when he was still about ten metres from them. 'I've never heard of anything so stupid. You force open the gate and start up the drive. You're lucky neither of you got hurt.'

Brunetti recognized bluster when he heard it. 'Do you always greet visitors that way, Signor Lorenzoni?'

'When they break open my gates, I do,' the young man answered, coming to a stop directly in front of them.

'Nothing's broken,' Brunetti said.

'The code is,' Maurizio shot back. 'The only people who know the code to the gate are members of the family. And whoever broke into the villa.'

'And the men who took Roberto,' Brunetti added in an entirely conversational voice.

Maurizio didn't have time to disguise his astonishment. 'What?' he demanded.

'I think you heard me, Signore. The men who kidnapped Roberto.'

'I don't understand what you mean,' Lorenzoni said.

'The rock,' Brunetti explained.

'I don't know what you're talking about.'

'The rock that blocked the gates. It weighed more than ten kilos.'

'I still don't understand you.'

Instead of explaining, Brunetti asked casually, 'Do you have a licence to carry a revolver, Signor Lorenzoni?'

'Of course not,' he said, making no attempt to disguise his mounting anger. 'But I do have a hunting licence.'

That, Brunetti realized, would explain the thick shower of pebbles that had spurted up at Vianello's feet. 'And so you used a shotgun? To shoot at people.'

'To shoot *towards* people,' he corrected. 'No one was hurt. Besides, a man has a right to defend his property.'

'And is the villa your property?' Brunetti asked with bland politeness.

As he watched, he saw Lorenzoni bite back a sharp response. When he did speak, all he said was, 'It's my uncle's property. You know that.'

From back towards the gates, they heard an engine roar into life and then the sound of a vehicle driving away, no doubt the *Carabiniere,* tired of waiting to see what would happen, and happy to leave it to the Venetian police.

The pause served to give Lorenzoni time to recover his self-possession. 'How did you get in?' he demanded of Brunetti.

'With the code. It was in the report of your cousin's kidnapping.'

'You've got no right to come in here, not without a judge's order.'

'That sort of ruling is usually applied only when the police pursue a suspect illegally, Signor Lorenzoni. I see no suspect here. Do you?' Brunetti's smile was entirely natural. 'I assume your shotgun is registered with the local police and the tax paid on your hunting licence?'

'I'm not sure that's any of your business,' Lorenzoni shot back.

'I don't like being shot at, Signor Lorenzoni.'

'I told you I wasn't shooting at you, only towards you, to warn you off.'

During all of this, Brunetti had been thinking ahead to Patta's inevitable response, should he come to learn that Brunetti had been caught making an illegal entry onto the property of a wealthy and influential businessman. 'Perhaps we're both in the wrong, Signor Lorenzoni,' he finally said.

It was evident that Lorenzoni didn't know whether or not to read this as an apology. Brunetti turned away from him and asked Vianello, 'What do you think, Sergeant? You over your fright?'

But before the sergeant could answer, Lorenzoni suddenly stepped forward and put his hand on Brunetti's forearm. His smile made him look much younger. 'I'm sorry, Commissario. I was alone here, and it frightened me when the gates opened.'

'Didn't you think it might be someone in your family?'

'It couldn't be my uncle. I spoke to him in Venice twenty minutes ago. And he's the only one who knows the code now.' He dropped his hand to his side, stepped back from Brunetti and added, 'And I kept thinking of what happened to Roberto. I thought they'd come back, but for me this time.'

Fear has its own logic, Brunetti knew, and so it was possible the young man was telling the truth. 'We're sorry to have frightened you, Signor Lorenzoni,' he said. 'We came out to have a look at the place where the kidnapping happened.' Vianello, reading Brunetti's mood, added his own encouraging nod to this.

'Why?' Lorenzoni asked.

'To see if anything's been overlooked.'

'Like what?'

'Like the fact that there have been three robberies here.' When Lorenzoni offered no comment, Brunetti asked, 'When did they happen, before or after the kidnapping?'

'One happened before. The other two happened after. The last one was only two months ago.'

'What was taken?'

'The first time all they got was some silver from the dining room. One of the gardeners saw a light and came in to see what was going on. They went over the wall.'

'And the other two times?' Brunetti asked.

'The second happened during the kidnapping. That is, after Roberto disappeared but before the notes stopped coming. We were all in Venice. Whoever it was must have come in over the wall, and this time they got some paintings. There's a safe in the floor of one of the bedrooms, but they never found it. So I doubt that they were professionals. Probably drug addicts.'

'And the third time?'

'That happened two months ago. We were all out here, my uncle and aunt and I. I woke up in the middle of the night—I don't know why, perhaps something I heard. I went to the top of the steps and could hear someone moving around downstairs. So I went down to my uncle's study and got the shotgun.'

'The same one you used today?' Brunetti asked.

'Yes. It wasn't loaded, but I didn't know it at the time.' Lorenzoni gave an embarrassed smile at this confession and went on, 'I went to the top of the stairs, turned on the downstairs lights, and shouted down to them, to whoever it was. Then I went down the stairs, holding the gun in front of me.'

'That was brave of you,' Brunetti said, meaning it.

'I thought the gun was loaded.'

'What happened?'

'Nothing.'

'When I got halfway down the steps, I heard a door slam, then there were noises out in the garden.'

'What sort of noises?'

Lorenzoni started to answer, paused for a moment, and then said, 'I don't know. I was so frightened I had no idea of what I heard.' When neither Brunetti nor Vianello expressed surprise at this, he added, 'I had to sit down on the steps, I was so frightened.'

Brunetti's smile was gentle. 'It's a good thing you didn't know the gun wasn't loaded.'

Lorenzoni seemed uncertain just how to take this until Brunetti put a hand on his shoulder and said, 'There aren't many people who would have had the courage to come down those stairs, believe me.'

'My aunt and uncle have been very good to me,' Lorenzoni said by way of explanation.

'Did you ever find out who it was?' Brunetti asked.

Lorenzoni shook his head. 'Never. The *Carabiniere* came out and looked around, even made some plaster casts of footprints they found under the wall. But you know how it is,' he said with a sigh. 'Hopeless.' Suddenly realizing who he was talking to, Lorenzoni added, 'I don't mean that.'

Brunetti, who believed he did, waved the remark away and asked, 'What made you think we might be the kidnappers? Come back, that is?'

All the time they were speaking, Lorenzoni had been slowly leading them back towards the villa. As they rounded the final bend in the driveway, it suddenly came into view, a central three-storey structure with two lower wings flung out to either side. The blocks of stone out of which it had been built glowed a soft rose in the weak sun; the tall windows cast back what little light there was.

Suddenly remembering his position as host, Lorenzoni said, 'Can I offer you something?'

Out of the corner of his eye, Brunetti caught Vianello's badly disguised astonishment. First he tries to kill us, and then he offers us a drink.

'That's very kind of you, but no. What I would like you to do is tell me anything you can about your cousin.'

'About Roberto?'

'Yes.'

'What sort of things?'

'What sort of man he was. What sort of jokes he liked. What sort of work he did for the company. Things like that.' Though it sounded like an odd list of questions to Brunetti himself, Lorenzoni seemed not at all surprised at them. 'He was . . .' Lorenzoni began. 'I'm not sure how to say this gracefully. He was not at all a complicated person.' He stopped. Brunetti waited, curious to see what other euphemisms the young man would use.

'He was useful to the company in that he always presented *una bella figura*, so my uncle could always send him anywhere to represent the company.'

'In negotiations?' Brunetti asked.

'Oh, no,' Lorenzoni answered immediately. 'Roberto was better at social things, like taking clients to dinner or showing them around the city.'

'What other things did he do?'

Lorenzoni thought about this for a few moments. 'My uncle would often send him to deliver important papers: if he had to be sure a contract would get somewhere in a hurry, Roberto would take it.'

'And then spend a few days there?'

'Yes, sometimes,' Lorenzoni answered.

'Did he attend university?'

'He was enrolled in the *facoltà* of *economia commerciale*.'

'Where?'

'Here, at Cà Foscari.'

'How long had he been enrolled?'

'Three years.'

'And how many exams had he taken?'

The truth, if Lorenzoni knew it, never made it past his lips. 'I don't know.' This last question had broken whatever rapport Brunetti had established by his response to

Lorenzoni's confession of fear. 'Why do you want to know all this?' Lorenzoni asked.

'I want to get an idea of what sort of person he was,' Brunetti answered truthfully.

'What difference is that supposed to make? After all this time?'

Brunetti shrugged. 'I don't know if it will make any difference at all. But if I'm going to spend the next few months of my life with him, I want to know something about him.'

'Months?' Lorenzoni asked.

'Yes.'

'Does that mean the investigation of the kidnapping is going to be reopened?'

'It's not just kidnapping any more. It's murder.'

Lorenzoni winced at the word but said nothing.

'Is there anything else you can think of to tell me about him that might be important?'

Lorenzoni shook his head and turned towards the steps that led to the front door of the villa.

'Anything about the way he was behaving before he was kidnapped?'

Lorenzoni shook his head again but then stopped and turned back to Brunetti. 'I think he was sick.'

'Why do you say that?'

'He was tired all the time and said he didn't feel right. I think he said he was having trouble with his stomach, diarrhoea. And he looked like he had lost some weight.'

'Did he say anything else about this?'

'No, no, he didn't. Roberto and I hadn't been all that close in the last few years.'

'Since you started to work for the business?'

The look Lorenzoni gave him was as devoid of friendliness as it was of surprise. 'What do you mean by that?'

'It would seem perfectly natural to me if he resented your presence in the business, especially if your uncle seemed to find you useful or placed trust in you or your judgement.'

Brunetti was expecting Lorenzoni to comment on this, but the young man surprised him by turning away silently and starting up the three broad steps that led to the villa. To his retreating back, Brunetti called, 'Is there anyone else I could talk to about him?'

At the top of the steps, Lorenzoni turned towards them. 'No. No one knew him. No one can help.' He turned back towards the door and went into the villa, closing the door behind him.

# 18

Because the following day was Sunday, Brunetti left the Lorenzonis to themselves and returned his attention to the family only the next morning, when he attended Roberto's funeral, a rite as solemn as it was grim. The mass was celebrated in the church of San Salvador, which stood beyond one end of Campo San Bartolomeo and which, because of its proximity to Rialto, received a constant flux of tourists during the day and hence during the mass. Brunetti, seated at the back of the church, was conscious of their invasive arrival, overheard the buzz of their exchanged whispers as they discussed how to photograph the Titian *Annunciation* and the tomb of Caterina Cornaro. But during a funeral? Perhaps, if they were very, very quiet and didn't use the flash.

The priest ignored their whispers and continued the millennium-old ritual, speaking of the transitory nature of our time upon this earth and of the sadness which must surround the parents and family of this child of God, cut off so soon from this earthly life. But then he enjoined his listeners to think of the joy which awaited the faithful and the good, gone to find their home with their Heavenly Father, He the source of all love. Only once was the priest distracted from his duties: a crash sounded from the back of the church as a chair fell over, this followed by a muttered exclamation in a language other than Italian.

Ritual swallowed up the interruption; the priest and his servers walked slowly around the closed coffin, chanting prayers and sprinkling it with holy water. Brunetti wondered if he were the only one moved to consider the physical state of what lay beneath that elaborately carved mahogany lid. No one within the church had actually seen it: Roberto's identity rested upon nothing more than some dental X-rays and a gold ring, recognition of which, Commissario Barzan had told Brunetti, reduced the Count to choking sobs. Brunetti himself, even though he had studied the autopsy report, had no idea of how much of the physical substance that had once been Roberto Lorenzoni actually lay there at the front of the church. To have lived twenty-one years and to have left so little behind save parents burdened with grief, a girlfriend who had already borne another man's child, and a cousin who had quickly manoeuvred himself into the position as heir. Of Roberto, son to both earthly and heavenly fathers, so little seemed to remain. He had been a common type, the indulged only son of wealthy parents, a boy of whom little had been asked and less expected. And now he lay, a pile of clean bones and tatters of flesh, in a box in a church, and even the policeman sent to find his killer could summon up no real grief at his early death.

Brunetti was spared from further reflection by the end of the ceremony. Four middle-aged men carried the coffin from the altar towards the back of the church. Close behind them followed Count Ludovico and Maurizio, the Contessa supported between them. Francesca Salviati was not present. Brunetti was saddened to realize that almost all of the mourners who trailed out of the church were elderly people, apparently friends of the parents. It was as if Roberto had been robbed not only of his future life but of his past, for he had left behind no friends to come and wish him farewell or to say some prayer for his long-departed spirit. How immeasurably sad, to have mattered so little, to have his passing marked by no more than a mother's tears. His own death, Brunetti realized, would pass unmarked even by those: his mother, bound within her madness, was long beyond the time when she could distinguish between son or father, life or death. And what if the coffin were to hold all that remained of his own son?

Brunetti stepped suddenly into the aisle and joined the trickle of people making towards the door of the church. On the steps, he was surprised to see the sunlight pouring down on the *campo*, the people trailing past on their way to Campo San Luca or Rialto, utterly unmoved by thoughts of Roberto Lorenzoni or his death.

He decided not to follow the coffin to the water's edge and see it placed upon the boat that would carry it to the cemetery. Instead, he went back towards San Lio and the Questura, stopping on the way for a coffee and a brioche. He finished the coffee but could eat only one bite of the brioche. He put it down on the counter, paid, and left.

He went up to his office, where he found a postcard from his brother on his desk. On the front was a photo of the Fountain of Trevi and on the back, in Sergio's neat square lettering, this message: 'Paper a success, both of us heroes,' followed by his scrawled name, and then a scribbled addition: 'Rome dreadful, squalid.'

Brunetti tried to see if the cancellation of the stamp bore a date. If it did, it was too smeared for him to be able to read it. He marvelled that the postcard could have arrived from Rome in less than a week, he had had letters take three to get to him from Torino. But perhaps the post office gave priority to postcards, or perhaps they preferred them, as they were smaller and lighter. He read through the rest of his mail, some of it important, none of it interesting.

Signorina Elettra was at the table by her window, arranging irises in a tall vase that stood in a bar of light that splashed across the table and the floor. She wore a sweater almost the same colour as the flowers, stood as slim and straight as they.

'They're very beautiful,' he said as he came in.

'Yes, they are, aren't they? But I've always wondered why the cultivated ones have no scent.'

'Don't they?'

'Very little,' she answered. 'Just smell them.' She moved to one side.

Brunetti bent forward. They had no scent at all, other than a faintly generic odour of vegetable.

Before he could remark on this, however, a voice behind him asked, 'Is that a new investigative technique, Commissario?'

Lieutenant Scarpa's voice purred with curiosity. When Brunetti straightened up and glanced towards him, Scarpa's face was a mask of respectful attention.

'Yes, Lieutenant,' he answered. 'Signorina Elettra was just telling me that, because they're so pretty, it's very difficult to tell when they're rotten. So you have to smell them. And then you know.'

'And are they rotten?' Lieutenant Scarpa asked with every appearance of interest.

'Not yet,' interrupted Signorina Elettra, moving in front of the Lieutenant and back towards her desk. She paused a short distance from Scarpa and ran her eyes up and down his uniform. 'It's harder to tell with flowers.' She stepped past him and went back to her desk. Then, with a smile as false as his, she asked, 'And was there something you wanted, Lieutenant?'

'The Vice-Questore asked me to come up,' he answered, voice thick with emotion.

'Then by all means go in,' she said, waving towards the door to Patta's office. Saying nothing, Scarpa walked in front of Brunetti, knocked once on the door, and went in without waiting to be told to do so.

Brunetti waited for the door to close before saying, 'You should be careful of him.'

'Him?' she asked, no attempt made to disguise her contempt.

'Yes, of him,' Brunetti repeated. 'He's got the Vice-Questore's ear.'

She reached forward and picked up a brown leather notebook. 'And I've got his appointment book. That cancels things out.'

'I wouldn't be so sure,' Brunetti insisted. 'He could be dangerous.'

'Take his gun away and he's no different from any other "*terron maleducato*".'

Brunetti wasn't sure if it was correct for him to countenance both disrespect for a lieutenant's rank and racist remarks about his place of origin. Then he recalled that it was Scarpa they were talking about and let it pass. 'Signorina, did you ever speak to your boyfriend's brother about Roberto Lorenzoni?'

'Yes, I did, Dottore. I'm sorry but I forgot to tell you.'

Brunetti found it interesting that she appeared more troubled by this than about her comments on Lieutenant Scarpa. 'What did he say?'

'Not much. Maybe that's why I forget. All he said was that Roberto was lazy and spoiled and that he got through school by reading other students' notes.'

'Nothing else?'

'Only that Edoardo told me Roberto was always getting into trouble because he kept putting his nose into other people's business—you know, going to other students' houses and opening drawers and looking through their things. He sounded almost proud of him. He said once Roberto arranged to get locked into the school building after school one day and went through all the teachers' desks.'

'Why did he do that, to steal things?'

'Oh, no. He just wanted to see what they had.'

'Were they still in touch when Roberto was kidnapped?'

'No, not really. Edoardo was doing his military service. In Modena. He said they hadn't seen one another for more than a year when it happened. But he said he liked him.'

Brunetti had no idea what to make of any of this, but he thanked Signorina Elettra for the information, decided against warning her again about Lieutenant Scarpa, and went back up to his office.

He looked down at the letters and reports on his desk and pushed them aside. He sat and pulled the bottom drawer open with the toe of his right foot, then crossed his feet on top of it. He folded his arms on his chest and glanced off at the space above the wooden wardrobe that stood against one wall. He tried to summon up some emotion for Roberto, and it was at the thought of him locked into school and poking through his teachers' desks that Brunetti finally began to have a real sense of this dead boy. It took no more than that, a consciousness of his inexplicable humanity, and Brunetti finally found himself moved to that terrible pity for the dead with which his life was too often filled. He thought of the things that could have happened in Roberto's life; he might have found work he liked, a woman to love; he might have had a son.

The family died with him; at least the direct line from Count Ludovico. Brunetti knew that the Lorenzonis could trace themselves back into the dim centuries where history and myth blended and became one, and he wondered what it must be to see it end. Antigone, he remembered, said that the chief horror of her brothers' deaths lay in the fact that her parents could never again have children, and so the family died with those bodies rotting under the walls of Thebes.

He turned his thoughts to Maurizio, now the presumptive heir to the Lorenzoni empire. Though the boys had been raised together, there was no evidence of any great affection or love between them. Maurizio's devotion seemed entirely directed at his aunt and uncle. That would make it unlikely he would deliver such a terrible blow as to rob them of their only child. But Brunetti had heard enough of the limitless self-justification of criminals to know that it would be the work of an instant for Maurizio to convince himself it would be an act of charity and love to provide them with a diligent, devoted, hard-working heir, someone who would so fully live up to their expectations of what a son should be, that the loss of Roberto would soon cease to pain them. Brunetti had heard worse.

He called down to Signorina Elettra to ask if she had found the name of the girl whose hand Maurizio had broken. She told him it was given on a separate page at the end of the list of the Lorenzoni financial holdings. Brunetti turned to the final pages. Maria Teresa Bonamini, with an address in Castello.

He called the number and asked for Signorina Bonamini, and the woman who answered said she was at work. When asked, making no attempt to discover who was calling, she told Brunetti that she worked as a salesgirl at Coin, in women's clothing.

He decided he would prefer to speak to her in person and so, telling no one what he was doing, he left the Questura and headed back in the direction of the department store.

Since the fire, almost ten years ago now, he had found it difficult to enter the store; the daughter of a friend of his had been one of the victims killed when a careless worker set fire to sheets of plastic that had, within minutes, turned the entire building into a smoke-filled hell. At the time, the fact that the girl had died from smoke inhalation and not from fire had seemed some consolation; years later, only the fact of her death remained.

He took the escalator to the second floor and found himself enveloped in brown, Coin's choice that year for summer's colour: blouses, skirts, dresses, hats—all blended together in a swirl of earth tones. The saleswomen, unfortunately, had decided or been told to wear the same colours, so they blended in, almost invisible in this sea of umber, chocolate, mahogany, chestnut. Luckily, one of them moved towards him, distinguishing herself from the rack of dresses in front of which she had been standing. 'Could you tell me where I might find Teresa Bonamini?' Brunetti asked.

She turned and pointed towards the back of the store. 'In furs,' she said and moved off towards a woman in a suede jacket who raised a hand in her direction.

Brunetti followed her gesture and found himself moving between racks of fur coats and jackets, a hecatomb of fauna, the sale of which was apparently not affected by the season. There was long-furred fox, glossy mink, and one particularly dense pelt he couldn't identify. Some years ago, a wave of social consciousness had swept the Italian fashion industry, and for a season women had been enjoined to buy 'la peilliccia ecologica', wildly patterned and coloured furs that made no attempt to disguise the fact that they were fake. But no matter how inventive the design or high the price, they could never be made to cost as much as real furs, and so the call of vanity was not sufficiently satisfied. They were symbols of principle, not of status, and they quickly passed out of fashion and were given to cleaning ladies or sent to refugees in Bosnia. Worse, they had turned into an ecological nightmare, vast swatches of bioundegradable plastic. So real fur had returned to the racks.

'*Sì, Signore?*' the salesgirl who approached Brunetti asked, pulling him back from reflections upon the vanity of human wishes. She was blonde, blue-eyed, and almost as tall as he.

'Signorina Bonamini?'

'Yes,' she answered, giving Brunetti a careful look instead of a smile.

'I'd like to talk to you about Maurizio Lorenzoni, Signorina,' he explained.

The transformation of her face was immediate. From passive curiosity, it changed instantly to irritation, even alarm. 'All of that's settled. You can ask my lawyer.'

Brunetti stepped back from her and smiled politely. 'I'm sorry, Signorina, I should have introduced myself.' He took his wallet from his pocket and held it up so that she could see his photo. 'I'm Commissario Guido Brunetti, and I'd like to talk to you about Maurizio. There's no need of a lawyer. I merely want to ask you a few questions about him.'

'What sort of questions?' she asked, the alarm still in her voice.

'About what sort of man he is, what sort of character he has.'

'Why do you want to know?'

'As you probably know, his cousin's body has been found, and we've reopened the investigation of his kidnapping. So we have to start all over again, gathering information about the family.'

'It's not about my hand?' she asked.

'No, Signorina. I know about the incident, but I'm not here to talk about it.'

'I never made *una denuncia*, you know. It was an accident.'

'But your hand was broken, wasn't it?' Brunetti asked, resisting the impulse to look down at her hands, which hung at her sides.

Responding to his unspoken question, she raised her left hand and waved it in front of Brunetti, opening and closing the fingers. 'There's nothing at all wrong with it, is there?' she asked.

'No, nothing at all, I'm glad to see,' Brunetti said and smiled again. 'But why did you speak of a lawyer?'

'I signed a statement, after it happened, saying that I would never make a complaint, never bring charges against him. It really was an accident, you know,' she added warmly. 'I was getting out of the car on his side, and he closed the door before he knew I was there.'

'Then why did you need to sign that statement, if it was an accident?'

She shrugged. 'I don't know. His lawyer told him I should do it.'

'Was there any payment made?' Brunetti asked.

Her ease of manner disappeared with the question. 'It's not illegal,' she insisted with the authority of one who has been told as much by more than one lawyer.

'I know that, Signorina. I was merely curious. It has nothing at all to do with what I'd like to know about Maurizio.'

A voice spoke behind him, addressed to Bonamini. 'Do you have the fox in size forty?'

A smile flowed on to the girl's face. 'No, Signora. They've all been sold. But we have it in forty-four.'

'No, no,' the woman said vaguely and drifted away, back towards the skirts and blouses.

'Did you know his cousin?' Brunetti asked when Signorina Bonamini returned her attention to him.

'Roberto?'

'Yes.'

'No, I never met him, but Maurizio did talk about him once in a while.'

'What did he say about him? Can you remember?'

She considered this for a while. 'No, nothing specific.'

'Then can you tell me if, by the way Maurizio spoke about him, they seemed to like one another?'

'They were cousins,' she said, as if that were explanation enough.

'I know that, Signorina, but I wondered if you can remember Maurizio's ever saying something of Roberto or if you had some idea—I don't think it matters how you formed it—about what Maurizio thought about him.' Brunetti tried another smile.

Absently, she reached out and straightened a mink jacket. 'Well,' she said, paused awhile, and then continued, 'if I had to say, then I'd say that Maurizio was impatient with him.'

Brunetti knew better than to interrupt or question her.

'There was one time when they sent him—Roberto, that is—to Paris. I think it was Paris. A big city, anyway, where the Lorenzonis had some sort of business deal going. I never really understood what happened, but Roberto opened a package or something like that or saw what was in a contract, and he talked about it to someone he shouldn't have told about it. Anyway, the deal was cancelled.'

She glanced up at Brunetti and saw the look of disappointment on his face. 'I know, I know it doesn't sound like very much, but Maurizio was really angry when it happened.' She weighed up the next comment but decided to say it. 'And he's got a terrible temper, Maurizio.'

'Your hand?' Brunetti asked.

'No,' she answered instantly. 'That really was an accident. He didn't mean to do it. Believe me, if he had, I would have been down at the *Carabinieri* station the next morning, straight from the hospital.' She used the hand in question to adjust another fur. 'He just gets mad and shouts. I've never known him to *do* anything. But you can't talk to him when he's like that; it's like he becomes someone else.'

'And what is he like when he's being himself?'

'Oh, he's serious. That's why I stopped going out with him: he was always calling up and saying he had to stay and work, or we had to take other people to dinner, business people. And then this happened,' she said, waving the hand again, 'and so I told him I didn't want to see him any more.'

'How did he take that?'

'I think he was relieved, especially after I told him I'd still sign the paper for his lawyers.'

'Have you heard from him at all since then?'

'No. I see him on the street, the way you always do, and we say hello. No talk, nothing really, just "How are you?" and things like that.'

Brunetti pulled out his wallet again and took one of his cards from it. 'If you think of anything else, Signorina, would you call me at the Questura?'

She took the card and slipped it into the pocket of the brown sweater she was wearing. 'Of course,' she said neutrally, and he doubted that his card would survive the afternoon.

He extended his hand and shook hers, then made his way back through the racks of furs, towards the stairs. As he walked down towards the main exit, he wondered how many undeclared millions she had been given in return for her signature on that paper. But, as he so often reminded himself, tax evasion was not his business.

# 19

When he returned to work after lunch, Brunetti was told by the guard at the front door that Vice-Questore Patta wanted to see him. Fearing that this might be the repercussions of Signorina Elettra's behaviour towards Lieutenant Scarpa, he went up immediately.

If Lieutenant Scarpa had said anything, however, it was in no way apparent, for Brunetti found Patta in an uncharacteristically friendly mood. Brunetti was instantly on his guard.

'Have you made any progress on the Lorenzoni murder, Brunetti?' Patta asked after Brunetti had taken his seat in front of the Vice-Questore's desk.

'Nothing yet, sir, but I've got a number of interesting leads.' This measured lie, Brunetti thought, would suggest that enough was happening to keep him on the case, yet would not seem so successful as to prompt Patta to ask for details.

'Good, good,' Patta muttered, enough for Brunetti to infer that he was not at all interested in the Lorenzonis. He asked nothing; long experience had shown him that Patta preferred people to worm news out of him, rather than to tell them straightforwardly. Brunetti wasn't going to help him out.

'It's about this programme, Brunetti,' Patta finally said.

'Yes, sir?' Brunetti inquired politely.

'The one RAI is doing about the police.'

Brunetti remembered something about a police programme to be produced and edited in a film studio in Padova. He'd had a letter some weeks ago, asking if he would agree to serve as consultant, or was it commentator? He'd tossed the letter into his wastepaper basket and forgotten about it. 'Yes, sir?' he repeated, no less politely.

'They want you.'

'I beg your pardon, sir.'

'You. They want you to be the consultant and to give them a long interview about how the police system works.'

Brunetti thought of the work that waited for him, thought of the Lorenzoni investigation. 'But that's absurd.'

'That's what I told them,' Patta agreed. 'I told them they needed someone with broader experience, someone who has a wider vision of police work, can see it as a whole, not as a series of individual cases and crimes.'

One of the things Brunetti most disliked about Patta was the fact that the cheap melodrama of his life always had such bad scripts.

'And what did they say to this suggestion, sir?'

'They have to call Rome. That's where the original suggestion came from. They're supposed to get back to me tomorrow morning.' Patta's inflection turned this into a question and one that demanded an answer.

'I can't imagine who could have suggested me for this sort of thing, sir. It's not anything I like or anything I want to be involved with.'

'I've told them that,' Patta said, but when he caught Brunetti's look of sharp surprise, added, 'I knew you wouldn't want to be taken away from this Lorenzoni thing, not after having just reopened it.'

'And so?' Brunetti asked.

'And so I suggested that they choose someone else.'

'Someone with broader experience?'

'Yes.'

'Who?' Brunetti asked bluntly.

'Myself, of course,' Patta said, tone level and in the instructional mode, as if giving the boiling point of water.

Brunetti, though it was true that he wanted no part of a television programme, found himself unaccountably enraged by Patta's blithe assumption that he could take it for himself, just like that.

'It was TelePadova, wasn't it?' Brunetti asked.

'Yes. What's that got to do with anything?' Patta asked. Television was television to the Vice-Questore.

Caught in the grip of sheer perversity, Brunetti answered, 'Then perhaps they'll be aiming the programme at an audience in the Veneto, and they might like someone local. You know, sir, someone who speaks dialect or at least sounds like he's from the Veneto.'

All warmth disappeared from Patta's voice or manner. 'I don't see what difference that makes. Crime is a national problem and one that must be treated nationally, not divided up province by province, as you seem to think it should be.' His eyes narrowed and he asked, 'You aren't a member of this Lega Nord, are you?'

Brunetti, who wasn't, didn't believe that Patta had any right either to ask the question or get an answer to it. 'I didn't realize you'd called me in to have a political discussion, sir.'

It was with evident difficulty that Patta, the bright prize of a television appearance dancing before his eyes, reined in his anger. 'No, but I mention it to you to point out the dangers of that sort of thinking.' He straightened a folder on the top of his desk and asked, voice as calm as if the subject was just being introduced, 'Now, what are we going to do about this television thing?'

Brunetti, ever open to the seduction of language, was enchanted with Patta's use of the plural, as well as with his dismissal of the programme as a 'television thing'. He must want it desperately, Brunetti realized.

'When they call you, just tell them that I'm not interested.'

'And then what?' Patta asked, waiting to see what Brunetti was going to ask in exchange for this.

'Then make any suggestion you please, sir.' Patta's expression made it clear that he didn't believe a word of what Brunetti was saying. In the past, he'd had ample proof of his subordinate's instability: he'd once referred to a Canaletto his wife had hanging in the kitchen; Brunetti had himself turned down a promotion to work directly for the Minister of the Interior in Rome, and now this, proof of sovereign madness if ever Patta had seen it: the flat rejection of a chance to appear on television.

'Very well. If that's the way you feel about it, Brunetti, I'll tell them.' As was his habit, Patta moved some papers around on the surface of his desk, thus giving evidence of his labours. 'Now, what's happening with the Lorenzonis?'

'I've spoken to the nephew and to some people who know him.'

'Why?' Patta asked with real surprise.

'Because he's become the heir.' Brunetti didn't know this to be true, but in the absence of any other male Lorenzoni, he believed it a safe assumption.

'Are you suggesting he's responsible for his own cousin's murder?' Patta asked.

'No, sir. I'm suggesting he's the one person who appears to have profited the most from his cousin's death, and so I think he bears examination.'

Patta said nothing to this, and Brunetti wondered if he were busy contemplating the interesting new theory that personal profit might serve as a motive for crime to see if it might be helpful in police work.

'What else?'

'Very little,' Brunetti answered. 'There are a few other people I want to talk to, and then I'd like to speak to his parents again.'

'Roberto's?' Patta asked.

Brunetti bit back the temptation to answer that Maurizio's parents, one dead and one absent, would be difficult to speak to. 'Yes.'

'You realize who he is, of course?' Patta asked.

'Lorenzoni?'

'Count Lorenzoni,' Patta corrected automatically. Though the Italian government had done away with titles of nobility decades ago, Patta was among those who would always love a lord.

Brunetti let it pass. 'I'd like to speak to him again. And to his wife.'

Patta started to object, but then perhaps remembered TelePadova and so said only, 'Treat them well.'

'Yes, sir,' Brunetti said. He toyed for a moment with the idea of again bringing up Montisi's promotion but said nothing and got to his feet. Patta returned his attention to the papers on his desk and ignored Brunetti's departure.

Signorina Elettra was still not at her desk, so Brunetti went down to the officers' room, looking for Vianello. When he found the sergeant at his desk, Brunetti said, 'I think it's time we talked to those boys who stole Roberto's car.'

Vianello smiled and nodded towards some papers on his desk. Seeing the rigorously clear type of the laser printer, Brunetti asked, 'Elettra?'

'No, sir. I thought to call that girl who was going out with him—she complained about police harassment and said she'd already given them to you, but I still asked—I got their names and then found the addresses.'

Brunetti pointed to the paper, so different from the usual crabbed scrawl of Vianello's reports.

'She's teaching me how to use the computer,' Vianello said with pride he made no attempt to disguise.

Brunetti picked up the paper, holding it at arm's length to read the small print. 'Vianello, this is two names and addresses. You need a computer to get this?'

'Sir, if you'll look at the addresses, you'll see that one of them is in Genoa, doing his military service. The computer got me that.'

'Oh,' Brunetti said and looked more closely at the paper. 'And the other one?'

'He's here in Venice, and I've already spoken to him,' Vianello said sulkily.

'Good work,' Brunetti said, the only way he could think of to soothe Vianello's injured feelings. 'What did he say about the car? And about Roberto?'

Vianello looked up at Brunetti; the sulks disappeared. 'Just what everyone's been saying. That he was *un figlio di papà* with too much money and too little to do. I asked him about the car, and at first he denied it. But I told him there'd be no consequences, that we just wanted to know about it. So he told me that Roberto asked them to do it to get his father's attention. Well, Roberto didn't say that; it's what the boy said. In fact, he sounded sort of sorry for him, for Roberto.'

When he saw Brunetti start to speak, he clarified his remark. 'No, not that he's dead, or not only that he's dead. It seemed to me like he was sorry that Roberto had to go to such lengths to get his father's attention, that he could be so lonely, so lost.'

Brunetti grunted in assent, and Vianello went on.

'They drove the car to Verona and left it in a parking garage, then took the train home. Roberto gave them the money for it all, even took them to dinner afterwards.'

'They were still friends when he disappeared, weren't they?'

'It seems so, though this one—Niccolò Pertusi—I know his uncle, who says he's a good boy—but Niccolò said Roberto seemed like a different person the last few weeks before it happened. Tired, no more jokes, always talking about how bad he felt, and about the doctors he saw.'

'He was only twenty-one,' Brunetti said.

'I know. Strange, isn't it? I wonder if he was really sick.' Vianello laughed. 'My Aunt Lucia would say it was a warning. Only she'd say it was,' and here Vianello added creepy emphasis, '"A Warning".'

'No,' Brunetti said. 'It sounds to me like he really was sick.'

Neither of them had to say it. Brunetti nodded and went up to his office to make the call.

As usual, he lost ten minutes in explaining to various secretaries and nurses just who he was and what he wanted, then another five in assuring the specialist in Padova, Doctor Giovanni Montini, that the information about Roberto Lorenzoni was necessary. More time passed as the doctor had a nurse look for Roberto's file.

When he finally had it, the doctor told Brunetti what he'd already heard so often he was beginning to feel the same symptoms: lassitude, headache, and general malaise.

'And did you ever determine what the cause was, Doctor?' Brunetti asked. 'After all, it's surely unusual for a man in the prime of youth to have these symptoms?'

'It could have been depression,' the doctor suggested.

'Roberto Lorenzoni didn't sound like a depressive type to me, Doctor,' Brunetti said.

'No, perhaps not,' the doctor agreed. Brunetti could hear pages being turned. 'No, I've no idea what might have been wrong,' the doctor finally said. 'The lab results might have said.'

'Lab results?' Brunetti asked.

'Yes, he was a private patient and could pay for them himself. I ordered a whole battery of tests.' Brunetti could have asked if a patient with the same symptoms who was on the public health rolls would have been left untested. Instead, he asked,' "Might have said", Doctor?'

'Yes, I don't have them here in the file.'

'And why might that be?' Brunetti asked.

'Since he never called to make a follow-up appointment, I suppose we never requested the results from the lab.'

'Would it be possible to do that now, Doctor?'

The doctor's reluctance was audible. 'It's quite irregular.'

'But do you think you could get the results, Doctor?'

'I don't see any way that could help.'

'Doctor, at this point, any information we have about the boy might help us find the people who murdered him.' It had long been Brunetti's experience that, no matter how inured people might have become to the word 'death', all of them responded the same way to the word 'murder'.

After a long pause, the doctor asked, 'Isn't there some official way you can request them?'

'Yes, there is, but it's a slow and complicated process. Doctor, you could save us a lot of time and paperwork if you'd request them.'

'Well, I suppose so,' Doctor Montini said, reluctance again audible.

'Thank you, Doctor,' Brunetti said and gave him the fax number of the Questura.

Having been finessed into sending the fax, the doctor took the only revenge he could. 'By the end of the week, then,' and hung up before Brunetti could say anything.

# 20

Remembering Patta's admonition to treat the Lorenzonis well—whatever that meant—Brunetti called the number of Maurizio's cellular and asked if he could speak to the family that evening.

'I don't know if my aunt is able to see anyone,' Maurizio said, speaking over the noise of what sounded like street traffic.

'Then I need to speak to you and your uncle,' Brunetti said.

'We've already spoken to you, spoken to all kinds of police, for about two years, and what's it got us?' the young man asked. The words, Brunetti realized, came from the text of sarcasm, but they were spoken in the tones of grief.

'I can understand your feelings,' Brunetti said, knowing this was a lie, 'but I need to get more information from your uncle, and from you.'

'What sort of information?'

'About Roberto's friends. About a number of things. About the Lorenzoni businesses, for one.'

'What about the businesses?' Maurizio asked, this time having to raise his voice over the background noise. Whatever he said next was blotted out by a man's voice speaking over what sounded like a public address system.

'Where are you?' Brunetti asked.

'On the 82, just pulling into Rialto,' Maurizio answered, then repeated his question, 'What about the businesses?'

'The kidnapping could be related to them.'

'That's absurd,' Maurizio said heatedly, his next words drowned out by the repeated message that Rialto was the next stop.

'What time may I come and talk to you tonight?' Brunetti asked as if Lorenzoni had raised no objections.

There was a pause. Both of them listened to the voice on the public address system, this time in English, and then Maurizio said, 'Seven,' and broke the connection.

The idea that the Lorenzoni business interests might have been involved in the kidnapping was anything but absurd. Quite the contrary, the businesses were the source of the wealth that made the boy a target. From what he had heard about Roberto, it seemed unlikely to Brunetti that anyone would kidnap him for the pleasure of his company or the delights of his conversation. The thought had come unbidden, but Brunetti was ashamed at having entertained it even for an instant. For God's sake, he was only twenty-one years old, and he had been killed by a bullet through his head.

Some odd linkage of ideas in his mind had Brunetti remembering something Paola had once said, years ago, when he told her about the way Alvise, the dullest policeman on the force, had been suddenly transformed by love, raving on about the many charms of his girlfriend or wife—Brunetti could now no longer remember which. He recalled laughing at the very idea of Alvise in love, laughing until Paola had said, voice icy, 'Just because we're smarter than people doesn't mean our emotions are any finer, Guido.'

Embarrassed, he had tried to argue the point, but she had been, as she always was when intellectual truth was concerned, both rigorous and relentless. 'It's convenient for us to think that the nasty emotions, hate and anger, can adhere to the lower orders, as if they owned them by right. So that leaves us, not surprisingly, to lay claim to love and joy and all those high-souled things.' He'd tried to protest, but she'd cut him short with a gesture. 'They love, the stupid and the dull and the crude, quite as strongly as we do. They just can't dress their emotions up in pretty words the way we do.'

Part of him had known she was right, but it had taken him days to admit it. He thought of that now: no matter how arrogant the Count or how spoilt the Contessa might have been, they were parents whose only child had been murdered. That their blood and manners were noble did not exclude the fact that their grief was, too.

He arrived at seven, and this time a maid let him into the Lorenzonis' home. She led him to the same room as before, and he found himself in the company of the same people. Only they were not the same. The Count's face was drawn more tightly over the bones beneath it, the nose sharper and more aquiline than before. Maurizio had lost whatever glow of health or, if nothing else, youth he had possessed the last time and seemed to be wearing clothes a size too large for him.

But the worst was the Contessa. She sat in the same chair, but now she gave the impression that the chair was in the process of devouring her, so little of her body seemed to remain within its enveloping wings. Brunetti glanced at her and was shocked by the skull-like hollows in front of her ears, the tendons and bones visible in the hands that clutched the beads of a rosary.

None of them acknowledged his entrance, though the maid spoke his name when she led him in. Suddenly uncertain how to proceed, Brunetti spoke to a point somewhere between the Count and his nephew. 'I know this is painful for you, all of you, but I need to know more about why Roberto might have been taken and to discover who might have done it.'

**171**

The Countess said something so softly that Brunetti didn't hear her. He glanced down at her, but her eyes remained on her hands and on the beads that slipped through her thin fingers.

'I don't see why any of this is necessary,' the Count said, making no attempt to disguise his anger.

'Now that we know what has happened,' Brunetti began, 'we'll continue our investigation.'

'To what purpose?' the Count demanded.

'To find the people who are responsible for this.'

'What difference will that make?'

'Perhaps to prevent its happening again.'

'They can't kidnap my son again. They can't kill him again.'

Brunetti glanced down at the Countess to see if she was following what was being said, but she gave no sign of hearing. 'But they could be stopped from doing it again, to someone else, or to someone else's son.'

'That hardly matters to us,' the Count said, and Brunetti believed he meant it.

'Then to see that they are punished?' Brunetti suggested. Vengeance was usually attractive to the victims of crime.

The Count shrugged this away then turned towards his nephew. Because Brunetti was blocked from seeing the young man's face, he had no idea of what passed between them, but when the Count turned around, he asked, 'What sort of things do you want to know?'

'If you have ever had business dealings with . . .' and here Brunetti paused, not certain which euphemism to use. 'Have you ever dealt with companies or persons who later proved to be criminals?'

'Do you mean the Mafia?' the Count asked.

'Yes.'

'Then why not just say it, for God's sake?'

At his uncle's explosion, Maurizio took a step towards him, one hand raised to the level of his waist, but a glance from the Count stopped him. He lowered his hand and stepped back.

'The Mafia, then,' Brunetti said. 'Have you ever had dealings with it?'

'Not that I know of,' the Count answered.

'Have any companies you've done business with been involved in criminal activity?'

'Where do you live, on the moon?' the Count suddenly demanded, his face flushing red with anger. 'Of course I deal with companies involved in criminal activity. This is Italy. There's no other way to do business.'

'Could you be more specific, sir?' Brunetti asked.

The Count threw up his hands in what seemed like disgust at Brunetti's ignorance. 'I buy raw materials from a company that has been fined for dumping mercury into the Volga River. The president of one of my suppliers is in jail in Singapore for employing ten-year-olds and making them work fourteen-hour days. Another one, the vice-president of a refinery in Poland, has been arrested on drug charges.' As he spoke, the Count paced back and forth in front of the empty fireplace. He stopped in front of Brunetti and demanded, 'Do you want more?'

'They all seem very far away,' Brunetti said mildly.

'Far away?'

'Far away from here. I had something in mind a little closer, perhaps in Italy.'

The Count appeared utterly at a loss how to take what Brunetti said, whether to respond with anger or information. Maurizio chose this moment to interrupt. 'We had some trouble, about three years ago, with a supplier in Naples.' Brunetti gave him a quizzical glance and the young man continued. 'He was providing engine parts for our trucks, but they turned out to have been stolen from shipments made through the port of Naples.'

'What happened?'

'We changed supplier,' Maurizio explained.

'Was it a large contract?' Brunetti asked.

'Large enough,' the Count interrupted.

'How large?' Brunetti asked.

'About fifty million lire a month.'

'Were there bad feelings? Threats?' Brunetti asked.

The Count shrugged. 'There were words, but no threats.'

'Why?'

The Count took so long in answering this that Brunetti was finally prompted to repeat the question. 'Why?'

'I recommended him to another trucking company.'

'A competitor?' Brunetti asked.

'Everyone's a competitor,' the Count said.

'Was there ever any other trouble? Perhaps with an employee? Did one of them perhaps have connections to the Mafia?'

'No,' Maurizio interrupted before his uncle could answer.

Brunetti had been watching the Count when he asked the question, and he saw his surprise at the young man's response.

Calmly, he repeated the question directly to the Count. 'Were you aware of an employee who had criminal connections?'

He shook his head. 'No. No.'

Before Brunetti could ask another question, the Countess spoke. 'He was my baby. I loved him so much.' By the time he glanced down at her, she had stopped talking and was again pulling the smooth beads between her fingers.

The Count leaned down and caressed her thin cheek, but she gave no indication that she was aware of his touch, or of his presence. 'I think this has gone on long enough,' he said, straightening up.

There was still one thing Brunetti wanted. 'Do you have his passport?'

When the Count failed to answer, Maurizio asked, 'Roberto's?' At Brunetti's nod, he said, 'Of course.'

'Is it here?'

'Yes, it's in his room. I saw it there when we were . . . When we cleaned it.'

'Would you get it for me?'

Maurizio gave a puzzled glance at the Count, who remained motionless and silent.

Maurizio excused himself and for a full three minutes the two men listened to the whispered Ave Marias of the Countess, words repeated and repeated as the beads clicked together.

Maurizio returned and handed the passport to Brunetti.

'Would you like me to sign a receipt for this?' he asked.

The Count dismissed the suggestion with a wave, and Brunetti slipped the passport into the pocket of his jacket without bothering to examine it.

Suddenly the whispered voice of the Countess grew in volume. 'We gave him everything. He was everything to me,' she said, but this again was followed by a return to the words of the Ave Maria.

'I think this is more than enough for my wife,' the Count said, glancing towards her with eyes that tightened with grief, the first emotion Brunetti had seen the man display.

'Yes,' Brunetti agreed and turned to leave.

'I'll see you out,' the Count volunteered. Out of the corner of his eye, Brunetti saw Maurizio glance across at him sharply, but the Count seemed not to notice and turned towards the door, which he held open for Brunetti.

'Thank you,' Brunetti said, intending the remark for all of the people in the room, though he doubted that one of them had even known he was there.

The Count led him down the hall and opened the front door of the apartment.

'Is there anything else you can think of, Signor Conte? Anything that might help us?' Brunetti asked.

'No, nothing can help any more,' he answered, almost as if he were talking to himself.

'Should you think of anything or remember anything, I'd like you to call me.'

'There's nothing to remember,' he answered, pushing the door closed before Brunetti could say anything further.

Brunetti waited until after dinner to examine Roberto's passport. The first thing he noted was its thickness: an expandable accordion page was glued to the back and folded inside the cover. Brunetti pulled it open, pulled it out to his arm's length, and looked at the various visas, their many languages and designs. He turned it over and found more stamps on the back. He folded the paper back in place, then opened the passport to the front page.

Issued six years ago and renewed every year until Roberto's disappearance, the passport gave Roberto's date of birth, height, weight, and permanent residence. Brunetti turned to the first pages of the passport: there were of course no stamps from the EC member nations, but there were for the United States, followed by those for Mexico, Colombia, and Argentina. Then immediately following in chronological order, Poland, Bulgaria, and Romania. After that, chronological order broke down, as though the customs officers had simply stamped the document at any convenient page it happened to fall open to.

Brunetti went into the kitchen to get paper and pen, then began to list Roberto's trips in strict chronological order. After fifteen minutes, he had two sheets of paper covered with columns of places and dates, all complicated by the many insertions he had to make when he came upon stamps that had been made at random.

After noting down the places and dates of all of the stamps, he recopied the list in a more ordered form, this time covering three sheets of paper. The last place Roberto had visited, ten days before the date of his kidnapping, was Poland, which he had entered via Warsaw airport. His exit visa showed that he had stayed only a day. Before that, three weeks before his kidnapping, he had travelled to two countries whose names were given in Cyrillic letters and which Brunetti took to be Belorussia and Tadzhikistan.

He went down the corridor and stood at the door of Paola's study. She looked up at him over the top of her glasses. 'Yes?'

'How's your Russian?'

'Do you mean my boyfriend or my language?' she asked, setting down her pen and removing her glasses.

'No, what you do with your boyfriend is your own business,' he said with a smile. 'Your language.'

'Somewhere between Pushkin and road signs, I'd say.'

'City names?' he asked.

She stretched out her hand towards the passport he held up in front of him. He went over to the desk, handed her the passport, and went to stand behind her, absently brushing a piece of woollen thread from the shoulder of her sweater.

Taking the passport, she asked, 'Which one?'

'In the back, on that extra page.'

She opened the passport and pulled the page out to its full length. 'Brest.'

'Where is it?'

'Belorussia.'

'We have an atlas?' Brunetti asked.

'In Chiara's room, I think.'

177

By the time he was back, she had copied out the names of the cities and countries on a piece of paper. When he placed the book beside her, she said, 'Even before we bother to look, we ought to see what year it was printed.'

'Why?'

'Lots of the names have been changed. Not only countries, but cities.'

She took the book and opened it to the title page. 'Maybe this will do,' she said. 'It's last year's edition.' She turned to the index, looking for Belorussia, then flipped back to the map.

For a moment, they studied the map of the small country lodged in between Poland and Greater Russia. 'It's one of what are now called "breakaway republics".'

'Pity it's only the Russians who get to break away,' Brunetti said, imagining what glory it would be for northern Italy to be free of Rome.

Paola, used to this, ignored him. She replaced her glasses and bent down over the map. She placed a finger on a name, 'Here's the first one. On the border with Poland.' Keeping her finger there, she continued to study the map. After a few moments, she used her other hand to point to another place. 'Here's the second. It seems to be only a hundred kilometres from the other.'

Brunetti placed the open page of the passport beside her and looked again at the visas. The numbers and dates were written in Western style. 'Same day,' he said.

'Meaning?'

'That he went by land from Poland to Belorussia and stayed there only one day, perhaps even less, before coming back.'

'Is that strange? You said he was a sort of errand boy for the business. Maybe he had to deliver a contract or make a pick-up.'

'Hmm,' Brunetti agreed. He reached down and picked up the atlas and began to turn pages.

'What are you looking for?'

'I'd like to know what route he'd take to get back here,' he answered, studying the map of Eastern Europe and running his finger across the most likely route. 'Probably Poland and then Romania, if he was driving.'

Paola interrupted him. 'Roberto doesn't sound like someone who'd travel by bus.'

Brunetti grunted, finger still on the map. 'And then Austria and down through Tarvisio and Udine.'

'Do you think it's important?'

Brunetti shrugged.

Losing interest, Paola folded the long page back into the passport and handed it up to Brunetti. 'If it is important, then I'm sorry you'll never know. He'll never tell you,' she said and turned her attention to the book that lay open in front of her.

'There are more things in heaven and earth than are dreamt of in your philosophy, Horatio,' he dropped on her, a phrase she had used with him more than once.

'And what does that mean?' she asked, smiling up at him, glad he'd won a round.

'I mean that this is the age of plastic.'

'Plastic?' she repeated, lost.

'And computers.'

When Paola still failed to understand, he smiled and said, his voice the perfect imitation of a television announcer's, 'Never leave home without your American Express card.' As he saw comprehension dawning in her eyes, he added, 'And then I can follow your movements on . . .' and Paola, understanding at last, joined him in finishing the sentence, 'Signorina Elettra's computer.'

# 21

'Of course you can charge prostitutes on your credit card,' Signorina Elettra insisted to an astonished Brunetti. He stood beside her desk two days later, holding a four-page printout of the charges made to Roberto Lorenzoni's three credit cards in the two months before his kidnapping.

By any standards, these expenses were tremendous, a total in excess of fifty million lire, more than most people made in a year. The expenses had been converted into lire from a wide range of currencies, both familiar and strange: pounds, dollars, marks, lev, zloty, roubles.

Brunetti was on the third page, looking at the charges from a hotel in St Petersburg. In a period of two days, Roberto had run up more than four million lire in room service. It might have seemed the young man had never left his room, having all meals sent in to him, drinking nothing but champagne, were it not that the printout also listed enormous expenses from restaurants and what sounded like discos or night clubs: Pink Flamingo, Can Can, and Elvis.

'There's nothing else it could be,' Signorina Elettra insisted.

'But Visa?' Brunetti asked, unable to believe what seemed to be staring him in the face.

'The men from the bank did it all the time,' she said. 'In almost all the Eastern countries you can do that now. It goes down as room service or laundry or valet service, depending on how the hotel has decided to list it. But it's just a way they get a cut. And keep an eye on who goes into and out of the hotel.' Seeing that she had caught Brunetti's attention, she continued. 'The lobbies are full of them. They look just like us. Westernized, that is. Armani, Gucci, Gap, and really quite beautiful. One of the vice-presidents told me he'd been approached by one of them, in English. This must have been about four years ago. Perfect English, could have been an Oxford professor. And she was. A professor, that is, at the university there, not at Oxford. She made about fifty thousand lire a month, teaching English poetry. So she decided to supplement her income.'

'And improve her English?' Brunetti asked.

'Italian, in this case, I think, sir.'

Brunetti looked back down at the papers. His imagination superimposed upon the information contained in them the map of Eastern Europe which he and Paola had studied two nights before. He followed Roberto's path east, traced the purchase of petrol just at the edge of Czechoslovakia; a new tyre, shockingly expensive, somewhere in Poland, and then more petrol at the city where he'd obtained his entry visa to Belorussia. There was a charge for a hotel room in Minsk, far more expensive than in Rome or Milan, and a very expensive dinner. Three bottles of Burgundy were on the bill—the only word it contained that Brunetti could understand—so it must have been a dinner for more than Roberto alone, probably one of those business dinners he was so richly paid to extend to clients. But in Minsk?

Because this list was in chronological order, Brunetti could also trace Roberto's movements as he made his way back across the continent, following pretty much the path Brunetti had sketched out for him: Poland, Czechoslovakia, Austria, and then back down into Italy, where he'd bought fifty thousand lire in petrol in Tarvisio. Then, about three days before his kidnapping, the charges ended, but not before he had paid more than three hundred thousand lire at a pharmacy near his home.

'What do you think?' Brunetti asked.

'I think I wouldn't have liked him very much,' Elettra said coolly.

'Why not?'

'I usually don't like people who don't pay their own bills.'

'And didn't he?'

She flipped the report back to the first page and pointed to the third line, which gave the name of the person to whom the bill was to be sent. 'Lorenzoni Industries.'

'It's his company card, then.'

'For business expenses?' she asked.

Brunetti nodded. 'It seems like that to me.'

'Then what's this?' she asked, pointing to a charge for two million seven hundred thousand lire from a tailor in Milan. 'Or this?' This time she pointed to a receipt for a seven hundred thousand lire handbag from Bottega Veneta.

'It's his father's company,' Brunetti argued.

She shrugged.

Brunetti wondered why it was that Signorina Elettra, a woman from whom he had not come to expect conventional morality, would find Roberto's behaviour so objectionable.

'Don't you like rich people?' he finally asked. 'Is that it?'

She shook her head. 'No, that's not the case at all. Maybe I just don't like spoiled young men who spend their daddy's money on whores.' She pushed the papers towards him and turned back to her computer.

'Even if he's dead?' Brunetti asked.

'That changes nothing, Dottore.'

Brunetti made no attempt to hide his surprise, perhaps even his disappointment. He took the papers and left.

From the pharmacy he learned that the prescriptions had been written by Roberto's family doctor, no doubt part of the doctor's attempt to treat the symptoms of malaise and general lack of energy. No one in the pharmacy remembered Roberto, nor could they recall having filled the prescriptions.

Feeling himself at a dead end, possessed only of a sense that something was wildly wrong with both the kidnapping and the Lorenzoni family, Brunetti decided to make use of the family he had married into and dialled the Count's number. This time it was his father-in-law who answered.

'It's me,' Brunetti said.

'Yes?' the Count asked.

'I wondered if you'd heard anything else about the Lorenzonis since I spoke to you.'

'I've spoken to a number of people,' the Count said. 'They say the mother's in very bad shape.' In any other person, that would have been a request for gossip, not a statement of fact.

'Yes, I've seen her.'

'I'm sorry,' the Count said and then added, 'She was a lovely woman. I knew her years ago, before she was married. She was vibrant, funny, wonderfully beautiful.'

Surprised at himself for never having asked the history of the family, having allowed his vague sense that they were wealthy to suffice, Brunetti asked, 'Did you know him, as well?'

'No, not until later, after they were married.'

'But I thought the Lorenzonis were well known.'

The Count sighed.

'What?' Brunetti asked.

'It was Ludovico's father who gave the Jews to the Germans.'

'Yes, I know.'

'Everyone knew it, but there was no proof, so nothing happened to him after the war. But none of us would speak to him. Even his brothers wouldn't have anything to do with him.'

'And Ludovico?' Brunetti asked.

'He spent the war in Switzerland, with relatives. He was just a baby then.'

'And after the war?'

'His father didn't live long. Ludovico didn't see him, didn't come back to Venice until after he was dead. There wasn't much to inherit, the title and the *palazzo*, but nothing else. He came back and made peace with his uncles and aunts. Even then, it seemed like all he could think about was making the name so famous that everyone would forget about his father.'

'It seems he's succeeded,' Brunetti remarked.

'Yes, he has.' Brunetti knew enough about his father-in-law's interests to know that many of them overlapped, perhaps competed with, those of the Lorenzoni family, and so he accepted the Count's assessment of the other man.

'And now?' Brunetti asked.

'And now? And now all he has is a nephew.' Brunetti sensed them to be on very uncertain ground here. Count Orazio himself had no son to carry on the name, not even a nephew to carry on the family businesses. He had, instead, one daughter, and she was married, not to a man of rank as exalted as her own, but to a policeman who seemed destined never to rise above the rank of *commissario*. The same war that had led Ludovico's father to commit crimes against humanity had made Brunetti's father the captain of a regiment of infantry who had gone off to Russia in their paper-soled boots to fight against the enemies of Italy. Instead, they had fought a losing battle against the Russian winter, and those few who survived, Brunetti's father among them, had then disappeared for years into Stalin's gulags. The grey-haired man who walked back to Venice in 1949 was still a captain and lived out his remaining years with a captain's pension, but crimes had been done against his spirit, and Brunetti, as a boy, seldom saw in his father evidence of the playful, joyous young man his mother had married.

Shaking himself free of the grip of memory and of his involvement with the Lorenzonis, Brunetti said, 'I've tried to speak to Paola.'

'Tried?'

'It's not easy.'

'To tell someone you love them?'

Astonished that the Count would say something so close to passion, Brunetti said nothing.

'Guido?'

'Yes?' Brunetti braced himself for a long reproach from the Count, but instead he listened to a silence as long as his own had been.

'I understand. I didn't mean to snap.' The Count said nothing more, but Brunetti chose to interpret it as an apology. For twenty years, he and the Count had dodged around the fact that, though marriage had made them relatives, it had failed to make them friends, and yet here was the Count, seeming to offer him just that.

Another silence blossomed. Finally the Count ended it. 'Be careful with these people, Guido.'

'The Lorenzonis?'

'No. With whoever kidnapped that boy. There was no harm in him. And Lorenzoni could have given them the money. That was something else I was told.'

'What?'

'A friend of mine said that he'd heard a rumour that someone had offered to lend it to the Count.'

'All of it?'

'Yes, as much as he needed. There would have been considerable interest, of course. But the offer was made.'

'Who?'

'It doesn't matter.'

'Do you believe it?'

'Yes, it's true. But they still killed him. Lorenzoni could have got the money to them somehow; there's little doubt of that. But they killed him even before he had a chance to get it to them.'

'How would he have done it? There was police surveillance.' The file on the kidnapping had shown how closely the Lorenzonis and their assets had been watched.

'People are kidnapped all the time, Guido, and the ransoms are paid without the police ever being informed. It's not a difficult thing to arrange.'

Brunetti knew this was true. 'Did he, or whoever was going to lend him the money, hear from the kidnappers?'

'No. Nothing happened after the second note, so he never had to borrow it.'

The file had told Brunetti that the police had been completely at a loss about the crime. No leads, no rumours among their informers; the boy had been snatched into the void, and all trace of him had been lost until what remained of him turned up in a ditch.

'That's why I tell you to be careful, Guido. If they'd kill him, even knowing that they could easily have had the money, then they're dangerous people.'

'I'll be careful,' Brunetti said, struck by how often he had said the same thing to this man's daughter. 'And thank you.'

'It's nothing. I'll call you if I hear anything else.' With that, the Count hung up. Why kidnap someone and not collect the ransom? wondered Brunetti. The descriptions of Roberto's state of health in the weeks before his kidnapping hardly suggested that he could offer resistance or try to escape his kidnappers. So they had someone who would have been easy to keep captive. And yet they had killed him.

And the money. Despite the efforts of the government, it had been readily available to the Count, a man who certainly was clever and well connected enough to have found a way to get the money to the kidnappers.

And yet there had been no third note. Brunetti poked around in the pile of papers on his desk until he found the original report made by the Belluno police. He read the opening paragraphs again. The body, it stated, had been covered in parts by only a few centimetres of earth, one of the reasons there had been such extensive 'animal damage'. He turned to the back and opened the envelope that contained the many photos taken of the body. He pulled out those of the original site and spread them on his desk.

Yes, the bones were right there, close to the surface. In some of the photos, he could see what appeared to be fragments sticking up through the grass beside the furrow, in the part of the field that had not been ploughed. Roberto's burial had been a hasty and careless thing, as if his killers didn't care if the body was discovered.

And the ring. The ring. Perhaps, like his girlfriend, Roberto had attempted to hide it in the beginning, when he still might have thought it was only a robbery, shoved it into his pocket and forgotten about it. Like so much about Roberto's disappearance and death, there was no way to know what had happened.

Brunetti's reflections were interrupted by Vianello, who burst into his office, panting heavily at having run up the stairs from the floor below.

'What is it?'

'Lorenzoni,' the sergeant gasped.

'What?'

'He's killed his nephew.'

# 22

Vianello seemed undone by the news. He could barely speak for a few moments and leant an arm against the doorway, head hanging down while he pulled in deep breaths. Finally, when he had his breathing under control, Vianello went on, 'The call just came in.'

'Who called?'

'He did. Lorenzoni.'

'What happened?'

'I don't know. He spoke to Orsoni, told him the boy attacked him and that there'd been a fight.'

'Anything else?' Brunetti asked, moving past Vianello out into the corridor. Together they headed for the front door and the police launches. Brunetti raised an arm to get the attention of the guard. 'Where's Montisi?' he shouted. Heads turned at the urgency of his voice.

'Outside, sir.'

'I called him,' Vianello said, coming up behind.

'Tell me the rest,' said Brunetti, pushing open the heavy glass door.

With a nod to Montisi, Brunetti leaped on to the waiting launch and turned to pull Vianello on to the already-moving boat.

'What else?' Brunetti demanded.

'Nothing. That's all he said.'

'How did he attack him? With what?' Brunetti raised his voice over the roar of the boat's accelerating motor.

'I don't know, sir.'

'Didn't Orsoni ask?' Brunetti asked, directing his anger towards Vianello.

'He said he hung up. Just gave that message and hung up.'

Brunetti banged the open palm of his hand against the railing of the boat, and as if spurred by the blow, the boat soared out into the open waters of the Bacino, cutting across the wake of a taxi, slamming down with a jarring thump. Montisi hit the siren, and its dual-toned cry preceded them up the Grand Canal until they pulled in at the private dock of the Lorenzoni *palazzo*.

The water gate was open, but no one was there to greet them. Vianello was off the boat first, but his foot missed the top step and fell back on to the one below it, stepping into water that came above his ankle. He barely noticed, turned and half-pulled, half-held Brunetti as he made the longer jump to the higher step. Together they ran into the dark entrance hall and through an open door on the right that led to a lighted stairway. At the top stood the maid who had let Brunetti in the last time. Her face was white, and she kept her arms clasped around herself, as though she'd taken a hard blow to the stomach.

'Where is he?' Brunetti asked.

She pulled one arm loose and pointed to another staircase at the end of the hall. She gestured once, twice, with her extended hand.

The two men made towards the stairs and quickly went up them. At the first landing, they paused, listening, but they heard nothing, and so they continued up the next flight. As they approached the top, a slight sound, that of a single male voice, grew faintly audible. It came from an open door on their left.

Brunetti went directly into the room. Count Lorenzoni sat beside his wife, holding one of her hands in both of his, speaking softly to her. Anyone viewing the scene would believe that it spoke of domesticity and order: an elderly man sat in soft conversation with his wife, her hand held gently within his own. That is, until they glanced down and saw that the lower half of the man's trousers, and his shoes, were bathed in blood and that smatterings of it spotted his hands and cuffs.

'*Gesù bambino,*' Vianello whispered.

The Count glanced up at them, then back to his wife. 'Don't worry, dear, everything's all right now. I'm all right. Nothing's happened.'

As Brunetti watched, the Count released her hand, and Brunetti could hear a faint sucking sound as his blood-flecked hands pulled loose from hers. The Count got to his feet and moved away from her. Brunetti saw no sign that his wife realized that he had spoken to her or that he had left her.

'This way,' the Count said and led them from the room, back towards the steps, and down to the floor beneath. He went down the corridor, towards the room in which Brunetti had twice spoken to him. The Count pushed open the door but made no move to enter the room. He said nothing but shook his head when Brunetti gestured him into the room.

Brunetti stepped inside, closely followed by Vianello. What he saw made him understand the Count's refusal. The worst was the top of the curtains in front of the far window, which had absorbed whatever remained of the force of the pellets from the shot. They had also absorbed the bulk of the brain matter and blood that had exploded from Maurizio's head. The young man's body lay crumpled at the foot of the curtains, pulled, or collapsed, into a foetal position. Maurizio's face had escaped the force of the shot; the back of his head was gone. The barrel must have been just below his chin when the shot was fired. Brunetti saw this much before he turned away.

He went back into the corridor, thinking of what he must do, wondering whether anyone, in the wake of his sudden departure from the Questura, would have thought to send the crime team.

The Count was nowhere to be seen. Vianello came out behind him. His breath was as laboured and forced as it had been when he came into Brunetti's office. 'Will you call them and see if they've sent a team?' Brunetti asked.

Vianello started to talk but then stopped and nodded.

'There's got to be another phone,' Brunetti said. 'Try one of the bedrooms.'

Vianello nodded, 'You?'

Brunetti tilted his chin back towards the stairs. 'I'll go and talk to them.'

'Them?'

'Him.'

This time Vianello's nod signalled that he was again in control. He turned and went back down the corridor, not looking into the room where Maurizio's body lay.

Brunetti forced himself to go back to the door of the room and look inside. The shotgun lay to the right of the body, its glossy stock just a centimetre from the pool of blood that seeped towards it. Two small rugs lay unevenly bunched together, pushed up in parts, silent witnesses to the struggle that had taken place above them. A man's jacket lay in a heap just inside the door; Brunetti could see that the front was covered with blood.

He turned, pulling the door closed behind him, and went back to the stairs. He found the Count and Countess as he had left them, though there was no longer any blood on the Count's hands. When he went inside, the Count looked up at him again.

'Could I speak to you?' Brunetti asked. The Count nodded and again released his wife's hand.

In the hall, Brunetti said, 'Where can we go to talk?'

'Here's as good as anywhere,' the Count answered. 'I want to keep an eye on her.'

'Does she know what's happened?'

'She heard the shot,' the Count said.

'From up here?'

'Yes. Yes. But then she came downstairs.'

'To that room?' Brunetti asked, incapable of disguising his horror.

The Count nodded.

'Did she see . . . him?'

This time the Count shrugged. 'When I heard her coming —I could hear her slippers in the hall—I walked towards the door. I thought she'd see me, that I could block him out.'

Brunetti, remembering the jacket that lay inside the door downstairs, wondered what difference this would make.

The Count suddenly turned away. 'Maybe we had better go down here,' he said, leading Brunetti into the next room. There was a desk and chair and a bookcase filled with ledgers.

The Count sat just inside the door, lowering himself into a padded armchair. He rested his head against the back, closed his eyes momentarily, then opened them and looked at Brunetti. But he said nothing.

'Can you tell me what happened?'

'Last night, late, after my wife had gone to bed, I asked Maurizio if I could speak to him. He was nervous. So was I. I told him that I'd begun to rethink everything about the kidnapping, about how it happened and how the people who did it must have known a lot about the family and what Roberto was doing. To know to wait for him at the villa, they would have to know that he was going there that night.'

The Count bit his lip, looking off to the left. 'I told him, told Maurizio, that I no longer could believe that it was a kidnapping, that someone wanted money for Roberto.'

He stopped here until Brunetti prodded, 'What did he say?'

'He seemed not to understand me, said that ransom notes had come, that it had to be a kidnapping.' The Count pulled his head away from the back of the chair and sat up straight. 'He's lived with me most of his life. He and Roberto grew up together. He was my heir.'

As he pronounced that word, the Count's eyes filled with tears. 'That's why,' he said in a voice suddenly grown so soft that Brunetti had to strain to hear him. He said nothing else.

'What else happened last night?' Brunetti asked.

'I told him I wanted him to tell me what he did when Roberto disappeared.'

'It says in the file that he was here with you.'

'He was. But I remember that he cancelled a date that night, a business dinner. It was as if he wanted to be here, with us, that night.'

'Then he couldn't have done it,' Brunetti said.

'But he could have paid someone to do it,' the Count said, and Brunetti didn't doubt that this was what he believed.

'Did you tell him that?'

The Count nodded. 'I told him that I was going to give him time to think about this, what I suspected. That he could go to the police himself.' The Count sat up straighter. 'Or do the honourable thing.'

'Honourable?'

'Honourable,' the Count repeated but didn't bother to explain.

'And then?'

'He was gone all day yesterday. Not in the office, because I called and asked. Then tonight—my wife had already gone to bed—he came into the room—he must have gone up to the villa to get it—he came into the room with the gun. And he said . . . he said . . . that I was right. He said horrible things about Roberto, things that weren't true.' Here the Count could no longer contain his tears; they streamed down his face, but he made no attempt to wipe them away.

'He said Roberto was worthless, a spoiled playboy, and that he, Maurizio, was the only one who understood the business, the only one who was good enough to inherit it.' The Count looked at Brunetti to see if he could comprehend his own horror at having raised this monster.

'And then he came towards me with the gun. At first I couldn't believe him, didn't believe all the things he said. But then he said that it would have to look like I'd done it myself, out of grief for Roberto. And then I knew he meant it.'

Brunetti waited.

The Count swallowed and wiped at his face with the back of his sleeve, covering his cheeks with streaks of Maurizio's blood. 'He came up in front of me, holding the gun, and he put it against my chest. Then he raised it up under my chin, saying he'd thought about it, and it had to be done that way.' The Count paused, recalling the horror of the scene.

'When he said that, I must have gone mad. No, not because he would kill me, but that he would be so cold-blooded about it, could have planned it like that. And because of what he did to Roberto.'

The Count stopped talking, mind pulled away by this memory. Brunetti ventured a question. 'What happened?'

The Count shook his head. 'I don't know. I think I kicked him or pushed him. The only thing I remember is pushing the gun towards him and shoving at it with my shoulder. I hoped to knock him over on to the floor. But then the gun went off, and I felt it all over me, his blood. Other things.' He stopped talking and brushed violently at his chest, caught up in the memory of that violent cascade.

He looked at his hands, clean now. 'And then I heard my wife coming down the hall, towards the room, calling my name. I remember seeing her at the door, and I remember going towards her. But I don't remember anything else, at least not clearly.'

'Calling us?'

The Count nodded. 'Yes, I think so. But then you were here.'

'How did you and your wife get back upstairs?'

The Count shook his head. 'I don't remember. Really, I don't remember much between when I saw her at the door and when you came in.'

Brunetti looked at the man, saw him for the first time stripped of all the trappings of wealth and position, and what he saw was a tall, gaunt old man, face covered with tears and mucus, his shirt damp with human blood.

'If you want to clean yourself,' Brunetti suggested, the only thing he could think of to say. Even as he said it, he knew it was entirely unprofessional and that the Count should be made to keep those clothes on until the crime squad had photographed him in them. But the idea revolted Brunetti, and so he said again, 'Perhaps you'd like to change.'

At first, the Count appeared confused by Brunetti's remarks, but then he looked down at himself, and Brunetti watched his mouth twist with disgust at what he saw. 'Oh, my God,' he muttered and got to his feet, pushing himself up by the arms of the chair. He stood awkwardly, arms held clear of his body, as if afraid for his hands to come into contact with his soiled clothing.

He saw Brunetti watching him and turned away. Brunetti followed him out of the room and saw him stop once and tilt wildly towards the wall, but before Brunetti could move towards him, he had braced himself against it with an outstretched hand. The Count pushed himself away from the wall and, at the end of the hallway, went into a room on the right, not bothering to close the door after him. Brunetti followed down the hallway and paused at the door. At the sudden sound of rushing water, he looked in and saw the trail the Count's abandoned clothing had made across the floor as he made towards the door of what must be a guest bathroom.

Brunetti waited for at least five minutes, but the sound of the water continued to be the only thing he heard. He was still listening, undecided about whether to go and see if the Count was all right, when it stopped. It was then, in the silence that expanded towards him, that he heard the other sounds from below, the familiar thumps and clangs that told him the crime squad had arrived. Abandoning his role as protector of the Count, Brunetti went downstairs, back towards the room where the second heir of the Lorenzonis had met his grim death.

# 23

Brunetti passed through the next few hours in much the same way as the survivor of an accident remembers the arrival of the ambulance, being wheeled into the emergency room, perhaps even the descent of the mask bringing blessed anaesthesia. He stood in the room where Maurizio had died, he told people what to do, he answered questions and asked his own, but all the while he had the strange sensation of not being fully present.

He remembered the photographers, even remembered the vicious obscenity one of them muttered when his tripod collapsed, crashing the camera to the floor. And he remembered thinking, even then, how ridiculous it was to be offended by his language, in that place, in the midst of what was being photographed. He recalled the arrival of the Lorenzoni lawyer and then of a private nurse to take care of the Countess. He spoke to the lawyer, whom he had known for years, and explained that Maurizio's body would not be released for days, not until an autopsy could be performed.

And, as he explained this, he found himself thinking how absurd it was. The evidence of what had happened was all there, all over one side of the room: on the curtains, on the rugs, seeped already between the thin strips of parquet, just as it had been on the sordid clothes the Count had shed on his way to the shower. Brunetti had led the lab men to those clothes, told them to gather and label them, just as he had told them to test the Count's hands for any traces of graphite that might remain. And Maurizio's.

He had spoken to the Countess, or had tried to speak to her, but she responded to his every question by calling out the name of one of the mysteries of the rosary. He asked if she had heard anything, and she answered, 'Christ accepts his cross.' He asked if she had spoken to Maurizio, and she answered, 'Jesus is laid in his tomb.' He abandoned the attempt, left her to the nurse, and to her god.

Someone had thought to bring a tape recorder, and he used it as he led the Count slowly through the events of the previous day and of this afternoon. The Count had washed away only the physical signs of what had happened; his eyes still registered the moral cost of what he had done, of what Maurizio had tried to do. He told the story once, haltingly and with many long pauses during which he seemed to lose the thread of the story he was telling. Each time, Brunetti gently reminded him of where they were, asked what had happened next.

By nine, they were finished, and there was no longer a reason to remain in the *palazzo*. Brunetti sent the lab and camera crews back to the Questura and himself took his leave. The Count said goodbye but didn't seem able to remember that people shook hands upon leaving one another.

Vianello trailed along beside Brunetti, and together they went into the first bar they found. Each of them ordered a large glass of mineral water and then another. Neither of them wanted alcohol, and both of them turned their eyes away from the tired sandwiches lying in a glass case at one side of the bar.

'Go home, Lorenzo,' Brunetti finally said. 'There's nothing else we can do. Not tonight.'

'The poor man,' Vianello said, reaching into his pocket for a few thousand lire bills to put on the bar. 'And the woman. How old can she be? Not much past fifty. She looks like she's seventy. More. This will kill her.'

Brunetti nodded in sad agreement. 'Maybe he'll be able to do something.'

'Who? Lorenzoni?'

Brunetti nodded but said nothing.

Together they left the bar, neither of them bothering to answer the barman's farewell. At Rialto, Vianello said good-bye and went to get the boat that would take him towards Castello and home. The *traghetto* had stopped running at seven, thus leaving Brunetti no choice but to cross the bridge and then walk back up the other side of the Grand Canal towards his home.

The sight of Maurizio's body and the terrible evidence of the manner of his death that spread out on the wall behind him followed Brunetti down the *calle* that led to his house and up the stairs to his door. Inside, he heard the sound of the television: his family was gathered in front of a police series they watched every week, usually in company with him in his usual chair, pointing out the howlers and inaccuracies.

'*Ciao Papà*' rang out twice, and he forced himself to answer with a friendly greeting.

Chiara's head appeared in the doorway to the living room. 'Did you eat, *Papà*?'

'Yes, angel,' he lied, hanging up his jacket, careful to keep his back to her.

She paused there for a moment, then ducked back into the room. An instant later Paola appeared in the doorway, a hand stretched out towards him. 'What's wrong, Guido?' she asked, voice raw with fear.

He stayed near his jacket, fumbling at his pocket, as if looking for something. She put an arm around his waist.

'What did Chiara say?' he managed to ask.

'That something terrible's happened to you.' She pulled his busy hands from their useless hunt through the pockets of the jacket. 'What is it?' she asked, bringing one of his hands to her lips and kissing it.

'I can't talk about it now,' he said.

She nodded. Still holding his hands, she led him towards the back of the apartment and their room. 'Come to bed, Guido. Get into bed and I'll bring you a tisane.'

'I can't talk about it Paola,' he insisted.

Her face remained solemn. 'I don't want you to, Guido. I just want you to get into bed and drink something hot and go to sleep.'

'Yes,' he said, and he lapsed again into the strange sense of unreality. Later, undressed and under the covers, he drank the tisane—linden with honey—and held Paola's hand, or she held his, until he fell asleep.

He had a peaceful night, waking only twice and then to find himself wrapped in Paola's arms, his head on her shoulder. Both times, he didn't manage to come fully awake and was soothed back to sleep by the kisses she placed on his forehead and the sense that she was there, keeping him safe.

In the morning, after the children left for school, he told her part of what had happened. She let him tell his edited version of it, asking nothing, drinking her coffee and watching his face as he spoke.

When he finished, she asked, 'Is that the end of it, then?'

Brunetti shook his head. 'I don't know. There are still the kidnappers.'

'But if the nephew sent them, then he's the one really responsible.'

'That's just it,' Brunetti said.

'What is?' Paola asked, not following him.

'If he sent them.'

She knew him too well to waste words or time asking him what he meant. 'Hmm,' she said and nodded, then sipped at her coffee, waiting for him to say something more.

'It doesn't feel right,' Brunetti finally said. 'The nephew, he didn't seem capable of it.'

'"A man can smile and smile yet be a villain,"' Paola said in the voice she used for quotations, but Brunetti was too distracted to ask what it was.

'He seemed genuinely fond of Roberto, almost protective of him.' Brunetti shook his head. 'I'm not convinced.'

'Then who?' Paola asked. 'People don't kill their children like that; men don't kill their only sons.'

'I know, I know,' Brunetti said, acknowledging the unthinkable.

'Then who?'

'That's what's wrong. There's no other possibility.'

'Could you be wrong about the nephew?' she asked.

'Of course,' Brunetti admitted. 'I could be wrong about it all. I have no idea what happened. Or why.'

'To get money. Isn't that the reason for most kidnappings?' she asked.

'I don't know that it was a kidnapping, not any more,' Brunetti said.

'But you just spoke of the kidnappers.'

'Oh, yes, he was taken. And someone sent the ransom notes. But I don't think there was ever any intention to get money.' He told her about the offer of money that had been made to Count Lorenzoni.

'How did you learn of that?' she asked.

'Your father told me.'

She smiled for the first time. 'I like it that you keep all this in the family. When did you speak to him?'

'A week ago. And then yesterday.'

'About this?'

'Yes, and about other things.'

'What other things?' she asked, suddenly suspicious.

'He said you weren't happy.'

Brunetti waited to see how Paola would respond to this; it seemed the most honest way to get her to talk about whatever was wrong.

Paola said nothing for a long time, got up and poured them both more coffee, added hot milk and sugar, then sat back opposite him. 'Psychobabblers,' she said, 'call this projection.'

Brunetti sipped at his coffee, added more sugar, then looked at her.

'You know how people are always seeing their own problems in those around them.'

'What's he unhappy about?' he asked.

'What did he say I was unhappy about?'

'Our marriage.'

'Well, there you are,' she said simply.

'Has your mother said anything?'

She shook her head.

'You don't seem surprised,' Brunetti said.

'He's getting old, Guido, and he's beginning to realize it. So I think he's beginning to examine what is important to him, and what isn't.'

'And isn't his marriage?'

'Quite the opposite. I think he's beginning to see just how important it is to him, and how he's ignored that for years. Decades.'

They had never discussed her parents' marriage, though Brunetti had for years heard rumours of the Count's fondness for pretty women. Though it would have been easy for him to discover whatever truth lay behind those rumours, he had never asked the right questions.

Italian to the core, he did not for an instant doubt that a man could be passionately devoted to the wife he betrayed with other women. There was no question in his mind that the Count was in love with the Countess, and leaping from one title to the next, Brunetti realized that the same was blazingly true of Count Lorenzoni: the one thing that seemed fully human about him was his love of the Countess.

'I don't know,' he said, letting that profession of confusion serve for both Counts.

She leaned across the table and kissed his cheeks. 'So long as I'm with you, I could never be unhappy.'

Brunetti lowered his head and blushed.

# 24

Brunetti could have written the script. Patta was bound to speak that morning, putting in the sombre remarks about the double tragedy to strike this noble family, the terrible disregard for the most sacred bonds of humanity, the weakening of the fabric of Christian society, and so on endlessly, ringing the changes on home, hearth, and family. He could have captured the flatulent pomposity of Patta's every word, the carefully timed naturalness of his every gesture, even noted within small parentheses the places where he would pause and cover his eyes with his hand while speaking of this crime that dared not speak its name.

Just as easily could he have written the headlines that were sure to scream from every newsstand in the city: *Delitto in Famiglia; Caìno e Abèle; Figlio Addotivo-Assassino*. To avoid both, he called the Questura and said he would not be in until after lunch and refused to look at the papers that Paola had brought back to the house while he was still sleeping. Sensing that Brunetti had said all that he wanted to about the Lorenzonis, Paola abandoned the subject and left him alone while she went to Rialto to buy fish. Brunetti, finding himself with nothing to do for the first time in what seemed like weeks, decided to impose upon his books the order he was obviously incapable of imposing upon events and so went into the living room and stood in front of the ceiling-high bookcase. Years ago, there had been some distinction made according to language, but when that fell apart, he had attempted to impose the order of chronology. But the curiosity of the children had soon put an end to that, and so Petronius now stood next to St John Chrysostom, and Abelard sidled up to Emily Dickinson. He studied the ranked bindings, pulled down first one and then two more, and then another pair. But then just as suddenly, he lost all interest in the job, took all five books and jammed them indiscriminately in a space on the bottom shelf.

He pulled down his copy of Cicero's *On the Good Life* and turned to the section on duties, where Cicero writes of the divisions of moral goodness. 'The first is the ability to distinguish truth from falsity, and to understand the relationship between one phenomenon and another and the causes and consequences of each one. The second category is the ability to restrain the passions. And the third is to behave considerately and understandingly in our associations with other people.'

He closed the book and slid it back into the place the vagaries and whims of the Brunetti family had assigned it: John Donne to the right, Karl Marx to the left. 'To understand the relationship between one phenomenon and another and the causes and consequences of each one,' he said aloud, startling himself with the sound of his own voice. He went into the kitchen, wrote a note for Paola, and left the apartment, heading towards the Questura.

By the time he got there, well after eleven, the press had come, feasted, and gone, and so he was at least spared the necessity of listening to Patta's remarks. He took the back steps to his office, closed the door behind him, and sat at his desk. He opened the Lorenzoni folder and read through it all, page by page. Starting with the kidnapping two years ago, he listed a complete chronology of those things he knew. It took him four sheets of paper to list everything, ending with Maurizio's death.

He spread the four sheets in front of him, tarot cards filled with death. 'To distinguish the truth from falsity. To understand the relationship between one phenomenon and another and the causes and consequences of each one.' If Maurizio had been the organizer of the kidnapping, then all phenomena were explained, all relationships and consequences clear. Desire for wealth and power, perhaps even jealousy, would have led to the kidnapping. And that would lead to the attempted attack on his uncle. And thus to his own violent death, the blood on the jacket, the brain matter on the Fortuny curtains.

But if Maurizio were not the guilty person, there was no connection between the phenomena. Uncles might well kill their nephews, but fathers do not kill their sons, not in that peculiarly cold-blooded manner.

Brunetti raised his eyes and stared from the window of his office. On one side of the scale was his vague feeling that Maurizio did not have the makings of a killer, nor of the sender of killers. On the other, then, was a scenario in which Count Ludovico gunned down his nephew and, if that were true, then it would also contain the Count as his own son's murderer.

Brunetti had been wrong before in his assessment of people and their motives. Hadn't he just been misled by and about his father-in-law? So easily had he been willing to admit to his own wife's unhappiness, so quickly had he believed that it was his own marriage that was at risk, while the real solution had been but a question away, the truth to be found in Paola's simple protestation of love.

No matter how he shifted facts and possibilities from one side to the other on these terrible scales, the weight of the evidence always came down heavily on the side of Maurizio's guilt. Yet still Brunetti doubted.

He thought of the way Paola had kidded him for years about his intense reluctance ever to discard a piece of clothing —jacket, sweater, even a pair of socks—that he found especially comfortable. It had nothing to do with money or with the expense of replacing the old garment, but with his certainty that nothing new could ever be as comfortable, as comforting, as the old. And his present situation, he realized, was caused by the same sort of reluctance to dismiss the comfortable in favour of the new.

He picked up his notes and went down to Patta's office for one last try, but that turned out to be exactly as he would have written it in the script, with Patta rejecting out of hand the 'offensive delusional suggestion' that the Count could in any way be involved in what had happened. Patta did not go as far as ordering Brunetti to apologize to the Count; after all, Brunetti had done no more than speculate, but even the speculation offended something profound and atavistic in Patta, and it was with difficulty that he restrained his rage at Brunetti, though he did not restrain himself from ordering Brunetti out of his office.

Back upstairs, Brunetti slipped the four sheets of paper inside the folder and placed it in the drawer which he usually pulled out to prop his feet on. He kicked the drawer shut and turned his attention to a new folder which had been placed on his desk while he was in Patta's office: the motors had been stolen from four boats while their owners had dinner at the *trattoria* on the small island of Vignole.

The phone saved him from the contemplation of the full triviality of this report. '*Ciao*, Guido,' came his brother's voice. 'We just got back.'

'But,' Brunetti asked, 'weren't you supposed to stay longer?'

Sergio laughed at the question. 'Yes, but the people from New Zealand left after they gave their paper, so I decided to come back.'

'How was it?'

'If you promise you won't laugh, I'd say it was a triumph.'

Timing really is all. Had this call come some other afternoon, even had it pulled him from sound sleep some morning at three, Brunetti would have been happy to listen to his brother's account of the meeting in Rome, eager to follow his explanation of the substance of and reception given his paper. Instead, as Sergio talked about Roentgens and residual traces of this and that, Brunetti stared down at the serial numbers of four outboard motors. Sergio talked of deteriorated livers, and Brunetti considered the range of horsepower from five to fifteen. Sergio repeated a question someone had asked about the spleen, and Brunetti learned that only one of the motors was insured against theft and that for only half its value.

'Guido, are you listening?' Sergio asked.

'Yes, yes, I am,' Brunetti insisted with unnecessary emphasis. 'I think it's very interesting.'

Sergio laughed at this but resisted the impulse to ask Brunetti to repeat the last two things he'd heard. Instead, he asked, 'How's Paola, and the kids?'

'All fine.'

'Raffi still going out with that girl?'

'Yes. We all like her.'

'Pretty soon it'll be Chiara's turn.'

'For what?' Brunetti asked, not understanding.

'To find a boyfriend.'

Yes. Brunetti didn't know what to say.

Into the expanding silence, Sergio asked, 'Would you like to come over, all of you, this Friday night?'

Brunetti started to accept, but then he said, 'Let me ask Paola and see if the kids have anything planned.'

Voice suddenly serious, Sergio said, 'Who ever thought we'd see this, eh, Guido?'

'See what?'

'Checking with our wives, asking if our children have made other plans. It's middle age, Guido.'

'Yes, I suppose it is.' Other than Paola, Sergio was the only other person he could ask. 'Do you mind?'

'I'm not sure it makes any difference if I do or not; nothing we do can stop it. But why this serious tone today?'

By way of explanation, Brunetti asked, 'Have you been reading the papers?'

'Yes, on the train back. This thing with Lorenzoni?'

'Yes.'

'Yours?'

'Yes,' Brunetti answered and offered nothing further.

'Terrible. The poor people. First the son and then the nephew. It's hard to know which was worse.' But it was evident that Sergio, newly back from Rome and still aglow with the happiness of professional success, didn't want to speak of such things, and so Brunetti interrupted him.

'I'll ask Paola. She'll call Maria Grazia.'

# 25

Ambiguity might well be said to be the defining character-
istic of Italian justice or—that concept being elusive—of
the system of justice which the Italian state has created
for the protection of its citizens. To many it seems that,
during the time when the police are not labouring to bring
criminals before their appointed judges, they are arresting
or investigating those same judges. Convictions are hard
won and often overturned on appeal; killers make deals and
walk free; imprisoned parricides receive fan mail; official-
dom and Mafia dance hand in hand towards the ruin of the
state—indeed, to the ruin of the very concept of the state.
Rossini's Doctor Bartolo might have had the Italian appeals
court in mind when he sang, *'Qualche garbuglio si troverà.'*

During the next three days, Brunetti, cast down into
darkness of spirit by a deadening sense of the futility of his
labours, considered the nature of justice and, with Cicero a
voice that refused to cease, the nature of moral goodness.
All, it seemed to him, to no purpose.

Like the troll lurking under the bridge in a children's
tale he'd read decades ago, the list he'd made lurked in his
desk drawer, silent, not forgotten.

He attended Maurizio's funeral, feeling more disgust at
the hordes of ghouls with cameras than at the thought of
what lay in that heavy box, its edges sealed with lead against
the damp of the Lorenzoni family vault. The Countess did
not attend, though the Count, red-eyed and leaning on the

arm of a younger man, walked from the church behind the body of the man he'd killed. His presence and the nobility of his bearing hurled Italy into a paroxysm of sentimental admiration not seen since the parents of a murdered American boy donated his organs so that young Italians, children of the country of his murderer, could live. Brunetti stopped reading the papers, but not before they reported that the examining magistrate had decided to treat Maurizio's death as a case of justified self-defence.

He devoted himself, like a man with toothache who prods at the affected tooth with his tongue, to the motors. In a world with no sense, motors were as vital as life, and so why not find them? Alas, it proved too easy to do so—they were quickly discovered in the home of a fisherman on Burano, his neighbours so suspicious at having seen him bring them in, one after the other, from his boat that they called the police to report him.

Late in the day after this triumph, Signorina Elettra appeared at the door of this office. '*Buon giorno*, Dottore,' she said as she came in, her face hidden and her voice muffled by the immense bouquet of gladioli she carried in her arms.

'But what's this, Signorina?' he asked, getting up from his chair to steer her clear of the one that stood between her and his desk.

'Extra flowers,' she answered. 'Do you have a vase?' She set the bouquet down on the surface of his desk, then placed beside them a sheaf of papers that had suffered from both her grip and the water on the stems of the flowers.

'There might be one in the cupboard,' he answered, still confused as to why she would bring them up to him. And extra? Her flowers were usually delivered on Monday and Thursday; this was Wednesday.

She opened the door to the cupboard, rustled through the objects on the floor, came up with nothing. She waved a hand in his direction and went back towards the door, saying nothing.

Brunetti looked at the flowers, then at the papers that lay beside them, a fax from Doctor Montini in Padova. Roberto's lab results, then. He tossed them back on the desk. The flowers spoke of life and possibility and joy; he wanted nothing more to do with the dead boy and his dead feelings about him and his family.

Signorina Elettra was quickly back, carrying a Barouvier vase Brunetti had often admired when he saw it on her desk. 'I think this will be perfect for them,' she said, setting the waterfilled vase down beside the flowers. She started to pick them up, one by one, and slip them into the vase.

'How are they extra, Signorina?' Brunetti asked and then smiled, the only response, really, to the conjunction of Signorina Elettra and fresh flowers.

'I did the Vice-Questore's monthly expenses today, Dottore, and I saw that there was about five hundred thousand lire left.'

'From what?'

'From what he's authorized to spend on clerical supplies every month,' she answered, placing a red flower between two white ones. 'So since there's one day left in the month, I thought I'd order some flowers.'

'For me?'

'Yes, and for Sergeant Vianello, and some for Pucetti, and then some roses for the men down in the guard room.'

'And for the women in the Ufficio Stranieri?' he asked, wondering if Signorina Elettra was the sort to give flowers only to men.

'No,' she said. 'They've been getting them twice a week, with the regular order, for the last two months.' She finished the flowers and turned to him.

'Where would you like them?' she asked, setting them on the corner of his desk. 'Here?'

'No, perhaps on the window sill.'

Dutifully she carried them over and placed them in front of the central window. 'Here?' she asked, turning so that she could see Brunetti's expression.

'Yes,' he said, his face relaxing into a smile. 'They're perfect. Thank you, Signorina.'

'I'm glad you like them, Dottore.' Her smile answered his own.

He went back to his desk, thought of putting the papers into the file unread, but then smoothed them out with the side of his hand and began to read. And might as well have saved his time, for it was nothing more than a list of names and numbers. The names meant nothing to him, though he thought they must be the various tests the doctor had prescribed for the tired young man. The numbers, as well, might have referred to cricket scores or prices on the Tokyo exchange: it was meaningless to him. Anger at this latest impediment erupted, and as quickly disappeared. For a moment, Brunetti thought of tossing the papers away, but then he pulled the phone towards him and dialled Sergio's home number.

When he had said the right things to his sister-in-law and promised they'd be there for dinner Friday night, he asked to speak to his brother, who was already home from the laboratory. Tired of the exchange of pleasantries, Brunetti said without introduction, 'Sergio, do you know enough about lab tests to tell me what the results mean?'

His brother registered the urgency in Brunetti's voice and asked no questions. 'For most of them, yes.'

'Glucose, reading of seventy-four.'

'That's for diabetes. Nothing's wrong with it.'

'Triglycerides. Reading of, I think, two-fifty.'

'Cholesterol. A bit high but nothing worth bothering about.'

'White cells, reading of one thousand.'

'What?'

Brunetti repeated the number.

'Are you sure?' Sergio asked.

Brunetti looked closer at the typed numbers. 'Yes, one thousand.'

'Hmm. That's hard to believe. Are you feeling all right? Do you get dizzy?' Sergio's concern, and something else, was audible.

'What?'

'When did you have these tests done?' Sergio asked.

'No, no. They're not mine. They're someone else's.'

'Ah. Good.' Sergio paused to consider this, then asked, 'What else?'

'What does that one mean?' Brunetti insisted, troubled by Sergio's questions.

'I won't be sure, not until I hear the others.'

Brunetti read him the remaining list of tests and the numbers to the right of them. He finished. 'That's it.'

'Anything else?'

'At the bottom, there's a note that says spleen function seems to be reduced. And something about . . ' Brunetti paused and peered closely at the doctor's scrawl. 'Something that looks like "hyaline" something. "Membranes", it looks like.'

After a long pause, Sergio asked, 'How old was this person?'

'Twenty-one,' and then, when he registered what Sergio had said, 'Why do you say "was"?'

'Because no one survives with levels like that.'

'Levels of what?' Brunetti asked.

214

But instead of answering, Sergio demanded, 'Did he smoke?'

Brunetti recalled what Francesca Salviati had said, that Roberto was worse than an American in the way he complained about smoking. 'No.'

'Drink?'

'Everyone drinks, Sergio.'

A sudden note of anger flashed out in Sergio's voice. 'Don't be stupid, Guido. You know what I mean. Did he drink a lot?'

'Probably more than normal.'

'Any diseases?'

'Not that I know of. He was in perfect health, well in very good health, until about two weeks before he died.'

'What did he die of?'

'He was shot.'

'Was he alive when he was shot?' Sergio asked.

'Of cour . . ' Brunetti started to say, but then he stopped. He didn't know. 'We've assumed so.'

'I'd check,' Sergio said.

'I don't know that we can,' Brunetti said.

'Why? Don't you have the body?'

'There wasn't much of it left.'

'The Lorenzoni boy?'

'Yes,' Brunetti answered, and into the expanding silence he finally asked, 'What does all that mean, the numbers I gave you for those tests?'

'You know I'm not a doctor,' Sergio began, but Brunetti cut him off.

'Sergio, this isn't a trial. I just want to know. Me, for myself. What do they mean, all those tests?'

'I think it's radiation poisoning,' Sergio said. When Brunetti didn't respond, he explained, 'The spleen. It can't have been that damaged if he had no organic disease. And the blood count is horribly low. And the lung capacity. Was much of them left?'

Brunetti remembered the doctor saying that they looked like the lungs of a heavy smoker, of a man far older than Roberto, who had smoked for decades. At the time, Brunetti had not questioned or pursued the contradiction between that and the fact that Roberto didn't smoke. He explained this to Sergio, then asked, 'What else?'

'All of it—the spleen, the blood, the lungs.'

'Are you sure, Sergio?' he asked, forgetting that this was his older brother, just back from a triumph at an international congress about radioactive contamination at Chernobyl.

'Yes.'

Brunetti's mind was off far from Venice, following the trail of Roberto's credit cards across the face of Europe. Eastern Europe. To the breakaway republics of the former Soviet Union, rich in natural resources that lay hidden beneath their soil and just as rich in the armaments which the hastily departing Russians had left behind as they fled in advance of their collapsing empire.

'*Madre di Dio,*' he whispered, afraid at what he understood.

'What is it, Guido?' his brother asked.

'How do you transport that stuff?' Brunetti asked.

'What stuff?'

'Radioactive things. Material, whatever it's called.'

'That depends.'

'On what?'

'On how much of it there is and what kind it is.'

'Give me an example,' Brunetti demanded and then, hearing his own insistent voice, added, 'It's important.'

'If it's the sort we use, for radiotherapy, it's shipped in individual containers.'

'How big?'

'The size of a suitcase. Perhaps even smaller if it's for a smaller machine or dosage.'

'Do you know anything about the other kind?'

'There are lots of other kinds, Guido.'

'The kind for bombs. He'd been in Belorussia.'

No sound came through the phone, only the well-crafted silence achieved by Telecom's new laser network, but Brunetti thought he could hear the gears meshing in Sergio's mind.

'Ah,' was all his brother said. And then, 'So long as the container is lined with enough lead, it can be very small. A briefcase or suitcase. It'd be heavy, but it can be small.'

This time it was from Brunetti's lips that the sigh escaped. 'That would be enough?'

'I'm not sure what you've got in mind, Guido, but if you mean enough for a bomb, then yes, that would be more than enough.'

That left very little for either of them to say. After a long pause, Sergio suggested, 'I'd check the place where he was found with a Geiger counter. And the body.'

'Is this possible?' Brunetti asked, not having to explain what he meant.

'I think so, yes,' Sergio's voice blended the certainty of the expert and the sadness of the man. 'The Russians left them nothing else to sell.'

'God help us all, then,' said Brunetti.

# 26

Brunetti's work had long accustomed him to horror and the various indignities humans inflict upon one another, indeed, upon anything near them, but nothing in his experience had prepared him for this. To contemplate what his phone call to Sergio had revealed was to contemplate the unthinkable. It was not difficult for Brunetti to imagine traffic in armaments on however grand a scale; indeed, he could easily accept the fact that guns would be sold, even to those the sellers knew to be killers. But this, if what he suspected—or feared—was true, then it went beyond any potential for evil he had formerly witnessed.

Not for an instant did Brunetti doubt that the Lorenzonis were involved with the illegal transport of nuclear material, and not for an instant did he doubt that the material would be used for armaments: there is no such thing as an illegal X-ray machine. Further, it was impossible for him to believe that Roberto could have organized it. Everything he had learned about the boy spoke of his dullness and lack of initiative: he was hardly the sort to mastermind a traffic in nuclear material.

Who better to do so than Maurizio, the bright young nephew, the better choice of heir? He was ambitious, a young man who looked forward to the commercial possibilities of the next millennium, to the vast new markets and suppliers in the East. The only obstacles to his leading the Lorenzoni business and fortunes to new triumphs was his dull cousin Roberto, the boy who could be sent to fetch and carry, rather in the manner of the friendly family dog.

The only doubt Brunetti had was the extent of the Count's involvement in the business. Brunetti doubted that something like this, an endeavour which could put the entire Lorenzoni empire at risk, could have been carried out without his knowledge and consent. Had he chosen to send his son to Belorussia to bring back the deadly material? Who better and more invisible than the playboy with the credit-card whores? If he drank enough champagne, would anyone question what he had in his briefcase? Who inspects the luggage of a fool?

Brunetti doubted that Roberto would even have known what he was carrying. His picture of the boy did not permit that. How, then, had it happened that he was exposed to the deadly emanation of the materials?

Brunetti tried to imagine this boy he had never seen, pictured him in some flashy hotel, whores gone home, alone in his room with the suitcase he was to take back to the West. If there had been some leakage, he would never have known, would have brought back with him no more than the strange symptoms of malaise that had driven him from doctor to doctor.

He would have spoken, not to his father, but to his cousin, the boy who had shared youth and innocence with him. And Maurizio would certainly have come quickly to suspect what Roberto was describing, would have recognized the symptoms for what they were: Roberto's death sentence.

For a long time, Brunetti sat at his desk and looked at the door to his office, thinking about moral goodness and beginning to understand the relationships between one phenomenon and another and the consequences of each. What he did not understand, not yet, was how the Count had come to learn of this.

Cicero advised that the passions be restrained. If someone murdered Raffi, his own son, in cold blood, Brunetti knew he would not be able to restrain his passions, that he would be savage, relentless, ruthless, would forget all policeman, be only father, and hunt them down and destroy them. He would seek vengeance at any cost. Cicero allowed no exceptions to his rules concerning moral goodness, but surely a crime like this would free a father from the injunction to behave considerately and understandingly and would give him the human right to seek vengeance.

Brunetti pondered all of this as the sun set, taking with it what little light filtered into his office. When it was almost fully dark in the room, Brunetti switched on the light. He went back to his desk, pulled out the folder from the bottom drawer, and read through it again, very slowly. He took no notes, though he often glanced up from it and across at the now-darkened windows, as if he could see reflected therein the new shapes and patterns that his reading was creating. It took him a half hour to read it all, and when it was finished, he placed it back in the drawer, closed the drawer softly, with his hand, not his foot. Then he left the Questura, heading towards Rialto and the Lorenzoni *palazzo*.

The maid who answered the door said that the Count was not receiving visitors. Brunetti asked her to carry up his name. When she came back, her face tight with irritation at this interruption upon familial grief, she said the Count had repeated his message: he was not receiving visitors.

Brunetti asked, then told, the maid to carry up the message that he was now in possession of important information concerning Roberto's murder and wanted to speak to the Count before reopening the official investigation of his death which, if the Count still refused to speak to him, would begin the following morning.

As he expected, this time the maid, when she returned, told him to follow her, and she led him, an Ariadne without a string, up the staircases and through the corridors to a new part of the *palazzo*, a part Brunetti had never seen before.

The Count was alone in what must have been an office, perhaps Maurizio's, for it was filled with computer terminals, a photocopier, and four telephones. The clear plastic tables on which all of these machines stood seemed out of place with the velvet curtains, with the view from the ogival windows and the rooftops that lay beyond those windows.

The Count sat behind one of the desks, a computer terminal to his left. He looked up when Brunetti came in and asked, 'What is it?' not bothering to stand or offer Brunetti a seat.

'I've come to discuss some new information with you,' Brunetti answered.

The Count sat rigid, hands before him. 'There is no new information. My son is dead. My nephew killed him. And now he's dead. After that, nothing follows. There's nothing more I want to know.'

Brunetti gave him a long look, making no attempt to disguise his scepticism at what he'd just heard. 'The information I have might shed light on why all of this happened.'

'I don't care why any of it happened,' the Count shot back. 'For me and my wife, it is enough that it did happen. I want nothing more to do with it.'

'I'm afraid that's no longer possible,' Brunetti said.

'What do you mean, not possible?'

'There's evidence that something far more complicated than kidnapping was going on.'

Suddenly remembering his duties as host, the Count waved Brunetti to a seat and switched off the soft purr of the computer. Then he asked, 'What information?'

'Your company, or companies, have a great deal to do with Eastern Europe.'

'Is that a statement or a question?' the Count asked.

'I think it's both. I know you have dealings there, but I don't know how extensive they are.' Brunetti waited a moment, just until the Count was going to speak, and then added, 'Or just what sort of dealings they might be.'

'Signor . . . I'm sorry, I've forgotten your name,' the Count began.

'Brunetti.'

'Signor Brunetti, the police have been investigating my family for almost two years. Surely, that's enough time for them, even the police, to have discovered everything about the nature and extent of my dealings in Eastern Europe.' When Brunetti didn't respond to his provocation, the Count asked, 'Well, isn't that true?'

'We've discovered a great deal about your dealings there, yes, but I've learned something else, something that was never mentioned in any of the information you, or your nephew, supplied to us.'

'And what is that?' the Count demanded, dismissing with his tone any interest he might have in what this police-man could have to say.

'Traffic in nuclear arms,' Brunetti said calmly, and only as he heard himself say the words did he realize just how paltry was his evidence and how impulsive the haste with which he had come halfway across the city to confront this man. Sergio was not a doctor, Brunetti had not bothered to check either Roberto's remains or the place where they were found to see if there were traces of nuclear contamination, nor had he tried to learn more about the Lorenzonis' involvement in the East. No, he had jumped up, like a child at the sound of the bells of the ice cream truck in the street, and had come bustling across the city to posture and play policeman in front of this man.

The Count's chin shot up, his mouth tightened, and he started to speak, but then his eyes shifted away from Brunetti and to the left, to the door to the room, where his wife had suddenly and silently appeared. He stood and went towards her, and Brunetti got to his feet to acknowledge her presence. But when Brunetti looked more closely at the woman who stood in the door, he was not certain that this was the Countess, this bent, curved, frail old woman who supported herself with a wooden cane which she clutched in a hand that seemed a paw, or a claw. Brunetti could see that her eyes had gone cloudy, as if the sudden onslaught of grief had blown smoke into them.

'Ludovico?' she said in a tremulous voice.

'Yes, my dear?' he said, taking one arm and leading her a few steps into the room.

'Ludovico?' she said again.

'What is it, dear?' he asked, bending down over her, bending down more now that she seemed to have grown so small.

She paused, placed both hands on the top of the cane, and looked up at him. She glanced away, then back. 'I forget,' she said, started to smile, but then forgot about that, too. Suddenly her expression changed, and she looked at her husband as though he were a strange, ominous presence in the room. She raised one arm in front of her, her palm splayed open towards him as if to protect herself from a blow. But then she seemed to forget about that, as well, turned and, cane finding the way for her, left the room. Both men listened to the tap of the cane as it disappeared down the corridor. Then a door closed and they were conscious of being alone again.

The Count went back to his seat behind the desk, but, when he sat down and faced Brunetti, it seemed that the Countess had somehow managed to infect him with her age, for his eyes had grown duller, his mouth less firm than when she came in.

'She knows,' the Count said, voice black with despair. 'But how did you learn?' he asked Brunetti in a voice as tired as his wife's had been.

Brunetti sat down again and dismissed the question with a wave of his hand. 'It doesn't matter.'

'I told you that,' the Count said. When he saw Brunetti's puzzled expression, he said, 'Nothing matters.'

'Why Roberto died matters,' Brunetti said. The only response he got for this was a quick shrug of one shoulder, but he continued, 'Why he died matters because then we can find the people who did it.'

'You know who did it,' the Count said.

'Yes, I know who sent them. We both know that. But I want them,' Brunetti said, half rising from his chair and surprising himself with the passion with which he spoke but unable to restrain it. 'I want their names.' Again that fervent tone. He lowered himself back into his chair and looked down, embarrassed at his own anger.

'Paolo Frasetti and Elvio Mascarini,' the Count said simply.

For a moment, Brunetti didn't know what he was hearing, and then when he understood, he didn't believe; and then when he believed, the entire pattern of the Lorenzoni killings that had started to form with the discovery of those tattered remains in a ditch shifted again and came into a strange new focus, one far more grotesque and horrible than those rotting fragments of his son. Brunetti reacted instantly, but instead of staring up at the Count in astonishment, he pulled his notebook from the inner pocket of his jacket and made a note of the names. 'Where can we find them?' He forced his voice to remain calm, entirely casual, while his mind raced ahead to all the questions he had to ask before the Count realized how fatal his misunderstanding had been.

'Frasetti lives over near Santa Marta. I don't know about the other one.'

Brunetti had sufficient control over his emotions and his face, and so he looked up and across at the Count. 'How did you find them?'

'They did a job for me four years ago. I used them again.'

This was not the time to ask about that other job; he had only to find out about the kidnapping, about Roberto. 'When did you learn about the contamination?' There could be no other reason.

'Soon after he got back from Belorussia.'

'How did it happen?'

The Count folded his hands in front of him and looked down at them. 'In a hotel. It was raining, and Roberto didn't want to go out. He couldn't understand the television: it was all in Russian or German. And this hotel couldn't—or wouldn't—find him a woman. So he had nothing to do, and so he started to think about what we had sent him for.'

He glanced across at Brunetti. 'Do I have to tell you all of this?'

'I think I need to know about it,' Brunetti said.

The Count nodded, but really not in acknowledgement of what Brunetti said. He cleared his throat. 'He said—he told Maurizio this later—he said that he got curious, wondered why we'd bothered to send him halfway across Europe to bring back a suitcase and that he wanted to see what was in it. He thought it might be gold or precious stones. Because it was so heavy.' He paused, then said, 'It was lined with lead.' He stopped again, and Brunetti wondered what would make him continue.

'Did he want to steal them?' Brunetti asked.

The Count looked up. 'Oh, no, Roberto would never steal anything, and certainly not from me.'

'Then why?'

'He was curious. And I suppose he was jealous, thinking that I would trust Maurizio to know what was in the suitcase, but not him.'

'And so he opened it?'

The Count nodded. 'He said he used the old-fashioned sort of can opener they had in the hotel, you know, the sort with the triangular point, the kind we used to use for opening beer.'

Brunetti nodded.

'If it hadn't been in the room, he wouldn't have been able to open the suitcase, and then none of this would ever have happened. But it was Belorussia, and that's the kind they have. So he forced the lock and opened the suitcase.'

'What was inside?'

The Count looked across at him, surprised. 'You just told me what was in it.'

'I know, but I want to know how it was being shipped. What form was it in?'

'Small blue pellets. They look like rabbit droppings, only smaller.' The Count held up the first two fingers of his right hand to indicate the correct size to Brunetti and repeated, 'Rabbit droppings.'

Brunetti said nothing; experience had taught him that there was a time when people had to be left alone to go ahead on their own, at their own pace, or they would simply stop.

Eventually the Count continued. 'He closed the suitcase again after that, but he had left it open long enough.' It wasn't necessary for the Count to explain long enough for what. Brunetti had read the symptoms of what that exposure had done to him.

'When did you find out that he had opened it?'

'When we sent the material on, to our buyer. He called me to tell me that the lock had been tampered with. But that didn't happen for almost two weeks. It went by ship.'

Brunetti let that go for now. 'And how soon did he begin to have trouble?'

'Trouble?'

'Symptoms.'

The Count nodded. 'Ah.' After a short pause, he continued, 'About a week. At first I thought it was influenza or something like that. We still hadn't heard from our buyer. But then he got worse. And then I found out that the suitcase had been opened. There was only one thing that could have happened.'

'Did you ask him?'

'No, no. There was no need for that.'

'Did he tell anyone?'

'Yes, he told Maurizio, but not until he was very bad.'

'And then?'

The Count looked down at his hands, measured a small distance with the fingers of his right, as if again measuring out the size of the pellets that had killed his son, or that had led to the killing of his son. He looked up. 'And then I decided what I had to do.'

'Had to do?' Brunetti asked before he could stop himself.

'Yes.' At first, he thought the Count wouldn't explain this, but he went on. 'If it had come out, what was wrong with him, then all the rest would have come out, too, about the shipments.'

'I see,' Brunetti said, nodding.

'It would have ruined us, and it would have disgraced us. I couldn't let that happen. Not after all these years. These centuries.'

'Ah, yes,' Brunetti whispered.

'So I decided what had to be done, and I spoke to those men, Frasetti and Mascarini.'

'Whose idea was it about how it should be done?'

The Count shook this aside as unimportant. 'I told them what to do. But the important thing was that my wife not be made to suffer. If she had learned what Roberto was doing, what had caused his death . . . I don't know what would have happened to her.' He looked at Brunetti, then down at his hands. 'But now she knows.'

'How?'

'She saw me with Maurizio.'

Brunetti thought of the curved bird-woman, her tiny hands grasped around the handle of her cane. The Count wanted to spare her from suffering, spare her from shame. Ah, yes.

'And the kidnapping? Why didn't they send a third note?'

'He died,' the Count said in a barren voice.

'Roberto? He died?'

'That's what they told me.'

Brunetti nodded, as if he understood this and as if he were following with sympathy the twisted path the Count was taking him down. 'And so?' he asked.

'And so I told them they had to shoot him, to make it look like that's what killed him.' As the Count continued to explain all of this, Brunetti began to understand that the man was persuaded of the inner logic of everything that had been done, of the rightness of it. There was no doubt in that voice, no uncertainty.

'But why did they bury him there, near Belluno?'

'One of them has a small house in the woods, for the hunting season. They kept Roberto there, and when he died, I told them to bury him up there.' The Count's face softened momentarily. 'But I told them to bury him in

**228**

a shallow grave. With his ring.' Seeing Brunetti's confusion, he explained, 'So that he would be found, and for his mother. She would have to know. I couldn't think of her not knowing, of never knowing whether he was alive or dead. It would have killed her.'

'Yes, I see,' Brunetti whispered, and in a lunatic way he did. 'And Maurizio?'

The Count cocked his head to one side, perhaps recalling that other young man, dead now too. 'He didn't know any of it. But then when it all began again, when you started asking questions . . . well, he began to ask questions about Roberto and about the kidnapping. He wanted to go to the police and tell what had happened.' The Count shook his head here at the young man's weakness and folly. 'But then my wife would know. If he went to the police, she'd know what had happened, what was going on.'

'And you couldn't permit that?' Brunetti asked levelly.

'No, of course not. It would have been too much for her.'

'I see.'

The Count stretched out one hand towards Brunetti, the same hand that had measured out those small balls of radium, or plutonium, or uranium.

If he had turned a dial and adjusted the clarity of a television screen, or suddenly removed some sort of static interference from a radio reception, the change could have been no more apparent, for it was at this point that the Count began to lie. There was no change in his voice as it went seamlessly from his agitation at the thought of his wife's pain to what he next began to explain, but it was as audible and evident to Brunetti as if the Count had suddenly jumped on the desk and begun to tear off his clothing.

'He came to me that night and said he understood what I'd done. He threatened me. With the shotgun.' The Count couldn't keep himself from looking over towards Brunetti to see how he received this, but Brunetti gave no indication that he was at all aware of what was happening.

'He came in with the shotgun,' the Count continued. 'And he pointed it at me and told me he was going to go to the police. I tried to reason with him, but then he came closer and put the gun up against my face. And I think, then, that I did go a little bit crazy because I don't remember what happened. Just that the gun went off.'

Brunetti nodded, but what he nodded at was the correctness of his belief that anything the Count said from now on would be a lie.

'And your client?' he asked. 'The person who bought the materials?'

The Count's hesitation was infinitesimal. 'Only Maurizio knew who he was. He arranged everything.'

Brunetti got to his feet. 'I think that's enough, Signore. If you'd like, you can call your lawyer. But then I'd like you to come to the Questura with me.'

The Count was visibly surprised by this. 'Why there?'

'Because I'm arresting you, Ludovico Lorenzoni, for the murder of your son and the murder of your nephew.'

The confusion on the Count's face could not have been more real. 'But I just told you. Roberto died of natural causes. And Maurizio tried to murder me.' He pushed himself to his feet but stayed behind his desk. He reached down, moved a paper from one side to the other, pushed the computer keyboard a bit more to the left. But he found nothing further to say.

'As I told you, you can call your lawyer, but then you must come with me.'

He saw the Count give in, a change as subtle as that which marked the beginning of the lies, though Brunetti knew that they would never stop now.

'May I say goodbye to my wife?' he asked.

'Yes. Of course.'

Wordlessly, the Count came around the desk, walked in front of Brunetti, and left the room.

Brunetti went over to the window behind the desk and looked out over the rooftops. He hoped the Count would do the honourable thing. He had let him go, uncertain about what other guns might be in the house. The Count was trapped by his own admission, his wife knew him to be a killer, his reputation and that of his family was soon to be in ruins, and a weapon might be somewhere in the house. If he were an honourable man, the Count would do the honourable thing.

Yet Brunetti knew he would not.

# 27

'But what does it matter if he's punished or not?' Paola asked him three nights later, after the feeding frenzy of the press that had greeted the Count's arrest had quieted down. 'His son is dead. His nephew's dead. His wife knows he killed them. His reputation is ruined. He's an old man, and he'll die in prison.' She sat on the side of the bed, wearing one of Brunetti's old bathrobes and a heavy woollen sweater on top of it. 'What else do you want to happen to him?'

Brunetti was sitting in bed, covers drawn up to his chest, and had been reading when she came into the room, bringing him a large mug of heavily honeyed tea. She handed him the mug, nodded to tell him that, yes, she'd thought to add cognac and lemon, and sat down beside him.

As he took his first sip, she pushed aside the newspapers that lay scattered on the floor beside their bed. The Count's face looked up from page four, pushed there by a Mafia killing in Palermo, the first in weeks. In the time that had elapsed since the Count's arrest, Brunetti had not spoken of him, and Paola had respected his silence. But now she wanted him to talk, not because she relished discussing a parent who murdered a child, but because she knew from long experience that it would help Brunetti to rid himself of the pain of the case.

She asked him what he thought would happen to the Count, and as he answered, she took the mug from him now and again and sipped at the hot liquid as he explained the manoeuvres of the Count's lawyers, now three of them, and his general feeling about what was likely to happen. It was impossible for him to disguise, especially from Paola, his disgust at the thought that the two murders would most likely go unpunished and the Count to jail only for the transport of illegal substances, for he now claimed that Maurizio had masterminded the kidnapping.

Already the force of the paid press had been called into action, and every front page in the country, not to mention what passes for editorial comment in Italy, had carried stories lamenting the sad fate of this nobleman, this noble man, to have been so deceived by a person of his own blood, and what crueller fate could there be than to have nursed this viper in the bosom of his family for more than a decade, only to have him turn and bite, strike to the heart. And gradually, popular feeling responded to the prevailing wind of words. The idea of traffic in nuclear armaments faded, smothered under the weight of euphemism that transmuted the crime into 'trafficking in illegal substances', as though those deadly pellets, strong enough to vaporize a city, were the equivalent of, say, Iranian caviare or ivory statuettes. Roberto's temporary grave was checked by a team of men carrying Geiger counters, but no trace of contamination was found.

The books and records of the Lorenzoni companies had been sequestered, and a team of police accountants and computer experts had pored over them for days, trying to trace the shipment that would have taken the contents of the suitcase on to the client the Count still said he couldn't identify. The only shipment they found that seemed at all suspicious was ten thousand plastic syringes sent from Venice to Istanbul by ship two weeks before Roberto's disappearance. The Turkish police sent back word that the company in Istanbul had records which showed that the syringes had been sent on by truck to Tehran, where the trail ended.

'He did it,' Brunetti insisted, his voice and his feelings no less fierce than they had been days ago, when he'd taken the Count to the Questura. Even then, at the very beginning, he'd been out manoeuvred, for the Count had insisted that a police launch be sent for him: Lorenzonis do not walk, not even to prison. When Brunetti had refused, the Count had called a water taxi, and he and the policeman who arrested him arrived at the Questura a half hour later. There they found the press already in place. No one ever discovered who made the call.

From the very beginning, the whole affair had been presented to appeal to pity, replete with the sort of vacuous sentimentality Brunetti so disliked in his countrymen. Photos had appeared, summoned up by the magician's hand of cheap emotion: Roberto at his eighteenth birthday party, sitting with his arm around his father's shoulder; a decades' old photo of the Countess dancing in the arms of her husband, both of them sleek and gleaming with youth and wealth; and even poor Maurizio managed to get his face shown, walking along the Riva degli Schiavoni, a poignant three steps behind his cousin Roberto.

Frasetti and Mascarini had presented themselves at the Questura two days after the Count's arrest, accompanied there by two of Conte Lorenzoni's lawyers. Yes, it was Maurizio who had hired them, Maurizio who had planned the kidnapping and told them what to do. They insisted that Roberto had died of natural causes; it was Maurizio who had ordered them to shoot his dead cousin and thus disguise the cause of death. And they had both insisted that they be given complete medical exams to determine if they had suffered contamination during their time with their victim. The tests were negative.

'He did it,' Brunetti repeated, taking the mug back and finishing the tea. He turned to the side and reached out to place it on the table beside the bed, but Paola took it from him and cradled the still-warm mug in her hands.

'And he'll go to jail,' Paola said.

'I don't care about that,' Brunetti said.

'Then what do you care about?'

Brunetti sank lower on the bed, hiked the covers up closer to his chin. 'Would you laugh if I said I cared about the truth?' he asked.

She shook her head. 'No, of course not. But does it matter?'

He slipped one hand out from under the covers, took the mug from her and placed it on the table, then took her hands in his. 'It matters to me, I think.'

'Why?' she asked, though she probably knew.

'Because I hate to see people like this, people like him, going through life and never having to pay for what they do.'

'Don't you think the death of his son and his nephew is enough?'

'Paola, he sent the men to kill the boy, to kidnap him and then kill him. And he killed his nephew in cold blood.'

'You don't know that,' she answered.

He shook his head. 'I can't prove it, and I'll never be able to prove it. But I know it as well as if I had been there.' Paola said nothing to this, and their conversation stopped for a minute or so.

Finally Brunetti said, 'The boy was going to die. But think of what happened to him before that, the terror, the uncertainty about what was going to happen to him. That's what I'll never forgive him.'

'It's not your place to forgive, is it, Guido?' she asked, but her voice was kind.

He smiled at this and shook his head. 'No, it's not. But you know what I mean.' When Paola didn't answer, he asked, 'Don't you?'

She nodded and squeezed his hand. 'Yes.' And then again, 'Yes.'

'What would you do?' he asked her suddenly.

Paola released his hand and brushed back a lock of hair that had fallen across her eyes. 'What do you mean? If I were a judge? Or if I were Roberto's mother? Or if I were you?'

He smiled again. 'That sounds like you're telling me to leave it alone, doesn't it?'

Paola stood and then bent to pick up the newspapers. She folded and stacked them, then turned to the bed. 'I've been thinking lately about the Bible,' she said, amazing Brunetti, who knew her to be the most unreligious of people.

'That part about an eye for an eye,' she continued. He nodded, and she went on. 'In the past, I always looked at it as one of the worst things that particularly unpleasant god had to say, crying for vengeance, thirsting after blood.' She pulled the papers towards her breast and glanced away from him, considering how to phrase this.

She looked down at him. 'But recently it's occurred to me that what it might be enjoining us to is just the opposite.'

'I don't understand,' he said.

'That instead of demanding an eye and a tooth, it's really telling us that there are limits; that, if we lose an eye, we can't ask anything more than a eye, and if we lose a tooth, then all we can get is a tooth, not a hand or,' and here she paused again, 'a heart.' She smiled again, bent down and kissed his cheek, the newspapers crinkling in protest.

When she stood, she said, 'I'll tie these into a bundle. Is the string in the kitchen?'

'Yes, it is,' he answered.

She nodded and left the room.

Brunetti picked up his glasses and his copy of Cicero and went back to reading. More than an hour later, the phone rang, but someone picked it up before he could answer it.

He waited for a minute, but Paola didn't call him. He returned his attention to Cicero; there was no one who could call that he wanted to talk to.

A few minutes later, Paola came into the bedroom. 'Guido,' she said, 'that was Vianello.'

Brunetti put his book face down on the covers and peered at her over the top of his glasses. 'What?' he asked.

'Countess Lorenzoni,' Paola began, then closed her eyes and stopped.

'What?'

'She's hanged herself.'

Before giving it thought, Brunetti whispered, 'Ah, the poor man.'

# A Noble Radiance

# Donna Leon

## ABOUT THIS GUIDE

We hope that these discussion questions will enhance
your reading group's exploration of Donna Leon's *A Noble
Radiance*. They are meant to stimulate discussion, offer new
viewpoints, and enrich your enjoyment of the book.

More reading group guides and additional information,
including summaries, author tours, and author sites
for other fine Grove Press titles may be found on our
Web site, www.groveatlantic.com.

## QUESTIONS FOR DISCUSSION

1. By the late twentieth century, the Lorenzoni family, whose long and illustrious history was woven into the fabric of its native city since the eleventh century, had become notorious primarily for what recent act by one of its members? What was the effect, if any, on the extended family's standing in Venice? Did noble roots provide any immunity against the taint of collaboration?

2. What were the circumstances of Roberto Lorenzoni's kidnapping? Why were the family's funds frozen, and what other avenues did the family have for trying to secure the young man's return?

3. When Brunetti begins to re-interview Roberto Lorenzoni's friends and family about his behavior leading up to the kidnapping, what kind of a portrait emerges? Which details seem to surface again and again?

4. How would you describe the dynamic between Brunetti and his father-in-law, Count Falier? To what extent do their differences in class, temperament, and profession dictate the terms of their relationship?

5. Why is it important to Brunetti that justice be carried out? What is the difference between bad things and

illegal things, and should the former be the province of law enforcement officials?

6. Why does Brunetti refuse to recommend Lieutenant Scarpa for promotion? What are the consequences of his decision? How adept is Brunetti at playing office politics, and where does he draw the line?

7. Brunetti "knew that the rigor of the law was most often exercised on the weak and the poor, and he knew further that the law's severity was no impediment to crime." Yet he is not immune to the desire for more punitive laws. Is there a cultural component to this impulse—grounded in the broader tradition of an eye for an eye—or is this a universally human response to certain types of crime?

8. What sort of young man is Maurizio Lorenzoni? What are his feelings toward his late cousin, and toward his aunt and uncle? Why does he shoot at Brunetti and Vianello, and what kind of impression does he leave on the commissario?

9. When Brunetti questions Count Lorenzoni about his business activities, the Count is blunt: "Of course I deal with companies involved in criminal activity. This is Italy. There's no other way to do business." To what extent is his statement true, and to what extent is it self-serving?

10. How does Signorina Elettra account for the astronomical charges on Roberto Lorenzoni's credit cards during his trips abroad? How do the hotels benefit by serving as the facilitators and middlemen of various transactions?

11. Why does Count Falier warn Brunetti to be careful when dealing with the people who kidnapped Lorenzoni? What about the kidnapping and disposal of the victim's body seem odd to Brunetti?

12. What are the circumstances of Maurizio Lorenzoni's death? How does Brunetti treat the Count when he arrives at the scene of the crime? Why does Brunetti begin to doubt the Count's version of events?

13. What is unusual about the results of the medical tests carried out in Padova for Roberto Lorenzoni shortly before his death? Which original assumptions about the case does Brunetti begin to question?

14. What does Count Lorenzoni reveal to Brunetti when the policeman confronts him with his newfound suspicions about the family business? Why does he confess as much as he does, and what does he choose to lie about?

15. Why does Brunetti say he doesn't care whether Count Lorenzoni goes to jail? What kind of a resolution does he crave, and is it possible to achieve?